TREE OF LIFE · BOOK 5

Now That I Know You

Olivia Newport

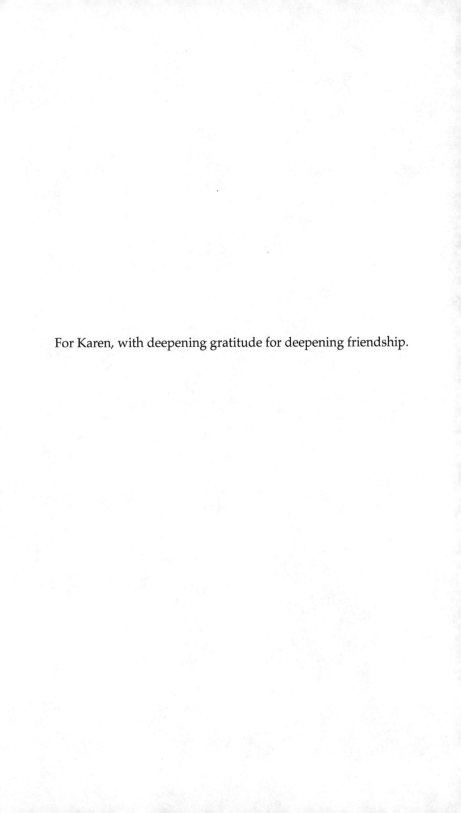

For Karen, with deepening gratitude for deepening friendship.

CHAPTER ONE

SOME DAYS THE DECISION to sync all her devices seemed like the worst decision Jillian Parisi-Duffy had ever made.

Text messages dinging in on her iPhone, chiming on her iPad, and popping up in the corner of her computer monitor, all within seconds of each other, normally didn't distract her. She'd been running her own business as a genealogist out of the house since right after college, and routines and habits served her well. Certain tasks called for Mozart in her ears to keep her focused and marching forward in rhythm with a symphony. Others allowed the occasional sing-a-long with the favorite pop artists of her high school years or movie scores that took her on a journey of vast brave courage and quiet tender revelations, all in ninety minutes. And Jillian knew when to work in utter silence, when to get up and stretch, or go for a run to clear her head, or rummage in the refrigerator for leftovers—preferably from one of her father's delectable endeavors rather than one of her own more mundane offerings. Counting how many cups of coffee she consumed in a day was not allowed, not by her nor by her dad—though he tried when he was home. Her barista-quality setup in the kitchen kept the caffeine coming as much as she wanted it, whether to bear down on a deadline or simply for the warmth and comfort of a favorite sweet concoction.

Never before had the thought crossed Jillian's mind that perhaps she should simply drop all her electronics out the window in her office and watch them bang against the gray-blue siding and white trim of the old Victorian on their way down to the ground. For the last couple of days, the vision had been growing in its detail. Perhaps one of the pieces would even chip a chunk of red accent paint.

She couldn't simply turn off texting because she had long-standing clients who communicated with her by text. And her father had a way of freaking out if he texted and she didn't answer, even though she was twenty-nine.

And there was Drew. He had his own ring tone, his own text alert sound. Short of being in the middle of a client video call, Jillian would stop anything for him. Their conversations might start in the morning and be the last thing she typed before bed, even if they managed to squeeze in a phone call and she savored his voice.

But she had to find a way to make this incessant, relentless barrage stop.

Surely by any standard, eighteen texts in one day was too many from somebody she barely knew. Cate Butler allegedly had her own job. Her texts weren't saying any of the things Jillian expected from a person she met under the circumstances that brought them together. And then there were the voice messages—six just today. Jillian hadn't even listened to the last two yet.

Jillian glanced across the office at the antique clock that had been her mother's. She had to pick up the pace and clear up the detritus of her work day before dinner. Both her physical desktop and her computer desktop were littered with documents that required safekeeping in proper folders, and she needed a fresh to-do list for tomorrow. She'd been too ambitious in her goals, which often happened on a Monday. Something about the start of a new week made her think she was going to attack everything with the energy and resources of a team of five. A handpicked group of other genealogists helped with research on a large project involving stolen babies from the middle of the twentieth century, and Jillian coordinated their efforts, but generally she was on her own. She should know better by now.

On a fresh narrow-ruled yellow legal pad, she began a new list, this time spreading tasks out over the next several days. Everything would still be accomplished in an orderly fashion and on time while allowing for October runs to clear her mind before the mountain weather changed and she'd have to hang up her shoes for the winter.

And Drew. Time for Drew, definitely.

The list was almost finished when another round of text noises began. Somewhere over the weekend Jillian had given Cate Butler a unique alert sound—a dark, gloomy melody—so she knew she did not have to respond with more than sighing now. The message wasn't her dad or Drew or any of her friends in Canyon Mines.

Cate Butler was the fourth cousin Jillian was so sure she wanted to find. She did want to find her. She just hadn't thought it was going to be like this. It would be a shame to have to block her number now.

Jillian turned her phone face down. Her iPad was already on top of the bookcase across the room. She closed the message app on her computer so she could finish cleaning up her work without feeling guilty that she hadn't even read the last seven messages.

How do you tell someone, I really wanted to find you, but could you please not bother me so much?

"There's always a way." That's what her father would say. Easy for him. He was a professional mediator. Jillian hadn't inherited that gene. She preferred avoiding conflict and simply helping people research family trees or insurance companies find lost beneficiaries. Finding her own relative wasn't supposed to cause regret.

It wasn't regret, exactly. Not at all, in fact.

The Duffy side of her family tree was well leafed out. Jillian had grown up knowing the stories of generations of her father's family. Where they'd come from in Ireland, why they'd come to America, how they eventually settled in and around Denver, the marriages, the children. She hadn't had to be a particular expert genealogist to fill in the few gaps. Organizing the Duffy tree as a teenager had sparked wonderment in history, in untold stories that pass with the generations that don't tell them or the ones no one listens to. She'd realized treasure troves of photos and personal belongings can end up in a trash bin because no one knows what to do with them after the last person who knew their significance was gone.

It was the Parisi side of Jillian's family tree that trembled tenuously like a solo dry, crinkled fall leaf losing its grip on a bare, brittle branch. She'd known her grandparents, both only children. But before that? Nothing more than a couple of names. Only a few months ago had she figured out that the coat her mother used to play in actually had a name sewn into it.

Aldo Parisi, her great-grandfather.

Jillian was only fourteen when her mother died—before she was curious enough to ask all the questions no one was around to answer now.

Except now there was this distant cousin.

Like the cobbler's child who has no shoes, Jillian the genealogist had finally spit in a tube and sent off her own DNA a few months ago, and just three weeks ago the first match came.

Cate Butler, a fourth cousin, once removed.

Their great-grandfathers had been cousins. Or first cousins once removed. Jillian was fuzzy on that point. But they had both been Parisis, and Jillian had never had a Parisi cousin of any variety. According to Cate, there were plenty.

And a bunch of them were in southern Colorado, practically right under Jillian's nose.

Jillian dragged a few loose documents into their proper folders on her computer to make sure they wouldn't miss the automatic overnight backup cycle and then started tidying the papers on her desk.

From her first-floor office just off the kitchen, it was easy to hear when the back door opened and her dad dropped his keys into the copper bowl on the counter as he always did.

"Jilly?"

"Coming." Grabbing a hair band to wrangle her mass of black curly hair, Jillian padded into the kitchen.

Nolan wiggled one eyebrow at her when she ignored the text alert sound on her phone—which she left behind in her office.

"Not taking calls this afternoon?" Nolan eased out of his suit jacket and hung it on the back of one of the stools at the bar.

"It's been even worse today, Dad."

"I run a boundaries workshop every now and then. Family discount for two or more members."

"Very funny." Jillian slid into a stool. "She's a stranger. Somehow she thinks I'm not."

"My child needs a meal." Nolan began rolling up his shirtsleeves.

"I'm not sure I can eat."

"Ah, but that's what you often say in situations that cause you stress. We both know you feel better after you do."

Jillian couldn't argue with him. "I should have started something for dinner."

"Nonsense. We have...what do we have?"

"Dad."

"Fine. Have it your way. I will create something out of nothing."

"You're on the late side getting home. Long meeting?"

"Accident on the interstate before I even got out of Denver." Nolan stuck his head in the refrigerator. "I believe we have sufficient resources for those veggie patties your young man taught me to make."

"Admit it. You like Drew too."

"I gladly admit it. He cooks masterfully. He sings like an angel. He loves my daughter ardently. What's not to like?"

Jillian pretended not to notice that her father pretended not to notice that her cheeks heated at his mention of Drew's affection.

Nolan spread vegetables around the breakfast bar and contemplated his selection of knives. "Now, talk to me about the Cate dilemma."

"Why can't I find her, Dad?"

"What do you mean? You spit in a tube and found her."

"A DNA company says we're a match of fourth or fifth cousins. But when I go digging around on my own, I can't find a Cate Butler with connections to Colorado. And I'm pretty good at my job."

"Yes, you are."

"Zero records."

"You've tried your name variants trick?"

"All the ones I can think of. A dozen spellings of Catelyn or Catherine. Maiden names, married names. Nothing that is the right age to be her. And she doesn't even have a tree going with the DNA company. Nothing to give me any clues about who she really is. All I have to go on is that they say we're a match."

"You tell people all the time that these companies are very good at what they do and the results are credible." Nolan dropped a knife through an onion and diced it swiftly.

"I believe that. And her early emails seemed like she does know things about the Parisis. When I said Sal was my ancestor, she knew his name already and that his brother was Lou, who is her ancestor. I just find it strange that even with all the ways I know to get around limits to public information, I can't find a Cate Butler who seems to match the way she presents herself."

Nolan moved on to shopping mushrooms. "Are you having doubts about going any further with her?"

"Dad, she texted me eighteen—no, nineteen—times today. And the unending voice messages. Who does that?"

"Somebody who is super excited to find a distant cousin?"

"Cut it out. Don't take her side."

"Got it. Mediator hat off. Dad hat on." Nolan touched fingers to his temple and then arranged a carrot beneath his knife. "What exactly is she asking for today?"

"I stopped reading the texts after lunch. I guess I'll get my phone and see."

Jillian returned a minute later scrolling through messages. "'So cool to find someone like you. You are just the right kind of person.' And this one. 'I just know you are going to be able to help me.' And here. 'Give me a call and I can give you all the details.' That sounds like a sales pitch for a multilevel marketing company."

"I don't disagree." Nolan stirred leftover brown rice into his vegetable mixture.

"It goes on like that. 'I was floundering to know what to do, and then the match came. This is going to be perfect.' They're all like that, Dad. She wants something. If we're long-lost parts of the same family tree, shouldn't we be talking about that? I should have stuck to email until we knew each other better. I don't know what possessed me to give her my phone number."

"You were caught up in the excitement of finding a Parisi cousin." Nolan dumped in a can of black beans and took a large skillet out from a lower cabinet. "It's not so hard to imagine."

"I certainly didn't imagine this. She wants something from me before we even know each other, Dad."

"And that's disappointing."

"Yes, it is." Jillian's voice hitched. She couldn't help it. "But somebody spat in that tube and produced those DNA results that matched mine. Whoever this Cate Butler is, and why I can't find her apart from our DNA match, she's the only lead I have to any living Parisi relatives. The absolute only one. Can I really walk away from that because she's an annoying texter with a scam up her sleeve?"

CHAPTER TWO

WHEN SOMEONE RANG A DOORBELL three successive times, it was plain impolite. It certainly wasn't the UPS delivery person leaving a package.

"I'm sorry, Raúl. Just give me a sec."

Jillian typed a quick text to Nolan, who was working in his office upstairs on Tuesday, as he usually did. ON A VIDEO CALL. CAN YOU GET THE DOOR?

She popped up to close her office door before focusing again on the image on her monitor. "Where were we?"

"I don't think you'll have to travel," Raúl said, "but if you do, it would be on the usual terms."

"Of course. What's the time frame?"

"Naturally the person who uncovered the policy is eager to collect, but inheritance laws do apply. So we're more interested in being thorough and certain than swift."

The doorbell rang again simultaneously with Nolan's rapid footsteps down the front stairs. Tucked into the mountainside, in Canyon Mines these days the greatest attraction was tourism. The doorbell ringing at the home Jillian shared with her father without previous warning that a friend was dropping by almost never happened. If someone they knew was having an emergency, their phones would be ringing, not the doorbell.

Back to Raúl. His insurance company had been a client for years, hiring Jillian to track down lost heirs or clarify identities to ensure they were paying out properly on old life insurance policies with unclear succession of beneficiaries. Jillian depended on him for steady work. He deserved her full attention.

"How did the policy surface?"

"A young man, Travis, was going through his great-uncle's things after he passed," Raúl said. "They'd been close his whole life. No one has seen the uncle's daughter for decades. She showed up once, addicted

11

to drugs, long enough to leave a child for her parents to raise and never came back."

"Then what about that child?"

"Also gone."

"Where?"

"Not sure. When she was seventeen, she had a big blow-up with her grandparents—the great-uncle of Travis—and took off the week before her high school graduation. She was enough older than Travis that he barely remembers her."

"How big is the policy?"

Raúl named the number, and Jillian blew a low whistle. If the company paid out that amount of money to the wrong beneficiary, there could be trouble.

"Seems like Travis is the one who deserves the pay-out, if anybody gets it," Jillian said. "He stuck with his great-uncle to the end."

From the living room, she heard the muffled voices. She couldn't make out the unidentified female voice, but it seemed like the pitch of the conversation was rising despite Nolan's efforts to tamp it down.

"If only policies could be written to the person who exhibited the most loyalty," Raúl said. "But it specifically names his daughter and any children she might have."

"Children. Plural."

"We have to do due diligence to rule that out. She was a young woman when she left her first child. And that girl would be next in line. But it's been a long time, plenty of years in which she could have had more children—if she's even still alive."

"We'll find them. I'll have to know everything you know. Can I interview Travis?"

The rap on Jillian's office door was followed immediately by Nolan sticking his head in. "I'm afraid I need you, Jillian."

"I'm in a meeting."

"I know." Nolan waved at the monitor. "Hello, Raúl. Sorry to interrupt, but we have a situation here."

"We're just about finished," Raúl said. "We can circle back later, Jillian. I'll email the pertinent files to get you launched. And I have another project that may mean digging into some old census records. It seems like it would be up your alley."

"Definitely. So sorry for this interruption."

"No problem."

Raúl signed out, and Jillian turned toward Nolan.

"Dad!"

"I know. I broke a cardinal rule about the two of us conducting business from home. But we really do have a situation."

Jillian puffed her cheeks and followed Nolan down the hall and into the living room.

"Jillian," Nolan said, "this is Cate Butler. She'd like to talk to you. Fortunately she likes her coffee black, so I can be trusted with that. Be right back with coffee and scones."

Jillian bugged her eyes at Nolan, but he left the room anyway.

"Cate! Hi!"

"Jillian." Cate jumped out of the purple chair, usually Jillian's favorite place to sit. "I can't tell you what it means to me to meet you."

The texts she hadn't read. The messages she hadn't listened to. Had Cate said anything about planning to drive up to Canyon Mines?

Shake her hand.

"It's nice to meet you too." Jillian offered a hand, but her eyes were on Cate's face.

"It seemed like meeting in person was the best idea." Cate shook Jillian's hand and then held it a moment as if what she really wanted to do was hug.

Jillian swallowed her nerves. She would have preferred the option of agreeing to this meeting in advance. "You must have left really early." It was only ten in the morning now.

"Six o'clock, on the road." Cate ran a hand through her hair. Dark hair. Curly hair. Wild hair.

Jillian resisted the urge to mimic the gesture with her own dark, curly, wild hair.

Cate smiled. "I couldn't believe there was a DNA match out there I didn't know about."

Jillian nodded. Was that her own mother's crinkle around Cate's eyes? Grandpa Steve's turned-up lip on one side of Cate's smile? Was Jillian truly staring into the face of someone she shared Parisi genes with, even if it was five generations ago?

"Oh, here's your coffee," Jillian said as Nolan traversed the dining room. "Please make yourself comfortable."

Cate sank back into the purple seat. "This chair is amazing."

"I know." Jillian rounded the coffee table to sit at one end of the navy sofa, eyeing the stranger-cousin in her favorite chair. Grandpa Steve used to like that chair.

Nolan set down a tray with blueberry scones, two mugs of black coffee, and a latte. He liked to pretend he didn't know how to operate Jillian's setup that warmed and frothed milk and produced flavored hot beverages, but in moments when it mattered, he came through.

He had made himself a cup. *Please, Dad, stay.* Jillian positioned herself on the sofa across the room from Cate.

"Jillian has been very curious to find a Parisi cousin," Nolan said. "She has a large, loud family on the Duffy side, but her mother didn't have any siblings or first cousins."

"I assure you," Cate said, picking up the second black coffee, "all she has to do is scoot over one branch on the family tree, and she has plenty of relatives."

"Let's see," Nolan said, settling into an armchair, "that would be the brother Lou instead of the brother Sal?"

"Technically. Except we don't talk about Lou the gangster much. We don't really know much about him. But we like to claim Uncle Sal as our own, too, because he's the one who took Geppetto under his wing."

"I'm sure Jillian will draw me a family tree when the two of you get it sorted out. Please have a scone—they're homemade."

"Are you kidding? They look great. I know someone who is a great baker, but that is not me."

"I'm sure you have other skills," Jillian said. "Your emails sounded like you have interesting work."

This was a weak description of Cate's undertaking, but since Jillian hadn't studied the details, she couldn't find a better word under pressure.

Scone in hand, Cate nodded. "That's something else amazing about finding you. You can understand my dilemma. Maybe even help me."

Jillian sipped her latte. "I'm a genealogist."

"I know. But that's a kind of historian. A cousin to historian, like we're cousins. You'll understand."

"What is it you do?" Nolan asked.

"I think of myself as an independent museum curator. I have

funding from a foundation grant to develop a traveling exhibit about the lives of women and children during the coal strike in southern Colorado during 1913 and 1914."

"That sounds ambitious."

"Too many museums romanticize history." Cate set down her coffee and scones. Her fists exploded into ten splayed fingers, as if creating light out of nothing. "They just make stuff up to make people feel good about themselves instead of understanding what life was really like. My exhibit is going to tell the truth."

"About women and children. Not just the strikers?"

"Families. That's the heart of things, isn't it? That's why you do what you do, right, Jillian? And that's why you decided to see if you had distant relatives out there, isn't it?"

"I suppose so, yes," Jillian said.

"But we have to be honest. We have to tell the truth even to children, especially about other children. That's what I'm going to do. But someone is trying to tell some pretty big lies that are going to be nicer to hear than the truth. I need help to stop it."

Jillian glanced at Nolan. "I don't understand what you think I can do, Cate." It seemed to Jillian that Cate's family's decision to claim her Uncle Saul and not talk about the gangster Lou was telling the pretty parts of their family's history.

"I need someone on my side," Cate said. "Come down and see what I'm working on. Be in my corner. Give me some advice. Your reputation will count for something."

Cate's plea was vague and heavy at the same time. How could Jillian possibly live up to it?

"I'm sure you're doing a wonderful job." Jillian drummed two fingers against her mug as she offered another toothless encouragement. "The foundation wouldn't have given you the grant if you weren't."

"That was before the trouble started. I could lose everything."

"That can't be true," Jillian said. Now would be a good time for one of her father's invigorating speeches or an insightful comment about what Cate was really upset about. Instead he sipped his coffee. *Dad*!

"It is true!" Cate had lost all interest in her refreshments and scooted to the front of that chair Jillian wished she were sitting in. "I don't really know people who can possibly understand—except you."

Jillian's phone buzzed in her hip pocket. "I'm sorry. I was supposed to call a client."

"See. That's what I mean. You're a professional. You know about professional standards."

"It's just a phone call," Jillian said.

"I bet you always call your clients back."

"She does," Nolan said.

"And keep good records."

"Impeccable," Nolan said.

Jillian side-eyed Nolan. Her father could be charming, and he could be annoying. He wasn't picking his moments especially well.

"Did you have other business in Denver today?" Jillian asked.

"You want to know if I drove four hours just to see you without an appointment."

"Well ... I was wondering."

"I texted a bunch of times yesterday. I left messages. You didn't pick up."

"As you pointed out," Nolan said, "Jillian is running a business."

About time, Dad.

"It just that I don't have anyone else."

You don't actually have me.

"I'm not sure that I see how your grand project overlaps with what I'm good at," Jillian said.

"Come down and see for yourself. If you come down to that part of the state, you'll feel it for yourself. The reason it matters to get it right."

"I don't doubt it matters to get it right. But I'm sure you know better than I do what right is in this situation."

"Please, Jillian."

Jillian had stared at her coffee an awful lot the last few minutes. And she'd glanced at her dad. What she hadn't done was look Cate in the eye. Something about the bones of her face echoed her own mother's like a ripple across time, bent across generations but still ringing true through the canyon.

And that's what did in Jillian when the plain facts of the case made no sense.

"Thursday," she said. "I could come on Thursday."

Cate launched across the room and into Jillian's unexpecting arms.

"Thank you. Thank you!" Cate whipped out her phone. "I'm sending you my office address now. It's easy to find, not too far off the main street in Trinidad. You can see what I'm doing and why it matters so much to the area to tell the truth."

"More coffee?" Nolan asked.

Cate shook her head. "I shouldn't. I have a three o'clock shift. I have just enough time to get back to work it. Just tell me what time you'll be there. I'll be waiting."

Nolan closed the door behind Cate, and Jillian watched out the front window as Cate's vehicle pulled away from the curb.

"She drives a truck," Jillian said. "Not a new one."

"A woman after my own heart."

"What just happened here, Dad?"

"I didn't expect to see any resemblance, but I do," Nolan said. "She reminds me of your Grandpa Steve. There must be a Parisi jaw line."

"It kind of knocks you over." Jillian caught the last sight of Cate's truck finishing a three-point turn to go back the way she came into town. "What did she mean about having to work a shift?"

"A mysterious statement, to be sure, for a young woman in charge of a grant."

Jillian turned to catch her father's eye. "Please tell me you can rearrange your schedule and come with me on Thursday."

"Sorry, Jilly. I'm due in family court in the morning and have a mediation in the afternoon." Nolan started stacking dishes on the tray. "I'll be in Denver all day."

Her shoulders dropped. "So not even if I stick my lip out and look really pitiful?"

"Not even."

"Nuts. I guess I'll have to go begging and see if Nia or Kris can go with me. I really don't want to go alone."

"It's really too bad you don't know anyone who lives down in that neck of the woods who would move the moon to please you."

"Drew? You really think I should drag him into this?"

"It wasn't that long ago that he brought his DNA results to you to be sure he'd really found his own fourth cousin, and look what that led to."

"Dad, you're a hopeless romantic."

"I don't deny it. Call him."

CHAPTER THREE

September 19, 1913
Outside Pueblo, Colorado

RUBBING HER THUMB AND FOREFINGER together produced a constant smudge. Caterina never quite had the self-control to handle the newspaper at the edges. Her English had come a long way from the days when her family spoke only Italian and she didn't know anyone who didn't speak Italian. Now she still wrote letters to her family in Italian, but she read the English newspapers—with her habit of dragging a finger under the line she was reading, picking up the black ink, and transferring the smudge to her thumb while she thought about what she read.

Caterina rubbed her thumb hard. "Geppetto!"

Her husband emerged from the small bedroom of their little red house. "Shh. Giuseppe finally went back to sleep."

"Thank you for settling him down." Their little boy had recently decided he was opposed to sleeping both at night and during naps, but a busy almost-two-year-old needed rest. So did his parents. Caterina thumped the newspaper.

"What have you read today?" Geppetto lifted the coffee pot, hopeful.

"I'm sorry. I drank the last of it." Caterina winced. She had meant to make more.

"No trouble. Carrick will have some in a flask when we start up again for the afternoon." Geppetto kissed the top of Caterina's head. "Now what is making you get your fingers so black today?"

"Did you read this paper?"

"No. I just brought it to you as usual, after I was sure Carrick and Ela were through with it."

"It's yesterday's paper, Geppetto," Caterina said.

He dropped into a chair beside her and studied her face. "It always is."

"The strike, Geppetto. They are going to do it. They had their meeting two days ago. That Mother Jones was in Trinidad. A unanimous vote."

Geppetto's gaze fell to his half-eaten sandwich.

"I'm sorry," Caterina said. "You came for lunch, and I let you use all your time trying to get Peppy to sleep."

"I like seeing him in the middle of the day. Besides, Ela will be waiting for you as soon as he wakes up again. Eat." Geppetto nudged the plate toward Caterina.

She shook her head. "I can't. Not when there is news of a strike."

"We knew it was coming. Everyone said it would happen."

"A strike, Geppetto. What will happen? The paper says they 'shouted, danced about the room, vowed vengeance on the operators and pledged themselves to stay with the strike until they won or dropped into their graves.'"

"The operators drew first blood a month ago when they killed George Lippiatt."

"Geppetto! This is not the Italian mob where revenge is all that matters. Your father sent you to your Uncle Salvatore in Denver to get you out of that kind of danger in New Orleans."

"And I am not in danger now, am I?"

"I hope not. But our friends could be. What is to become of Chiara and Celestrino?"

"Did they set a date for the strike?"

"Four days from now."

"Then the union must be preparing even now."

"Geppetto."

"I know, Caterina. I know." Geppetto pushed his chair back. "I hope Peppy gives you a good break. Carrick will be waiting for me. He's worried one of the cows is poorly. I may have to call for the veterinarian, and we still have a lot of hay to get in."

Geppetto took his broad-brimmed hat and left the house. Before they moved here from Denver, shortly after they married, Geppetto had never ridden a horse. Now he left one tied outside their cozy home whenever he had a chance to drop in during the day. Many days he didn't. Moving the herds between pastures, keeping up with constant fence repairs, seeding and irrigating the fields where they grew the food that would see the herds through the winter, and, like now, making sure hay cut and baled in the fields was stored in the barns before it got wet and molded—the work was never-ending. Carrick had an automobile truck with an open bed for using around the ranch, but he and Geppetto agreed that most of the time the horses were more nimble.

For her part, Caterina's days flowed with the rhythms of the main house. Everyone called it the "main house" because it was the biggest dwelling on the ranch and because the owners, Carrick and Ela Kyp, lived in it. It wasn't a mansion, though the Kyps had already made one addition and talked about adding more rooms for their growing family. They planned to always live here, it seemed.

When Caterina met him in Denver, Geppetto Parisi was the manager of a narrow four-story hotel. He hadn't had much choice. His father wanted to send him from New Orleans to Denver, and his Uncle Salvatore found him a job. He did well in the work, though. Everyone thought so. The hotel's owner had been stunned to learn Geppetto planned to leave the city to work on a ranch outside of Pueblo for someone he'd met at the hotel.

Caterina had only ever lived in cities, the same as Geppetto. Her parents talked about the Italian countryside, but in America finding work meant living in the cities. They told Caterina every day of her life how fortunate they were to be in America, no matter how back-breaking the work might be. When she found a nice Italian man to marry, they let out their breath. Someday they would have beautiful Italian *nipoti*—and now they had Peppy. Of course, they did not see him as often as they wished. They reminded Caterina of this in every letter. And it was true that the hundred and thirty miles between the ranch and Denver were not convenient to close on a regular basis, and Giuseppe was growing up fast!

Still, Caterina would go wherever Geppetto wanted to go. And she gave thanks every day that he had never wanted to go into the coal mines.

Not like Chiara's husband.

Even the steel mills in Pueblo would be better than the coal mines that kept the steel mills in business.

Did Geppetto miss the hotel in Denver? If he did, he never said. Caterina supposed not. They could always go back to Denver. His aunt and uncle would be just as thrilled to have little Peppy nearby as her parents, but Geppetto didn't bring it up. He only promised they would find the time to visit more often. It wasn't so far by train. Ela often said her parents were welcome at the ranch, but Caterina had a hard time imagining her mother would make the trip. It would be up to her to make more visits to Denver.

The unsaid truth was that little Giuseppe would never meet Geppetto's parents. It was as if he'd never lived in Louisiana. Even Uncle Sal never spoke of it.

She cleared the dishes and got out her mending basket, settling into a chair in the front room across from the wall featuring the stone fireplace flanked by bookshelves. Carrick's sister, Wilhelmina, and her husband, Charles, had first occupied the little red house. They'd only moved out six months ago with their own little boy to a home in Pueblo. Ela immediately offered the little red house to the Parisis. It was a step up from the building everyone called the "hut," where they'd lived since arriving on the ranch. It wasn't a hut. Caterina didn't know why it had that name. But it was only one large room with a bed, a small table and chairs, and a stove for heating and cooking. The little red house was so much homier.

When the whimpering from the bedroom began, Caterina tightened her lips and poked her needle through the cuff of Geppetto's favorite denim shirt, determined to make it last a little longer by constraining the fray.

"Mama!"

Eight quick neat stitches.

"Mama!"

Caterina shoved everything back into the basket. She could tell from Giuseppe's pitch that the nap was over, and if she didn't respond to his summons he would only start climbing out of his crib. They wouldn't be able to leave him in there much longer.

"Hello, my Peppito." Caterina cooed as she lifted the boy.

He popped his thumb out of his mouth and grinned. "Mama!"

"Oh, Peppito! Your papa changed you, and look at you. Already leaking everywhere."

"Wet."

"Very wet."

If Caterina's mother were there, she would wag her finger and say that she should be speaking Italian to her child. There would be time to learn English later, but he might never learn Italian if he did not learn it now.

"*Bagnato*," Caterina said, as she started to put him into a dry diaper.

Peppy giggled. "Wet!"

Caterina laughed. "At least you understand Italian. Your Nonna would be very happy about that."

"Nonna!"

"She would love to hear you say Nonna." The word would sound equally beautiful in English or Italian. "Are you hungry?"

"See Dot."

"First lunch, then Dottie and Mina."

"See Dot!"

Every day was the same. The first thing Peppy wanted after his nap was to go to the main house and see Dottie and Mina. Sometimes Caterina wondered if this excitement contributed to the growing abbreviation of his naps.

Caterina fastened his trousers. "First you must eat your lunch—all of it." Stalling was necessary. The little girls were still reliable nappers. She and Giuseppe would walk up to the main house, and it was no short walk for a child as small as Peppy. When he was younger, he would fall asleep anywhere. Those days were gone, but he still had a napping spot at the main house if Caterina could ever convince him to use it. Even the hike up would not tucker him out. As soon as he was anywhere near Ela's children his mind would only be on rolling and giggling—whether or not the girls noticed this is what he was interested in doing.

Back in the kitchen, Caterina cut some cheese into bites and an apple into thin slices she could be sure Peppy would not choke on. If he seemed to want more, she had bread she had baked only yesterday. She poured milk into a tin cup with two handles, something he managed well on his own. When he'd had his fill, she wrangled him into a jacket and shoes, both of which he disliked. But Caterina had been outside earlier in the day, and the bright sunshine was deceptive. She didn't like the color of the sky breaking around the mountains. Surely the weather was going to change soon.

They ambled up toward the main house, with its crisp white color and lovely green shutters. Carrick had let Ela pick out whatever she wanted for the house. Caterina wondered what that might feel like, but the red of their cottage, while Wilhelmina's choice, felt perfect for them. If she wanted more colors, all she had to do was step outside to any other part of the ranch and lift her eyes to the wide open beauty boundless on every side. So far Peppito had no idea what it felt like to live penned in, and she hoped he never would.

Chiara. She still didn't know what this felt like.

Eventually Caterina had to carry Peppy, as she knew she would, or Ela would wonder what had become of her. There was too much work to be done to spend the afternoon waiting on the short legs of a child not yet two.

Ela was in the vegetable garden behind the house and the girls, three and a half and one and a half, were on a blanket where she could keep an eye on them. Peppy wiggled down and hurtled himself toward them. Dottie threw a blue elephant at him in greeting. Mina offered a dour welcome.

Caterina's steps lagged.

Careful to keep the dirt on her glove off her face, Ela drew one wrist across her forehead. "Are you all right, Cat?"

Ela was the only one who called her that. She said it was because of the lanky, stealthy way Caterina walked.

Caterina met Ela's pale blue eyes. "Of course. What are we doing this afternoon?"

"I'm hunting for whatever we might have missed before it rots on the vine and checking on how the fall squash and pumpkins are coming along. I thought the girls could use some fresh air."

Caterina nodded. "Do you need help, or shall I go on inside?"

"It's a beautiful day. I don't think we have to rush inside to find carpets to beat, do you?"

"I should come early tomorrow," Caterina murmured. "There's canning to do. Fall fruit."

"I suppose. Cat, you don't seem yourself. What's wrong?"

"The strike."

"Yes, I read the papers too." Ela found a stray zucchini and dropped it in her basket.

"My friend Chiara."

"What about her? I realize Berwind will empty out. It's a company town, after all. But my understanding is the union sets up tent colonies when they vote to strike."

"Chiara is so sick. All her letters tell me this."

"Sick? You didn't tell me."

"Sick with child. She can only go to the company doctor, and he does nothing to help. Who will take care of her?"

"Won't the colony have a doctor?"

"I don't know. This is her first baby, and she is so sick. Every day. All day. And Celestrino, he goes to work. Her English is not very good. It is hard for her to make friends."

Ela dropped her clippers into the dirt. "Are you saying she hasn't had anyone properly looking after her?"

"She tells me she is all right, but I don't think so. Her letters. One is very short, like she does not have strength to write. The next is very long, like she is very lonely and has no one to hear her words. Now this. I do not like this."

"The working conditions for the men are very dangerous, Caterina. They have good reasons for the strike."

"I know this too. But for Chiara, I do not like this."

"But you said she didn't like the company doctor and wasn't allowed to see anyone else."

"I don't like this! None of it!" Caterina blew out her breath. "I'm sorry. I just worry."

"Go get her," Ela said.

"What do you mean?" Caterina's wandering eyes found focus on Ela's face.

"I mean, you and Geppetto get on a train and go down there and get Chiara and Celestrino."

CHAPTER FOUR

IF JILLIAN HAD A FAVORITE OPERA, Nolan would sing it for her now. Verdi. Rosini. Pucini. Scarlatti. He hadn't had a satisfying outburst of Scarlatti in a good long while, probably because he could never remember the words. Or the notes. Salieri. Cherubini. Donizetti.

Jillian said he just liked to prove he could name more Italian opera composers than anyone else in the room. She was not entirely wrong. Threatening to play "Name that Tune" with operas and a roomful of party guests was one of the quickest ways to exasperate his daughter. He had the good sense today not to try her patience.

Nolan cracked two eggs in one hand and dropped the contents into the sizzling skillet on the stove. At least he could offer a fortifying breakfast before sending his daughter off on her southward journey.

He called up the back stairs that she had tumbled down every morning since she was two years old when he and her mother had found this gem of a Victorian to renovate.

"Jilly? Are you coming? Breakfast awaits."

"Soon."

"Fried potatoes. Eggs. Toast. Some of Nia's jam."

"I'll be down in a minute."

Nolan gave the potatoes a stir. They were browning nicely, fast approaching that instant of golden perfection when outer crispness and inner warmth coincided after which they might as well be cold mush headed for mashing and reheating. Jillian's steps came just as Nolan scooped the eggs off the stove and the toast popped up. She wore her good jeans, not the soft, faded, comfortable ones she donned around town. Her usual work-at-home hoodie was upgraded to a bright blue long sleeve tee shirt and a reddish-something cardigan. Probably those hues had actual names. Whatever they were called, Nolan approved. It did her good to leave the house a little more often. And he was grateful Drew was meeting her at the other end of her drive.

"Sit," Nolan said. "A perfect breakfast for my perfect daughter."

"You're not doing penance because you feel guilty that you're not coming with me to Trinidad, are you?" Jillian set her phone on the granite breakfast bar, where they tended to take most of their casual meals if they were both home, before crossing the kitchen to the coffee station.

"Would you feel better if I said yes?" Nolan added five strawberries to Jillian's plate in a crescent smile and set it at her spot.

"Would you say yes if I said yes?" Jillian took her favorite mug down from the cupboard, the one that had been her mother's favorite years ago, and got her morning latte going. She barely had to look at the buttons to accomplish the task.

"It's too fine a morning for this circuitous conversation. Sit down and eat while your food is hot. I'll bring your coffee when it's ready."

The machine gurgled ahead of delivering its finest concoction, spraying anticipatory aroma of cinnamon almond something or other. Or almond cinnamon. Some grind Nia Dunston had persuaded Jillian to try. Or was it Kris Bryant? One of Jillian's girlfriends who appreciated the olfactory nuances of the blends Clark Addison offered at the Canary Cage Coffee Shop. Nolan stuck to strictly black coffee. Always had, always would. And he didn't require artsy flavor descriptions.

Jillian chewed the potatoes, closing her eyes for that few seconds of lovely savory pleasure.

Then she spoke. "Why are you even here?"

"That's a little blunt, don't you think?" Nolan set her concoction in front of her, sugar and steamed milk added. "I just made you this wonderful breakfast before sending you on your way. Am I not a thoughtful father? Is this not my legal residence?"

Jillian corralled a bit of fried egg—but not overdone—and scooped it into her mouth. "I meant, you told me you couldn't come with me to Trinidad because you had court."

"Oh that. I still do. The docket got pushed out a couple of hours, that's all. I'll be on my way to Denver right after you hit the road."

"Usually when you have court you leave really early. Get in the zone and all that."

"I made an exception." Nolan sat in front of his own breakfast now. "I know you're nervous about this day. I wish I'd had a good sausage to give you with your eggs."

"Thanks, but a sausage would not make this better."

"Might."

"Nope."

"Eat." Nolan spread his toast with jam. "When did Nia take up making jam?"

"First time. Pretty good, don't you think? She's trying to get Clark to sell it at the Cage."

"I would think Veronica would eagerly take some at the Victorium Emporium."

"Already on the counter." Jillian blew out her nerves. "Chit-chatting about jam doesn't really distract me, Dad."

"It was worth a try."

"Cate keeps going on about the old coal strikes. One e-mail after another keeps coming, full of links. She's going to be pretty disappointed that I haven't done all my homework, but honestly, I don't have time—"

Nolan reached into his pocket for his singing phone.

"When are you going to get rid of that obnoxious opera ring tone?"

"I don't find it the least bit obnoxious, Silly Jilly. I'll just be a minute."

This was not a call for Jillian's ears. Nolan made sure to kick the kitchen door closed behind him as he passed into the dining room and strode to the far side of the living room.

"Amico," he said.

"Nolan, are we a go today?"

"We are."

"I'm counting on you."

"I won't let you down. I just need a bit more time to organize things,"

"Okay. This is a ripe opportunity and I want to make sure we don't waste it."

"We won't, Amico."

Nolan ended the call and returned to the kitchen. Jillian was clearing dishes, and he rescued his plate from her grip just in time to get the last of the potatoes and wipe up the egg with the remains of his toast before letting her put the plate in the dishwasher.

"How much do you know about Mother Jones?" Jillian asked,

running water in the skillet.

"Admittedly a colorful historical figure."

"So your base of knowledge is essentially the same as mine." Jillian arranged the last of the breakfast evidence in the dishwasher. "Apparently she has something to do with the coal strike I am supposed to be educated about when I arrive in Trinidad. If you were going with me, I could study on the way down."

"No, no, no. We have fine Wi-fi here. You could—"

Nolan's phone was making noise again.

"Not again," Jillian said. "Do you have to take that call?"

"'Fraid so."

This time Nolan took the stairs two at a time and found a spot in the upstairs hall.

"Hello again."

"Kris is not picking up her phone. Can you make a point to talk to her?"

"Absolutely."

"None of this works without her."

"I shall impress that upon her with utmost severity."

"Well, don't go overboard. I'm not trying to scare anyone."

"I take offense! I do not go overboard. I am a professional mediator. I find the middle ground."

"There's no middle ground in this case, Nolan."

"I understand. The essence of your request has not changed?"

"Correct."

"Then I'll make sure I meet with her this morning and try to elicit the assurance you require."

"She can call me, and I wish she would, but obviously there is a certain window of availability today."

"Obviously."

"Does she know that?"

"I'm unsure. But you can count on me."

"I am."

"Gotta go." Nolan hit the button to end the call just as Jillian hit the top of the stairs. "Are you about ready to go, Jillian?"

"I'd better be. It's going to be a lot of driving. Alone."

Nolan fended off the dig in her tone. "You've done it before."

"I know. This time I should pay more attention to shifting from living in a silver mining part of the state to entering where coal was everything."

"I need to pack my briefcase." Nolan turned toward his office.

"I thought you said you had some extra time."

"Time to make you breakfast, but I still need to get ready for court."

"Are you sure we can't talk over another cup of coffee?" Jillian followed him into his office, where his briefcase sat open on a side chair.

Nolan shuffled through a stack of files on his desk and extracted what he needed. "You just said you should get going. What time is Drew expecting you?"

Jillian glanced at the digital clock on Nolan's desk. "You might feel prepared for your trial today, but I'm not prepared for mine."

"It's not a trial, Jillian. It's a conversation. You agreed to go down to Trinidad and learn about Cate's work. That's all."

"I know that and you know that, but she has hammered me with so much information she expects me to have read."

"Just be honest." Nolan flipped through a file of his own. "It was only day before yesterday that she was here. You had a full load of work to do. You're going down in person so she can have your full attention."

"Does that really work when you're not prepared?"

"Don't be ridiculous." Nolan dropped another file into his briefcase. "I'm never not prepared."

"Dad! That's not helpful."

Nolan's phone sang again. Jillian's eyes pled. He silenced the call. She would be on the road in a few minutes.

"What time is court?" she asked.

"Eleven thirty."

"I might be calling you before that."

"And I will of course do my best to take the call," Nolan said, "but Jillian, you are underestimating yourself. You know this, right?"

"So you tell me."

"You'll go down there and size up the situation just like you do every job you take."

Jillian fiddled with the desk clock. "I've tried to call Drew, but I keep getting his voice mail. I hope he hasn't forgotten about me."

"I doubt that is possible. You are ever on his mind."

"Don't get sappy. You know I don't like sappy."

"Noted."

"I still wish you were coming."

"You'll have Drew, and you can tell me all about it when you get home."

"I really want to like Cate."

Nolan met the green eyes that matched his. The rest of her face looked so much like Bella, but her eyes were his. "I think you do like her. That's why this is hard."

"She looks like Mom, doesn't she, Dad?"

He nodded. "Obviously she has other genes mixed in, but she surprised us both."

"And the hair."

He chuckled. "Definitely the Parisi hair."

"It was like looking at that old photograph of those little girls in New Orleans that was in Mom's trunk. You know the one?"

"I do. Under the Parisi Green Grocer's sign."

She nodded, eyes glistening.

Bella Parisi Duffy had been gone for fifteen years, and the pain of her absence was tempered by the years—most days. Nolan wished he could remember any scrap of information she'd ever spoken about that old photo tucked away in her trunk in the attic for the years of their life together. If she'd been sure of anything she would have written something on the back of the picture, but she hadn't. Jillian was on her own for clues.

"Have you told Cate about that photo?" Nolan said.

Jillian shook her head. "I guess I should, if I think those could be Lou's daughters." She pushed the air out of her lungs.

"You're feeling a lot of things, Jillian. Maybe more than most people feel when they find out they have a distant cousin because she does remind you of Mom and there's no one else."

She nodded again.

"Drew is waiting, and he loves you."

Jillian fake-coughed, her latest half-hearted response when Nolan said anything about Drew's affection that might embarrass her, even if it was true and she knew it.

"You know," Nolan said, "if Nia were here, she would be cooking up one of her children's sermons. I recall the one she told about God disturbing a little boy named Samuel's sleep. It took him three times before he figured it out and said yes to the calling."

"So I'm going to do this even if the reason on Cate's end is that she wants something I probably can't give her because I might miss a calling from God if I don't?"

It was Nolan's turn to nod. "Maybe. Phone me later." He kissed her cheek.

He kept an ear cocked as she gathered her things, left the house, and backed her compact SUV out of the garage.

"Bella, my love, I wish you could see our girl now," he said aloud. He had been the first to declare his love. Practical Bella made sure what she was getting into. Law school for Nolan. Years of a grueling schedule getting established in a practice. What shape her own artistic leanings might take. But Nolan waited. He knew he was the only one for Bella.

Nolan lifted his phone to return the call he'd silenced earlier. "Do you have further instructions? I'm starting to be pressed for time, but I'll stop by Kris's shop and make doubly sure she is clear on the nonnegotiables."

"Just make sure she knows she needs to take my calls."

CHAPTER FIVE

Pueblo, Colorado

THE TWO-LANE ROAD SHOT arrow-like off the highway out of Pueblo and across wide open grazing land. Jillian was getting close. The drive from Canyon Mines to the ranch where Drew's family had lived for over a century dropped five thousand feet in altitude, and this was about the point where Jillian usually was waiting for the pressure in her ears to finally pop. She stretched her jaw open to force the process. The black iron gate was open as it nearly always was. A couple of decades ago, when the ranch still was a working cattle operation, various gates around the property were closed more consistently. Now there was a lot less reason to worry about valuable animals going astray. The horses, including the white steed Drew had been astride the day Jillian first met him, had their own secure stable and fenced pasture, and a handful of other animals were housed deeper into the property also in fenced areas. These days the property belonged to a family foundation and was more sentimental and recreational than income generating. The family was in the process of parting with a few outlying acres to help support upkeep costs.

Early October was a favorite time of year for Jillian—still stunning cerulean skies but precipitation increasingly depositing layers of white in the mountains at higher elevations. At these lower flatlands, early winter storms were possible but generally transient. Instead, the rolling seasons relieved the air of true heat and left instead the hope of invigorating brisk refreshment—the best kind of running weather, in Jillian's opinion. When she'd first come to the ranch a few months earlier, a suspicious interloper chasing all the wrong theories on a genealogy case that started out more as a side favor to her father but soon consumed her mind, the creek bed was running with snow melt and the mule deer were migrating. With the views of the Wet Mountains and Sangre de Cristos, the setting could not be more enchanting. Now she'd been back several times as a welcome guest.

Jillian navigated down the unpaved ranch road to the trim simple frame structure whose color provided its moniker, the little red house. In front of it, a gravel area marked off parking sufficient for a several vehicles, and on either side of the door, two large green planters were nearly finished with the colorful yield of assorted flowers arranged with care.

Not by Drew. He'd made sure Jillian knew that. His great-aunt, Min, could be gruff around the edges at times, but she first started helping to plant flower beds outside the little red house when she was a girl and had never stopped. The green planters had been her idea a few years ago. The little red house might be over a hundred years old, but Jillian had been inside it several times in the last few months and knew it was well cared for and updated to be a place of warmth and solidity. It could have been transported to any neighborhood in Pueblo or Canyon Mines and done nicely for a cozy starter home. The barn-red color found more appeal in Jillian's eyes each time she visited.

Nolan said that was because of who lived inside.

Jillian set the brake on her small SUV because her muscles couldn't interrupt their habit after learning to drive in a mountain town even while her brain reminded her the vehicle had no chance of rolling anywhere on this flat patch of earth. Whatever gentle incline involved in reaching the main house from here did not affect parking a car in the gravel. But since she had set it, she left it alone and got out. Drew's truck filled the closest parking spot, and this eased her breath. They'd talked during her drive down and he'd promised to be waiting for her.

And here he was. His truck was right where it was supposed to be. Jillian pulled the messenger bag she'd packed with a narrow-lined legal pad for taking notes, a pro-size iPad that did everything a laptop did on the fly with less weight, and a hair brush. Somehow driving down to see someone who had the same untamed head of hair made her want to be prepared.

The door of the little red house, which Drew had recently decided to paint a cheery blue, opened and he smiled at her.

"By my calculations," he said, "it's been twenty-three miles since we spoke. Far too far."

Jillian grinned from the inside out. It was true she'd been on the phone with Drew for two lengthy stretches of the drive, but the relief of seeing his face let her shoulders release their tension. Drew opened his arms and Jillian walked into them, turning her face up for his kiss. To her delight, he obliged quite nicely, and with no one around to watch, they took their time with mouths eager to make up for time apart.

"Mmm," Jillian said. "Hello."

Drew kissed her again, slowly and purposefully. Jillian let a hand wander up the back of his neck to find the dark curls at his collar that had delighted her from the beginning.

"Aunt Min made us a coffee cake," he said softly.

Jillian laughed into his chest. "Aunt Min baked for you? She's aware of your credentials, isn't she?" Drew was a master dessert chef. When it came to food, anything he touched sparkled.

"She is not confident in my preparedness for guests. Remember the first time you were here?"

"Bottled tea and a bag of pita chips."

"In my defense, I was not expecting company."

"In your defense, I never expected to be invited in. I was trespassing."

"I remember." He kissed her yet again. "And Min turned up to throw you off the ranch."

"So now she likes me." She stroked the side of his face, her finger trailing to his single dimple, her eyes fixed on his gray orbs.

"Very much. The coffee should be ready."

Arms around each other, they turned to go inside.

At about eight hundred square feet, the little red house was more than sufficient for a bachelor on his own. The front room dominated the space, with a fireplace that no doubt was once the only source of heat and a wall of bookshelves. Drew had clarified early that the contents of the shelves represented family history and he wasn't supposed to re-arrange things drastically. Some of the clutter Jillian had first seen six months earlier had been sorted out—or at least hidden away—but the furnishings remained eclectic leftovers from decades of previous occu-pants or cast-offs from the main house. Min now lived there alone, but it had housed growing and shrinking families through the Kyp family history. Min had raised her own family there when she and her husband took over the ranch's operations from her grandparents and parents.

Drew set a latte—he'd invested in a machine just for Jillian's visits—and a slice of cake on the coffee table while Jillian settled in the couch.

"I know you're still nervous," he said, "but I'll be there, and I know the area. We'll find out what this Cate wants, and my guess is I can steer her to some local resources to help her."

"Do you really think so?" Jillian cupped her hands around her mug. "Maybe if I just listen and nod a lot, and you swoop in with ideas about who she really ought to be talking to, we can get past this awkwardness and just be cousins."

"She might have to do some listening too. Listen to what being a genealogist means and what the limitations are."

"Well, I wouldn't say there are limitations, exactly."

"Boundaries, then?"

Jillian nodded. "That's what my dad says. Boundaries. Except he's busy ignoring me, at least this morning."

Drew chewed slowly. "Probably has work on his mind."

"Whatever. I'll call him later."

"Good. Did you bring an overnight bag like I suggested?"

"Yep."

"Phew. Aunt Min is off helping to organize a church rummage sale in Pueblo, but she'll be back this evening, or at least in time for a visit in the morning before you head home."

"I'd like to see her too."

"Your room is ready at the main house. That's what she calls it. Jillian's room. I think she wants you to know it will always be there for you, but you know Min. She has trouble saying things like that."

Jillian gave a half-smile. "Min."

"How long do you think this meeting with Cate will take?"

"I have no idea. Considering that I didn't do my homework, she might make me stay after school."

"That is not happening. I'm telling you that right now."

"My knight in shining armor."

"Cate, me, Aunt Min. Your docket is full. Besides, no one can solve everything in one day."

"Thank you for coming with me."

He drew two fingers along her jaw. "You'll never have to ask me twice for something like this. Ever."

Jillian melted into his gray eyes. His dark hair always seemed to be just past time for a haircut and produced those curls at his collar. The dimple in one cheek was not a reason to love a man, but it sure did make her want to settle her eyes on him and soak up the affection that shone from his features.

She checked the time on her phone. "We should probably go. An hour to Trinidad?"

"Could be more from this side of Pueblo."

Jillian grimaced. "Then we really should go."

Drew reached for her coffee cup and paused to squeeze her hand. "We still have the ride down. We'll take my truck and you can relax."

"I should do some homework."

"Nah. She's going to tell you the important stuff anyway."

He was right. She freshened up, and they left. Knowing that she could come back to the ranch for the night, with Drew and Min, and wake up to its views had a remarkable effect on her awareness of stress. Listen, nod, redirect, and come out of it with a cousin. It was a good strategy.

The drive down, taking her deeper into southern Colorado than even her previous trips to Pueblo, reminded Jillian of how different the landscape and history of this part of the state were. Cate could get agitated. This was true. But she was curious and passionate about history. The two of them had that in common. Once Cate understood that someone else—perhaps someone local—could assist her better, Jillian might have a lot to learn from her generations-lost cousin.

Drew slowed as they approached a traditional main street in Trinidad, a municipality of eight or nine thousand people, and went looking for an address slightly off the beaten path.

"Here's the bookstore." Jillian pointed. "Cate said she's above that, in a shared suite."

Drew cruised for a good spot to leave the truck, and they walked hand-in-hand back toward the bookstore and the side entrance to the stairs that took them to the offices above.

"Number 207," Jillian said.

"Down here." Drew led the way to a door with four businesses listed on it.

"Butler Education Exhibits," Jillian said. "That's it."

"The business name is a little stuffy."

Jillian shrugged. "Maybe it's temporary."

Drew put a finger on one of the other names. "Epic EduKids. Now there's a name."

Jillian blew out breath.

"You ready?"

"As I'll ever be."

Drew opened the door onto a shared waiting area with four doors opening onto it. Someone had made an effort with a sofa, chairs, coffee table and lamps—the landlord, Jillian supposed, since the common space served all the offices. Each door had a repeat of the relevant business signs from the hall door, and there was no receptionist.

"I guess we just knock," Jillian said.

She rapped the door of Butler Education Exhibits, and a young blond woman answered.

"I'm sorry," Jillian said, "We were looking for Cate Butler."

"You're in the right place. I'm Patrice, her assistant. On my way out to buy more copy paper. Go on through."

"Come on in!" Cate's voice came from inside the office.

Jillian and Drew stepped in.

Cate dropped her pen. "Drew!"

"Rini!"

CHAPTER SIX

Tuesday, September 23, 1913
Berwind, Colorado

THEY HAD WASTED TWO WHOLE DAYS. The thought pulsed constantly through Caterina's mind until it erupted nearly unceasingly from her lips.

"You've said that, Caterina." Geppetto's patience was starting to fray like his shirt cuffs, tiny threads catching in his voice. "The train only moves so fast, and I can't make it go any faster."

"We should have come yesterday. Or the day before."

"You were still trying to reach Chiara on a telephone to tell her about the invitation."

"Someone cut the telephone lines, Geppetto. There is only one line for all the miners who live in Berwind, and someone cut the line."

"Probably."

"The other line, the one for the mine operators, that one probably still works."

"Yes, Caterina. Everything you say is true."

"The owner of Colorado Fuel and Iron does not want to talk about the strikers' demands. He said it would be a 'strike to the finish.' I do not like the way that sounds, Geppetto."

"I know. I also read the newspaper, and if Carrick hears other news, he tells me." Geppetto took her hand and moved it from her lap to his. "But I cannot change any of that for you. I would if I could. You know that."

"Today is the day. The strike day. We waited too long."

"We don't know that."

The train rumbled, and Caterina gave herself to its sway. If Giuseppe were with them, he would be enthralled and wiggling off her lap to explore the massive wonder that carried them from Pueblo to Walsenburg and then south. The gray foreboding sky above the ranch when she placed Peppy in Ela's arms had given way to rain that clattered against the steel of the passenger carriage in a taunting rhythm and bursts of fury. After a brief pause at the Ludlow Depot, the train finally cut westward into the Berwind Canyon on the last short leg of the journey to the company town that housed the families of the miners who blasted coal out of the mountains around the clock.

Caterina's spine straightened. "We should have gotten off."

"We're here now," Geppetto said. "The train will stop again in a minute."

"Back there, before the depot." Caterina craned her neck. "I was looking out the wrong side of the train and thinking how much I hated the rain on this day. I didn't think much of it."

"I also was looking at the mountains. And the pump station. Little Peppy would love to see the pump station."

"Yes, he would. But we missed it, Geppetto. They were putting up tents."

Their eyes met.

"For the strikers," he said.

The train stopped and the whistle blew.

"Chiara, where are you?" Caterina whispered.

"We will get off the train and make sure she is not still here." Geppetto stood and tugged Caterina's hand. "We don't even know if Celestrino will really strike."

Caterina scoffed. "It was a unanimous vote. Celestrino is no scab."

"They might still be packing. What is the address you have?"

Berwind had nearly two hundred homes, none as sound and snug as the little red house where the Parisi lived. With no charm to commend them or distinguish them from each other, houses in tight rows butted up against the rock canyon like a coal seam, a stone wall seemingly placed to keep them from sliding into the road that Caterina and Geppetto walked.

Caterina shivered. The damp air was colder than at home, and as she raised her scarf to cover her head the moisture she was blinking off her eyelids was snowflakes, not raindrops.

"Oh Geppetto, what a miserable day. We wanted to do a good thing, and Ela was so kind, and it is all so ugly."

"Button your coat, Caterina."

"Why is it snowing on September 23?"

"Because this is Colorado, not the south of Italy. It will be warm again soon enough."

"But this is the day we must find Chiara and Celestrino." Caterina stepped out of the way of a wagon. "They are leaving. The wagons. The carts." There were even a few trucks loading spindly furniture and bags of provisions that did not look promising to Caterina.

The only other people resisting the exodus were an occasional woman running back for a pot or children protesting in languages Caterina did not understand while gesticulating at toys left behind.

"The house number." Geppetto prodded her, and they pressed on the search. "We must be sure."

The front door of the house clattered open, caught in a gust.

"It always does that," Caterina said. "Chiara wrote me about it. The latch never holds."

Inside, the wooden A-frame house held a bare bed frame, a table, a stove, several chairs, some lamps. At most, the dwelling was half the size of the little red house at the ranch.

An electrical pole stood right outside, but when Geppetto flipped a light switch, no illumination resulted. "They have already cut the electricity."

"There are no photos, no clothes, no dishes." Caterina opened a wardrobe and then a cupboard to be sure. "They've left the things that belong to the company and taken what belonged to them. Geppetto, where have they gone?"

He wrapped her in his arms. "We will find her."

She swallowed hard and nodded. They were here to find Chiara and Celestrino and take them home. There would be time for tears later—tears of relief.

Outside Geppetto waved down people in the street and began asking, "Do you know the people who live in this house?"

He tried English.

He tried Italian.

He attempted Spanish, but even Caterina knew he wasn't getting it right.

All he got in return were puzzled stares and shakes of heads.

The miners came from so many countries. That was one of the

reasons that Chiara was so lonely. She spoke only Italian, and the other Italians were scattered all around Berwind instead of living near each other.

"We will just follow them," Geppetto said. "Wherever they are going is probably where Celestrino took Chiara."

"They don't even have a cart to call their own."

"Neither do we, Caterina."

"But we could, if we needed one. If we didn't live on the ranch. Carrick and Ela pay us more than Celestrino earns, and you don't have to buy your own wire to fix Carrick's fence, and I don't have to buy my own pot to help Ela cook. It's not the same."

"You're right, of course."

"We put a little aside every month, don't we?"

"Yes, we do. Every month."

"And we don't owe anybody anything. We earn our way."

"That's right."

"Ela and Carrick are very generous, but Geppetto, we work very hard."

"Yes, we do."

"Chiara says that if she were not already so sick because of the child, she would be sick unto death because of how much they owe the company store."

"I know, Caterina." Geppetto slung an arm around her shoulders. "We will find them, and we will take them to the ranch where they will be safe during the strike."

They walked without speaking for a few moments, hearing instead of their own words the amalgam of pitched voices around them churning with every turn of a cart wheel. Triumphed voices. Frenzied voices. Fearful voices. Exasperated voices. Sleepless voices.

Caterina understood all of that—without understanding any of the words. A Greek accent ahead of them, perhaps Hungarian behind, Spanish definitely, and Portuguese. Japanese even. Many others she could not identify. Surely there would be Italian or English eventually. They would need to find someone to talk to about Chiara, and she and Geppetto only spoke two languages.

The rain could not make up its mind whether to freeze. Caterina could not make up her mind whether it was worse when the rain pelted her face or when the snow was so frigid that she could not stop worrying whether Chiara had a warm coat.

She would give Chiara her coat.

When a line of women snaked past them, Caterina turned to them hopefully. "Chiara? Do you know Chiara?"

They shook their heads and hefted their sacks of meager household goods a little higher.

"Celestrino?" Geppetto said to the men.

They grunted past with their hand carts, a horse and wagon if they were lucky, children trotting to keep pace.

"¿Donde?" Geppetto asked. "¿A donde vamos?"

He didn't know much more Spanish than that, but if he could find out where they were headed, the effort would not be wasted.

Finally a man paused for breath. "Ludlow. La colonia."

"The colony. The tents," Caterina whispered. They were right.

Geppetto nodded.

"Will there be a train?"

He shook his head. "We should not count on that. But it's only a couple of miles. Three at most."

Caterina took his hand. "Then let's hurry."

A few feet ahead of them, a small boy stumbled and landed in the sodden dirt.

Geppetto released Caterina's hand and scooped up the child before he could catch his breath enough to squall.

A young woman—a very young woman—came running. "Niño."

"Mama!"

"He is fine."

"Gracias."

Caterina saw now that the woman—she was so young—carried a new babe along with struggling to keep a fist closed around the top of her bag of belongings.

"We will help." Caterina straightened the shawl sliding off the young mother's shoulders. "Carry him, Geppetto."

Geppetto opened his jacket and tucked the boy inside, just as he would have done for Peppy. His mother's eyes grew wide with gratitude.

Caterina gasped. The baby! Her own coat was off her shoulders and around the young woman's in an instant, and Caterina would accept no protest. Ela had insisted she wear a wool sweater over her woolen dress that morning because the sky felt so damp. Caterina wasn't warm, but she willed herself not to shiver in front of the mother who now wore her coat.

There must be a husband somewhere. A young woman alone with two very small children in a mining camp? The two women smiled at each other, the wordless language.

Caterina eyed the company store as they passed it, a two-story wooden structure with a front porch and a balcony, and tried to picture Chiara there. It looked locked up now, no more credit for the families of striking miners. Chiara detested that place. She needed it for everything that sustained their life, and she felt spat on every time she went through the doors.

A train whistled.

"Niño, Niño," the young mother said. She was already trying to shirk off Caterina's coat.

"No, you keep it." Caterina fastened the button at the woman's neck again.

The train whistled again.

"¡Niño!" She held her infant in one arm and reached for the boy with the other.

Geppetto put him in her arms, and she hitched him on her hip. "Gracias."

And she hustled away toward the train.

"Will they let us ride the train, Geppetto?" Caterina asked. Anyone unencumbered by carts or animals was scrambling aboard.

"I think we should walk." Geppetto transferred his jacket to Caterina. "The train is getting crowded already. I would hate for us to take space that a mining family should have."

Hot tears flooded Caterina's eyes as she plunged her hands into the deep pockets of her husband's barn jacket. He was right, of course. The miners were a woeful stream leaving the terrors they knew for the terrors they did not yet know, and she and Geppetto had a warm bed and good jobs waiting for them. But it was freezing and gray and snowing and miserable, and wherever Chiara was, she was at least two miles away.

CHAPTER SEVEN

Trinidad, Colorado

RINI? WHY WAS DREW staring at Cate Butler with such a pleasurable look of recognition? This was Jillian's fourth cousin, once removed. He'd seen her photo. Or had he? Jillian rapidly inventoried her intentions and actions and found the gap. She'd never forwarded to Drew the selfie with Cate when she visited Canyon Mines earlier in the week. Nolan had snapped it on Cate's phone, and Cate had immediately sent it to Jillian. Jillian meant to send it to Drew so he could see for himself what she'd told him about the two of them having the same family hair.

But she never had.

Something had interrupted her. Kris Bryant had showed up with a quart of chocolate chip cookie dough ice cream for Jillian and another of cherry chocolate chip chunk for Nolan just in time for dessert that night. That's what happened. Delectables from Kris's Ore the Mountain shop could distract a person from anything.

Now Cate Butler—Rini?—was coming around her desk with a wide, welcoming smile on her face aimed at Drew more than Jillian.

"I wasn't expecting you," Cate said. "Do you know my new cuz?"

"I do," he said. "Very well. I hope you don't mind if I crash the party."

He kissed both of Cate's cheeks, and she his, in a gesture that was alarmingly unsetting to Jillian. Just how well did he know Cate?

"Rini?" Jillian said, both the word and her face a question.

"Right," Drew said. "Jillian only told me her cousin's name was Cate."

"Close the door, please." Cate tone sobered.

Jillian complied.

"I'm not Rini when I'm here," Cate said. "I use the professional name Cate Butler. I live and work down here for a reason."

"What's going on, Rini?" Drew said.

"Drew, I know we go way back," Cate said, "but please humor me."

"I beg your pardon," he said. "Cate. But why?"

Cate Butler was not Cate Butler. She was Rini somebody. No wonder Jillian hadn't been able to find traces of Cate Butler in the preliminary digging she'd done. In her experience, though, most people who changed their names came to their new monikers by a method that was far from random.

"Jillian, I was going to tell you," Cate said. "Obviously. I know you want to meet my family—your family—so it's not like I could keep it a secret indefinitely."

"Okay." Jillian shifted her weight. "I'm not meeting them today so I can keep your secret."

"I'll pinky swear, if you want me to," Drew said.

"I just have to keep parts of my life separate right now," Cate said. "You probably didn't even know I was living down here."

"I did not," Drew said. "I see you often enough in Pueblo. You never mentioned it."

"Working in Pueblo is an unfortunate necessity, but it's worth the hour drive to come here to sleep, no matter how late it is."

Jillian was lost. Drew saw Cate—Rini—often in Pueblo? Why would that be?

"Patrice is going to be back soon with the copy paper. It's her job to make sure we never run out, but somehow we often do. We can't talk here, and she is only one reason."

Somehow confronting historical truth in a righteous way had morphed into cloak and dagger.

"I take it you have a better suggestion," Drew said.

"There's a restaurant down the street with a back room that doesn't get used much." Cate circled back to her desk to reach underneath for an oversized purse and pushed a folder into it.

A back room? Jillian was losing track of the reasons she was glad Drew was with her.

They turned to leave the office.

"Do you need to leave your assistant a note?" Jillian asked.

"She saw you arrive. She'll figure it out." Cate pulled the door closed behind her and checked the lock.

The space at the restaurant was indeed a back room. Possibly not all that long ago it had been a storeroom, but with a coat of pale green paint that hadn't yet lost the last of its odor, several eclectic but interesting lamps for ambient lighting, and three small square tables that offered flexible arrangement, it passed as a private meeting room with access to the establishment's full menu. The restaurant itself, decorated with enlarged photos of Trinidad's history, offered American fare with southwestern accents.

"Don't get your hopes up, Drew," Cate said. "We're not actually here because of the menu."

"Surely a decent sandwich?" he said.

"Chicken salad is passable. I keep trying to get them to lay off the salt and add some herbs instead, but I may have to bring some in to prove my point."

"That's a hearty endorsement."

"I don't mind the tomato soup. They do an open-faced cheese bread with it that they usually manage to brown just right."

"Wow," Jillian said, "I didn't realize you were another foodie."

"Not like Drew. I don't cook."

"But the herbs and chicken salad," Jillian said.

"Oh, not mine. Drew's. Have you never had it?"

Jillian pinched her eyebrows together. Just how often had Drew made Cate—Rini?—chicken salad?

"Why don't I go to the counter and order us all some soup and cheese bread," Drew said. "Then we can explain to Jillian how we know each other."

Yes. Please do. So many questions.

"It's not what you think," Cate said once Drew had left the room.

"I don't really think anything." Jillian arranged her messenger bag on the back of her chair. She was twenty-nine, and Drew was a little older. They both had pasts.

Of course, during the last six months she thought they'd covered significant past romances. She would have remembered if he'd mentioned an unusual name like Rini.

"We've known each other since we were young," Cate said.

"And you still see each other?" Jillian bit her own tongue, but it was too late. The words were out.

"It's hard not too. Given the situation."

"Excuse me." Jillian reached for a paper napkin to dab at her bleeding tongue.

"We don't go out of our way to see each other or anything."

Paper shredded in Jillian's mouth. This wasn't going well.

"Are you all right?" Cate said.

"Sorry. I bit my tongue."

"And it won't stop bleeding. That happens to me!" Cate smiled and her lip turned up the way Grandpa Steve's always had. Who else had the lopsided smile? Jillian didn't yet know the names of the ancestors they ultimately shared, parents of the Parisi brothers who had immigrated from Italy to Louisiana.

Jillian tried to spit out the bits of paper napkin.

"Sorry they haven't brought water glasses yet. There's a water fountain in the hall," Cate said, "if you think that would help."

"Probably. Thanks."

Managing to keep her papered tongue inside her mouth, Jillian left the private dining room/storeroom/reunion space for Drew and a woman from his past. She found the water fountain, swished out the remains of paper napkin without provoking more blood, and checked the time on her phone. So far this day seemed four days long. Was it really only this morning she'd been frustrated with her father's inattentiveness? Sometime since she and Drew had arrived in Trinidad, Nolan had sent a text.

ON A BREATHER FROM COURT. HOW'S IT GOING?

She shrugged as if he could see her and responded. IT'S GOING. By now he was probably back in court or on to his mediation. This was not a conversation for text messages.

Back in the private dining room/storeroom/reunion space for Drew and a woman from his past, Drew had returned with the soup and cheese bread—and was laughing with Cate as he laid out food on the table.

Jillian arranged her lips out in a wide smile. "This smells good."

"I talked them into slicing some green olives onto the bread before they broiled it," Drew said.

"Sounds delicious."

"It is!" Cate picked up a piece of bread and waved it under Jillian's nose. "Wait till you taste it."

So Cate, the woman from Drew's past, knew about his secret touch on cheese bread.

"Then let's eat." Jillian eyed Drew and sat beside him, hoping that's what he meant when he laid out the food that as he had.

"So what's with the name change?" Drew asked.

"It's not a change, exactly," Cate said. "More like a Pueblo name and a Trinidad name."

"That sounds confusing."

"Cate Butler and Rini Butler?" Jillian asked.

"Rini Polombo," Drew said.

"Caterina Polombo," Cate said. "My family always called me Rini, ever since I was little. Drew has known me forever because his family has always supported our restaurants even before he started working in them."

"Mary Lou's Kitchen is your family's restaurant?" Jillian said.

"We also have an Italian restaurant. Mary Lou's is named for my mother, Mary Lou Butler. Diversifying, my parents called it."

"Let me guess, she's not Italian."

"Nope. And neither is the restaurant. Upscale, modern, chic."

"Drew has told me about it. I just haven't been there yet."

"You probably knew he was working there more before he moved out to the ranch to help look after his aunt and the animals."

Jillian nodded. Drew had also wanted more flexibility to pursue opportunities for his singing career than the role of head chef and manager at a restaurant allowed. Now he focused on desserts and filled in when they needed him, if he was available.

So when Cate said she had to work a shift, she meant in one of the restaurants.

Jillian looked from Drew to Cate, her mouth drying from the effort to form words.

All these months of dating Drew, only to discover he had known generations of her family his entire life. Jillian had been down to the ranch outside Pueblo a few times. More often Drew visited Canyon Mines. A few times they'd met in Monument or Colorado Springs when neither of them could manage more than a day trip away from their responsibilities. Sometimes Jillian had traveled to where Drew was giving a concert with his incredible classically trained tenor voice. Even if she'd ever visited Mary Lou's Kitchen at some point, she wouldn't have known she had a connection to the Polombos. There must have been several name changes, brought about by marriage, since the original Parisi brothers.

Before Cate, Jillian hadn't had a single lead to work with. If she had seen a whisper of Grandpa Steve's smile in someone's face at the restaurant, she would only have thought she was imagining things. And the thick, black, curly hair she shared with Cate—many other Italian women also shared some version of it.

"I guess now you're really going to want to visit the restaurant," Cate said.

"I guess so." Jillian nodded.

"I'm still a little lost, Rini—Cate," Drew said. "Why not just be Cate Polombo if you felt like you outgrew your family nickname? Why Cate Butler?"

"You know what my family is like." Cate played with her bread without eating it. "How long did it take you to get them to believe you were going to stop working full-time?"

"A long time."

"And you weren't even family." Cate dropped her bread in her plate. "I don't want to go into the family business. I don't want to just be Vince and Mary Lou Polombo's daughter. I went to college. I earned a degree. I went to graduate school and earned another one."

"You landed a grant," Jillian added. "You've accomplished something."

"Not a very big grant, unfortunately. I still have to go back to Pueblo to work a couple of shifts a week at one of the restaurants to make ends meet. But I almost always drive back here to sleep in my own place, no matter how late it is."

"A grant is a strong professional start," Jillian said. "You'll get your career off the ground."

"If I don't get it kicked out from under me first. I have to start showing some results soon or I could lose it all. Somebody doesn't want me to succeed."

"Now we're getting down to business." Drew broke his bread in half.

"What do you mean, Cate?" Jillian asked.

"I told you that somebody is trying to tell some pretty big lies that will be a lot nicer than the truth I want to tell about what happened at Ludlow in 1913. What I didn't tell you the other day is that this other organization rented space in the same office suite where I am."

"Epic EduKids."

"Yep. They're getting hold of my information and want to use it in all the wrong ways."

Drew asked, "How would they be getting it?"

"I don't know. But they're pitching the idea of a permanent exhibit to the local museum in Trinidad that is very similar to what I'm trying to do—except it gets all the facts wrong. Just enough wrong to be more attractive and seem right if you watch enough badly researched historical television shows." Cate pushed her dishes away. She'd barely touched her food. "And there's nothing I can do to stop it."

Under the table, Drew reached for Jillian's hand and squeezed it.

"You should hear how they're trying to romanticize what life was like for children during the strike." Cate rolled her eyes. "I want to show the life of children, but not like that."

"Cate," Jillian said with care, "I'm sorry this is happening to you. I'm sure it's hard and feels unfair."

"It is unfair."

Jillian nodded. "I'm not sure what you think I can do."

"I need help. I'm not too proud to ask."

"Rini," Drew said, "do you think I make a good pastry?"

"What are you talking about, Drew? I have a problem here."

"Do I make a good pastry?"

"You make a great pastry. The best. I tell everybody I know that."

"A lot of people are satisfied with a good pastry, and you'll never convince them to pay what your parents charge for a great one."

"Get to the point, Drew."

"You want to make a great pastry with layers of pure butter. And patience. You can't control if some people are satisfied with something made out of lard and shortcuts."

"But if they're trying to make it by stealing my recipe and using cheap ingredients, I don't have to sit by and watch it happen." Cate sank against the back of her chair and fixed her eyes on Jillian. "I've done my research. I know you're respected all around the state—regionally, nationally even. I need someone with your kind of standing to help me."

CHAPTER EIGHT

TWO EGGS OR THREE? Nolan caught himself before cracking four. It wasn't a large skillet. He was on his own for supper tonight after having almost no time to get the details of Jillian's overnight trip to see Cate. She'd arrived home around lunch time on Friday and dived right back into her work schedule, and he'd had his own stack of files to plow through. Working from home offices didn't mean they didn't have to keep up with commitments and earn a living. Nolan thought they'd have the evening to debrief over a real dinner.

Then Nia Dunston showed up, in that way she tended to do, impromptu and insisting the gang was overdue for a gaggle and a casual supper at the Canary Cage. No discussion. And no Nolan. Just Nia, Veronica, Kris, and Jillian.

So here Nolan was, chopping vegetables and cracking eggs, for a simple frittata. He was tempted to also throw together a dessert Jillian would find irresistible so she would still sit and tell him about her trip to Trinidad. He wasn't just being nosy. If Jillian found her Italian family, that meant she would also find Bella's family. She might have answers Bella never had because her own father was never interested in the questions.

How proud Bella would be of the path their daughter had chosen for her life to help people mend the broken branches in their family trees, and how touched she would be that Jillian was at last climbing up through the generations of Parisis about which Bella had known so little. At least, Jillian would do it if she could navigate past whatever it was that agitated Cate Butler.

Nolan whisked his eggs as Jillian's phone exploded with another round of text alerts. Despite her effort to come home and focus on work, she must have been flustered. Jillian never forgot her phone. Almost never. Her driver's license, debit card, and emergency cash were tucked into its case. Normally that was the one thing she grabbed when she left the house, and she was ready for anything. No doubt she was getting quite the ribbing from her friends once they discovered her missing appendage.

But there it was, on the kitchen counter beside her gleaming fancy coffee machine, making noise. Since she was with her mainstay girl-friends, and none of her clients were after-hours incessant texters, this could only be Cate. Nolan was experiencing firsthand what Jillian had been moaning about for a week.

The vegetables in the small cast iron skillet—yellow onions, green and red peppers, spinach—were nicely sautéed. Nolan gave them one last stir, poured the whisked eggs over them, and dropped in some feta cheese.

Jillian's phone went off again, ringing with an incoming call for the third time since she'd left the house. Did she not know where the silence button was? He couldn't be sure it was Cate every time the phone rang, but considering the peace and quiet that typically characterized the Parisi-Duffy household, he had his suspicions. Nolan was on the brink of violating his rule of respecting his grown daughter's personal belongings. He waited for the call to roll into voice mail after the fourth ring.

Nolan set a plate out on the breakfast bar, ready to receive his meal in another couple of minutes, and filled a glass with peach tea. As long as he was on his own, he had time to sort the mail. Lately they'd both taken to retrieving it from the box and tossing it on the piano at the far end of the living room to look at later. This was later, so Nolan went to grab it.

He took his plate of food to the nook table in the kitchen—the breakfast bar was where he and Jillian liked to eat together so he pre-ferred not to eat there alone—and sorted junk from envelopes he might need to open, setting aside anything addressed to Jillian. She would roll her eyes at why he didn't pitch most of it straight into the recycling bin, and he would point out that was her prerogative. It had her name on it and he wasn't in the habit of making decisions for her. This was the game they played.

His appetite satisfied and the magazines they subscribed to by choice separated from the pure junk with his name on it and first class letters stacked off to one side, Nolan collected Jillian's mail and padded through the kitchen to leave it on the chair in her office.

Ding, ding, ding.

She'd left her computer on, with her email screen open. Nolan could see immediately that the clatter was coming from Cate Butler's gmail account.

Seven emails from Cate in the last ninety minutes. Three contained the words PLEASE HELP in the subject line. The last one was in all capital letters. URGENT.

Nolan glanced down at the dock running across the bottom of Jillian's computer monitor. He wasn't familiar with all the software she used in her work, but he knew the basics. Curiosity and the nosiness he tried to avoid were difficult to distinguish in the moment. The app for text messages, which she could receive on her computer as well as her phone, indicated sixteen unread messages. And of course there were the three phone calls.

"Well, Silly Jilly," Nolan said aloud in the empty room, "your father suddenly feels obliged to check on you."

In the kitchen, Nolan took his own car keys out of the copper bowl where he habitually left them so he would always know where they were, picked up Jillian's phone, grabbed a light jacket off a hook near the back door, and headed for the garage.

Even in a small town like Canyon Mines people were looking for something to do on a Friday night, and parking was enough of a bother to make Nolan wish he had just power walked the mile between home and the Cage. Finally someone pulled out of a spot in front of Candles & Cards. Nolan grabbed the spot just across the street from the coffee shop. Clark stayed open till nine thirty on Fridays, and he wouldn't boot people out even then as long as they were regular buying customers. It was still early enough that plenty of people were enjoying the sandwiches and soups Clark had on offer or inspected the baked goods case in pairs or small groups, savoring the expectation of an end-of-week treat along with their conversation.

But the Friendly Foursome were not there.

Nolan tried to catch the eye of Joanna Maddon, Clark's niece who had turned up last spring to collect on his offer of a job if she ever wanted to come to Colorado. She shrugged at him as if to say, If you want to talk to me, get in line and buy something. Even when the shop wasn't busy, she made Nolan pay for information.

"What can I get for you, Nolan?"

"I just finished my supper, thank you."

"Then what are you doing here during our dinner rush?"

For a young woman barely twenty years old, she was remarkably cheeky with the older crowd.

"How much is this going to cost me?"

"Depends on what you're buying." Jo tapped her fingers on the cash register. "Just doing my part to keep my uncle's joint profitable."

"A little job security scheme, if you ask me."

"All I asked you is what I can get you."

She had him there.

"A little information," he said.

"Ah. Sandwiches. Soup. Pastries. That's more what I had in mind."

"No coffee?"

"There you go." Jo hit a button on the register. "One extra large black coffee coming right up."

"You know I don't drink coffee at this hour."

"Because you're old, right?"

"You just lost your tip, young lady."

Clark came out of the kitchen with three plates of sandwiches and fruit cups.

"Is the help harassing you again, Nolan?" Clark looked over the gold-rimmed glasses parked halfway down his nose.

"Sometimes I think you imported a branch of the Chicago mafia," Nolan said.

"Hey, I'm standing right here." Jo punched buttons. "Canceling your order."

Clark raised his eyebrows.

"He didn't want it anyway." Jo took the sandwich plates from Clark and left the counter to deliver them to the waiting seated customers.

"What do you need, Nolan?" Clark asked.

"Looking for my daughter." In Nolan's pocket, Jillian's phone buzzed. She might not have turned the ringer off, but he finally had.

"In that case, you might have thought twice about offending the mafia," Clark said. "She's the last person on these premises seen talking with that bunch."

Nolan slapped his forehead. "This is going to cost me, isn't it."

"I would say so."

"I heard that." Jo was back. "Why Mr. Duffy, how kind of you to order six cupcakes to go and offer me a thirty percent tip!"

"Extortion. Pure extortion."

Joanna was already filling a box with the cupcakes. "They went to Nia's. Kris was going to swing by Ore the Mountain to grab a couple of quarts of ice cream and make sure the hired help has everything under control to close up and then meet everyone at the Inn. In the meantime, Nia is getting the jam ready."

"I'd think twice about crashing that party," Clark said.

"I'm afraid I have to." Nolan took the bag Joanna handed him in exchange for cash. "Maybe these will help."

The Inn at Hidden Run, the bed and breakfast Nia and Leo Dunston ran in the sprawling Victorian they had meticulously renovated, was only half a mile away, midway between the Cage and Nolan's home. Nolan parked in front and cradled his peace offering as he approached the porch that wrapped around most of the house.

Leo was in one of the rockers. "I basically got kicked out of my own house, Nolan. You think you're going to waltz in there because you have a sack from the Cage?"

"I'm going to try."

"What have you got in there?"

"Not for you, Leo."

"You might need me on your side."

"True, but some of those women might want more than one cupcake."

"Cupcakes! You know they get those from Ben's Bakery."

"I have to talk to Jillian."

"She'll be home in a while."

"I know. But I've come all the way over here."

"It's half a mile, Nolan."

"It's a ferocious half a mile. And I came by way of the Cage, so technically I've already come a mile and a half."

"You had to get past Jo to find out where they were, didn't you?"

Nolan nodded.

"Then you deserve entry." Leo got out of his rocker and opened the door to his home. "But I'm not going in with you."

Laughter rang from the kitchen.

"Hello?" Nolan pressed his inner amiable button and announced his presence.

Nia's dark head came through the dining room and into the hall.

"It's just Nolan. Not Dreamy Drew." Laughter gurgled from the kitchen.

Dreamy Drew? Did Drew know they called him this?

"Nolan. It's a girls' night. Jillian didn't mention you'd be by."

"She didn't know. It's important."

"I guess you can come through, then." Nia flipped her dark braid over her shoulder. "But there'd better be something in that bag I want."

Nolan surrendered his ticket in and followed Nia. In the kitchen, Kris, Veronica, and Jillian were all licking spoons.

"Dad, what are you doing here?"

"You forgot your phone."

"I'm down the street from home with my best friends and you thought you should bring me my phone?"

"You forgot it."

Jillian stuck her spoon in a quart container and pulled it out loaded with chocolate chip cookie dough ice cream.

"I didn't forget it, Dad. I left it." She stuffed the spoon in her mouth.

"On purpose?"

"On purpose." She mumbled past the frozen concoction between her teeth.

"You don't do that."

"Well, I did."

This was how desperate she was.

"I can't say that I blame you," Nolan said. "It's been going off nonstop. Your email on your computer too. 'Help!' 'Urgent!' I confess I got uncharacteristically nosy."

Veronica and Kris burst out laughing.

"What?" Nolan said.

"Nothing, nothing." Kris turned her head and snorted.

"It not like you've ever stepped over a line before." Veronica wiped both ice cream and a smirk off her face with a napkin.

"I think I do rather well at holding to boundaries." Nolan handed Jillian her phone. "But Jillian is having trouble with someone who isn't as respectful as I am, and I think things have escalated quite a bit."

Jillian paled. "Since twenty-four hours ago?"

"Find out what is making your phone explode and you tell me."

Jillian scrolled through the stream of texts. "They're all from Cate."

"I'm sorry I didn't take you more seriously when you said she was way over the line," Nolan said, "but my gut says we shouldn't ignore this."

"Jillian?" Nia said. "What's going on?"

"My long-lost cousin," Jillian said. "She's in trouble."

The room went quiet as Jillian listened to phone messages and groaned.

"Cate has gotten herself into some big trouble harassing people she sees as competition to her work."

"Legal trouble?" Nia asked.

Jillian nodded. "I was going to tell you about everything she told me, Dad. I just wanted a breather for a day while I thought about it—or had a few hours *not* to think about it. But she just couldn't wait. Now she's really gone and done it. It sounds like she could be in real trouble."

"Answer her."

"Dad!"

"Tell her to come to Canyon Mines immediately. Well, not immediately. She'll take that literally and show up in the middle of the night. But tomorrow."

"What? Dad!"

"Do it. She'll come."

"That's what I'm afraid of."

"I'm not. I promise not to leave you feeling so stranded." Nolan pointed to the sack Nia had set on the table. "And if you do it, you can have all the cupcakes."

CHAPTER NINE

Friday, September 23, 1913
Ludlow, Colorado

"GEPPETTO, YOU SHOULD HAVE YOUR JACKET BACK." Caterina tugged at the giant button she had sewn onto the coat herself, replacing all the buttons when he'd lost one somewhere along the ranch's fence line so they would all still match. "Please. I cannot stand having you cold."

"I am not cold. And we have arrived." Geppetto once again drew her shoulder into the niche under his own.

When he did that, Caterina was in her true home. Her shoulder nested under his, her head against his chest, his scent in her nostrils, the warmth of his breath cascading over her face.

They were both soaked to the skin. The rain and snow mix meant it didn't matter which of them wore the coat. A shiver ran through Caterina's spine.

"Name and mine?" A guard at the colony's entrance, his accent thick below his graying mustache, raised his dark eyes toward Geppetto and Caterina.

They looked at each other.

"We are looking for friends," Geppetto said. "From the Berwind mine. We want to know they are all right."

"Did he vote to strike?"

"He's a union man." Caterina pushed every ounce of certainty she had through her voice.

"But did he vote?"

"We weren't there!" she said. "But if he is a union man and the vote was unanimous, doesn't that mean he voted to strike?"

The man looked at Geppetto. "This is your wife?"

Geppetto nodded.

"She talks a lot."

Geppetto laughed softly. "But what she says is true, yes?"

The guard looked from husband to wife and then pointed. "The big tent is over there. They are assigning tent sites to miners. Someone can help you."

Arms around each other, Geppetto and Caterina trudged through the muddy ground toward the big tent. It wasn't hard to find. Steady traffic in and out identified its flaps as the center of activity, with both women and men buzzing. Some were as drenched from the rain-snow mix as the Parisis were, while others had rummaged layers of dry clothing from somewhere. Inside, farthest from the entrance, a table served as headquarters with men and papers behind it and pencils tangled into the curls above their ears. Warmth from the number of people crowded within the dimensions of the tent was instantaneous when Caterina stepped inside.

"Coffee is over here," a woman said. "You look like you could use some."

"We would be grateful," Geppetto said. "We are looking for friends. Is this the line to ask?"

The woman nodded.

Soon their chilled, stiff hands wrapped around hot mugs, and they inhaled the rising steam.

"I cannot stop shaking," Caterina said.

"This is why you must wear the jacket."

"It's like wearing a wet rag now, Geppetto."

He glanced around. "If you take it off while we wait in this line, you may not want to put it on again."

"Then it will be your turn."

"You are sneaky, Caterina. But take it off. It's warm in here. Maybe it will dry out just a little."

At the front of the line, a clatter of languages and interpreters managed the slow process of filling out forms, finding out what people needed, and giving them the papers that would assign them to their temporary homes. Impatient, tired, hungry children whimpered and squalled. Women filled sacks with used clothes and essential household items to replace whatever they might have had to leave behind in the company town.

"It looks like they are taking care of people," Geppetto said.

"I will feel better when I know whether Chiara is one of them."

Caterina gulped hot coffee. "What is this?"

Caterina squinted at a paper nailed to a post in the center of the tent and moved her lips silently as she read.

Wage Scale Adopted by Special Convention, Colorado Mine Workers, at Trinidad, Colo., September 16, 1913

We, the representatives of the mine workers of district 15, after repeated efforts to secure a conference with the operators for the purpose of establishing joint relations and a fair wage agreement, and having been denied such a conference—the operators ignoring our invitation entirely—and believing as we do that we have grievances of great moment that demand immediate adjudication, we submit the following as a basis of settlement:

First. We demand recognition of the union. (State law on this subject, but not complied with.)

Second. We demand a 10 per cent advance in wages on the tonnage rates and a day-wage scale which is practically in accord with the Wyoming day-wage scale. (The recent Colorado scale is the lowest paid in any of the Rocky Mountain States. Wage advance is justified.)

Third. We demand an eight-hour workday for all classes of labor in or around the coal mines and coke ovens. (State law on this subject, but not complied with.)

Fourth. We demand pay for all narrow work and dead work, which includes brushing, timbering, removing falls, handling impurities, etc. (Scale for this work in all other States.)

Fifth. We demand checkweighman at all mines to be elected by the miners without any interference by company officials in said election. (State law on this subject but not complied with.)

Sixth. We demand the right to trade in any store we please and the right to choose our own boarding and our own doctor. (State law on this subject but not complied with.)

Seventh. We demand the enforcement of the Colorado mining laws, and the abolition of the notorious and criminal guard system which has prevailed in the mining camps of Colorado for many years. (State laws on these subjects but not complied with.)

If you believe in the enforcement of law and a living wage, you will support the miners in this strike.

"Geppetto, I do not understand all these words." Adjudicating. Narrow work. Dead work. Checkweighman. "And notorious and criminal guard system—whatever that is, it does not sound good."

"Some of it means the kind of work that the miners do but are not paid for."

"That is not fair."

"They don't think so."

"'State laws on these subjects but not complied with.' Complied?"

"Mmm. Obeyed. The state has laws, but the mine owners do not obey them."

"And for this reason Chiara must be suffering."

Geppetto laid a hand against Caterina's face. "We will find her."

They inched forward in the line. Geppetto stepped out of the line to refill their coffee mugs. They moved ahead a few more steps. Behind them, more soggy but determined mining families entered to take up the space they had just occupied.

Finally their turn came.

"English?" Geppetto said. "Italiano?"

A man at the far end of the table raised a finger, and Caterina hustled over to explain who she and Geppetto were looking for.

The man flipped through papers, found a scrap of paper, and wrote some numbers and words on it. In a rapid round of Italian he gave instructions and explanations for where they should find the tent their friends were assigned. Carrying the still-damp coat between them, Caterina and Geppetto shot out of the tent.

"A tent and an oven and a bag of clothes," Caterina muttered. "What kind of a place is that for Chiara while she is so ill? She hardly owned anything of her own other than a few pots and a couple of books in Italian that she reads over and over."

"Shelter and a way to keep warm and cook food," Geppetto said. "It's a start."

"They will not need it, because they are coming home with us." Caterina raised a hand toward the snowy canyon. "What if this is just the beginning of cold weather that doesn't go away?"

Voices of men singing rose, and Caterina slowed slightly to try to make out the words. She didn't recognize this English tune.

We will win the fight today, boys
We'll win the fight today
Shouting the battle cry of union
We will rally from the coal mines,
We'll battle to the end,
Shouting the battle cry of union.

"Do they have to sing about fighting?" Caterina resumed her hurried pace. "Two times they say fight. Three times they say battle."

"I don't know who writes the song, Caterina." Geppetto glanced at the scrap of paper that was their only guide.

"Why do they make it sound like they want someone to get hurt?"

"I'm sure they don't want any of the miners to get hurt."

"I don't want anyone to get hurt."

"Here's the spot."

"Where?"

"Here." Geppetto stopped.

"There is no tent."

"I'm sure they are working on it and it will come soon."

"Geppetto!"

Behind them a woman moaned, falling to her knees to wretch in the white snow purposely packed against the wall of the nearest tent as if to tamp down and seal any air coming in from below the flaps. She wretched three times, each time with more force until even Caterina could hear the gurgling bile on its way up. On her hands and knees now, the contents of her stomach spewed a textured array of small yellow and orange chunks over a patch of glistening snow.

She was so thin from the back, and the luster of her jet black hair faded, that Caterina didn't recognize her at first. But they were at the right tent site and a young Italian woman was losing her lunch.

"Chiara!"

"Caterina!" Chiara wiped her mouth with a hankie from her skirt pocket. "What are you doing here?"

"I was trying to call you at Berwyn."

"They cut the wires even before the vote." Celestrino assisted his wife to a standing position. Out of his back pocket he took a small garden shovel and quickly covered over the sick with snow, then scuffed dirt over it for good measure. "The tent is not quite ready. We're waiting on the poles. Then she should have a place to rest."

"She needs a place to rest now, Celestrino," Caterina said. Chiara looked even worse than Caterina had imagined. For someone more than three months gone with a child, she looked like she hadn't been able to keep a single extra ounce on her frame. Gray circles under her eyes pooled out into half oceans of death water sloshing around islands of pallid skin. Nothing Chiara had written had prepared Caterina for this. There was no point in wasting another moment.

"We're here to take you back to the ranch with us," Caterina said. "The Kyps have offered the building very near our cabin. We used to live in it ourselves. You'll have quiet when you need it, but I'll be close enough to check frequently on what you need and bring you meals. You won't have to cook or do chores. Your job is to get well and take care of the *bambino*."

Chiara's eyes glistened.

"Do you have things you want to take with you? You can wait out the strike where it's safe—where you're safe—and come back strong when Celestrino is ready to go back to work."

Geppetto clapped a hand on Celestrino's back. "There is always work to do at the ranch for a strong man."

"When I went to that convention, I didn't dream it would come to a strike," Celestrino said. "I thought we could present our reasonable demands—many are state law already—and continue working before a single day's profit was missed. But one story after another of men in danger because of what the boss told them they must do convinced me. If the operators would not talk to us, hear us, follow the laws, we would have no choice."

"So you voted." Geppetto nodded.

"What choice did I have? This is no life for Chiara. She needs a different doctor. And what happens to her and the baby if I get hurt because the owners don't care if I am safe? Every coal mine in the state will be idle in the next two days. The strike will be huge."

"I have a train schedule somewhere," Caterina said, "but I think it's not too long before we can catch one. What have you done with your things?"

"This will be good for Chiara." Celestrino glanced over a shoulder. "Give me one moment."

"We will get you well." Caterina held Chiara in a firm embrace. "There is a good doctor in Pueblo."

"I have no money for pay him. They have only been paying Celestrino in scrip. It's not good anywhere outside the company town." Chiara held her handkerchief to her mouth as if to stifle another round of retching.

"Don't worry about the doctor's fee," Caterina said. "You need some water to sip. I saw a pump. Do you have a cup unpacked yet, or shall I go back to the main tent?"

Chiara waved her away. "I can't hold anything down."

"You have to try."

Chiara's breath was slow and shallow. "Not right now."

"Maybe on the train," Geppetto suggested.

Celestrino was back dragging a trunk through the mud.

"Where is your bag?" Chiara demanded.

"I will need my things here," he said.

Chiara sank against Caterina. "You can't send me away without you!"

"It's the right thing for you and the bambino," Celestrino said. "It will be such a weight off my mind knowing that you are with someone who can look after you so closely."

"I don't want to leave you! They have a new doctor here in the camp. They told us that. And all the tents around here will be Italian families. I will have friends."

Two men, muscles bulging, turned up with the poles, reading to erect the tent, ropes, stakes, cots, and an oven.

"See? In just a few minutes I'll be able to lie down. They made sure we had extra blankets at the main tent, and we can go down there for meals for a few days until we get more settled. Or at least Celestrino can. There is no reason he should starve just because I can't eat."

"The ranch will be so much better!" Caterina said. "Dry and warm. We have water coming right out of the faucet in our cabin, with a pump just outside as well. Ela is making up a place for the two of you right now."

"Not me." Celestrino shook his head. "I signed on to support the strike."

"There won't be anything to do," Chiara said. "No one will be mining. Isn't that the point?"

"The camp needs guarding. We must protect the people who stay here—they expect twelve hundred. I own my own Winchester. I can be ready to fight if necessary."

"Fight who?" Caterina said. "Surely the owners don't plan to shoot at you over this. I would think the worst they would do is fire you permanently. Find a way to get their scabs in to do the mining."

"No scabs are getting past us. If we scatter to wait out the strike, they win."

Geppetto said, "How will you get by?"

"The United Mine Workers Association pays a stipend of three dollars a week. Coal. Food. Clothing. We'll manage. But you must take Chiara with you. This is the answer I've been praying for."

"I won't go without you," Chiara said.

"You must go."

"I won't!"

"You must. This will all be over long before the baby comes. You need your strength."

"I won't go." Chiara knelt in the snow again and began to retch.

"She must go," Celestrino said softly to Geppetto. "I will go find someone with a cart to help with the trunk."

"I won't go!" Chiara threw up an odious green-yellow bile.

They were going to need a bowl or tin cup to take on the train.

CHAPTER TEN

"HERE SHE IS. JILLIAN CLICKED closed her favorite fine point blue pen with the smooth roller tip and set aside her notepad. She hadn't been able to concentrate all morning anyway. Now she'd have to be a proper hostess and offer the comfortable purple chair and ottoman to Cate. "Are you positive this was a good idea, Dad?"

"We can hardly send her away now," Nolan said. "It was our idea for her to drive all the way up her to sort this out."

"Our idea? Watch your pronouns, old man."

"I'll make her a cup of black coffee."

"You will remain in the room at all times."

"Are you frightened of your cousin?"

Cate was on the porch steps now.

"It's a legal matter," Jillian said. "That's your area of expertise, not mine."

"But I prepared refreshments."

"Which I will gladly serve." The bell rang, and Jillian pointed at the front door.

Nolan welcomed Cate Butler—Caterina Polombo, it turns out—into their home for second time and took the overnight bag slung over her shoulder.

"The guest room is ready for you," Nolan said. "I'm sure you're going to be very comfortable during your stay at Chez Duffy."

"You remember where the powder room is," Jillian says. "Feel free to freshen up. Would you like coffee or a cold drink?"

"Coffee, please. Black."

"I remember," Nolan said. "I have a nice aromatic blend going."

Jillian rolled her eyes. As if he cared about an aromatic blend.

Nolan took Cate's bag up the front stairs and came down the rear stairs to claim his tray of fancy party crackers dressed with swirly cheese and bits of vegetables. Jillian was pretty sure he had a pound cake tucked away somewhere. She filled the coffee mugs. If Cate hadn't stopped for lunch on the way up, she would be well fed now.

The three of them reconvened in the living room, Nolan and Jillian on the sofa and Cate in the purple chair with a plate of crackers and cheese and a polished apple at the ready.

"Okay, Miss Caterina Polombo, doing business as Cate Butler," Nolan said, "it seems you've gotten yourself into a pickle."

"I'm sorry, Nolan. I didn't mean to drag you into this mess." Cate swallowed a cracker nearly whole.

"In matters that are not strictly genealogically professional," he said, "when you get Jillian, you get me too. Her name is Parisi-Duffy for a reason."

"That's how it works?"

"That's how it works. Jillian is not a source of legal advice, but I am."

Cate groaned and set down her plate. "I know I went over the line."

"Every legal matter has two sides," Nolan said, "but when one party threatens formal suit because they believe they are being harassed and threatened by the other party, then yes, we need to examine the line. You have a lot to lose, it seems to me, if you do in fact get sued over something like this."

"But you just said there are two sides." Cate pushed back. "Don't you want to hear mine?"

"Of course. As soon as we establish that certain retaliatory behaviors lack wisdom and induce legal exposure that comes at a high price. Therefore, on advice of counsel, you will cease and desist. In other words, you'll stay approximately five miles away from the line we're talking about."

"I know, I know."

Jillian sipped her hazelnut latte from her spot on the couch. Maybe bringing Cate here for a face-to-face was right after all.

"I was impressed by your work on Thursday," Jillian said. "I like to think we both inherited the Parisi history buff gene." She had been impressed once she recovered from discovering Drew's own connection with her cousin.

"I like to think that too." Cate's shoulders squared in the purple chair.

"You're thorough, with high standards. The photographs you've gathered are compelling, and the angle of focusing on families rather than the miners themselves is a great connection point."

"That means a lot coming from you."

"I don't understand what happened." Jillian leaned forward. "I only got back to Canyon Mines myself twenty-four hours ago. I was going to get back to you after I had some time to think."

"And I was going to wait," Cate said. "I figured a weekend couldn't make a difference."

"So what happened?"

"I made my mother mad."

Jillian glanced at Nolan. "And that made you harass someone in Trinidad?"

"Not directly." Cate was eating fancy crackers again. "If I had just said yes when my mother wanted me to drop everything and drive up to Pueblo to work an emergency shift at the restaurant in the middle of the day, I would have never found out about the other stuff when I did, and then I would never have gone off the way I did."

"I see," Jillian said, because she did. "One of those moments that changes everything."

"Exactly!" Cate chewed and swallowed. "A whole string of moments. If Lisa's babysitter hadn't called and said she had to pick up her son because he was running a fever, and that's the rule—no fevers—and if Max wasn't already going to be out because of a root canal, and if my brother wasn't already away for the day to meet with a supplier. Well, you get the drift. Mom needed somebody. And she always thinks it should be me. But I said no. I live an hour away, and I have another job. They can fumble through a couple more hours short-staffed until someone is available."

"That doesn't sound entirely unreasonable," Nolan said.

"Well, she was pretty annoyed. I hoped using her maiden name in my business name would make her at least a little bit curious about what I do, but it hasn't. And then I couldn't concentrate, so I went down the street to get something to eat. I thought maybe the change of scenery would help."

"That same sandwich shop?" Jillian said.

Cate nodded. "I go there a lot. There were staff from the Trinidad museum having lunch. They know me, I know them. They told me the director is very excited about the latest version of a proposal for the children's exhibit."

"Let me guess," Jillian said. "It uses some of your ideas."

"Not just in the neighborhood of my ideas. Exactly my idea to use enlarged photos and a few artifacts to show how workload only got harder for women and girls, and life was more uncertain than ever for children, and create interactive activities that compare life of kids today to the strikers' kids."

"That's what you were describing in the back room on Thursday."

"I know what you're thinking," Cate said. "Someone from the sandwich shop must be a leak. But Drew went and got the food."

"No one even came in to see if we needed anything," Jillian said.

"The ideas in the proposal the museum has are too close to mine not to be copied. Only they'll rewrite the descriptions to make life in mining towns and camps sound just lovely. How am I supposed to explain to my board that once again I need more time to tweak my presentations before I can start trying to attract schools to use my traveling exhibit so I don't sound like the copycat?"

"I can understand your frustration." Nolan put his elbows on his knees and leaned in. "So this is what led to the perceived harassment?"

"I know exactly where the museum got that proposal." Cate pushed herself up out of the purple chair and started to pace. "The office door of the people who put it together is exactly sixteen feet from mine."

"So you confronted them," Jillian said.

"You better believe it." Cate pivoted. "Just like all the other times."

"Ah," Nolan said. "Therein lies the harassment."

"Well, what am supposed to do? They're stealing my work, watering it down just enough to make it irresponsible but keeping the basic appeal so that I have to keep reinventing it so it doesn't look like I'm the one doing the copying. I could lose my grant over this."

"So you have to figure out how Epic EduKids is getting your work," Nolan said.

Cate shrugged. "I'm the newcomer in town. All it takes is knowing somebody who knows the landlord, and bam, you have a key to my office."

"It's still illegal."

"I can't prove anything. That's why I need help."

"Cate," Jillian said, "it's horrible that this is happening to you, but I'm not a detective agency. You need the police."

Cate flopped back in the chair. "I shot myself in the foot then. I'm the harasser, remember? Epic EduKids is the righteous bunch."

"No matter how unfair it feels in this moment," Nolan said, "I cannot impress on you enough the need to contain any further outburst."

"I know, I know."

"We can make this go away as long as nothing else happens."

"I get it. I'll do better."

The doorbell rang, and Jillian glanced at Nolan. "Expecting anyone?"

"Nope." He got up to answer the door.

"I hope you don't mind that I dropped by." It was Carolyn, from Digger's Delight, the candy shop that adjoined Kris's ice cream shop.

"Never!" Nolan said.

"I had to come down to this end of the street anyway," Carolyn said, "so I thought I might as well come in person with my question. But I did bring some chocolate-covered cherries to smooth the way. Three milk chocolate and three dark to keep you both happy."

"Come in," Nolan said. "Meet Cate Butler."

"Cate is my ... cousin," Jillian said. "On my mother's side. Fourth cousin once removed, as near as I can figure."

"Goodness, that's remarkable," Carolyn said.

"We've only discovered each other recently."

"I won't intrude. I just need an address. Drew's aunt emailed me about some chocolates, but I'm afraid I can't find the email and don't know where to send them. Can I trouble you for the mailing address for the ranch?"

"Min?" Jillian said. "She ordered chocolates?"

"She did indeed. Drew has taken samples home a few times. She says he has spoiled her now for anything she can get locally."

Jillian laughed. "I wish I'd known. I was just down there a couple days ago. I could have taken some." She took a sheet from her notepad, still sitting on the coffee table, and wrote out the address for Carolyn.

"Let's see," Carolyn said, "fourth cousin once removed. You'd have to go back quite a ways to find a common ancestor, wouldn't you?"

Jillian nodded as she handed Carolyn the address. "My ancestor and Cate's were brothers who immigrated from Sicily in the late 1800s."

"Lou and Sal," Cate said. "Of course, my family claims Uncle Salvatore as ours also. His name means savior, and we figure that since Lou sent Geppetto to Denver and Sal took him in, he lived up to his name. Geppetto might not have survived in New Orleans, and if he hadn't come to Denver, none of us would be here either."

"I'm sure Jillian is glad you are here," Carolyn said. "She has always wanted an Italian cousin."

"There was a third brother," Cate said, "but we think he didn't have any offspring, so bringing Jillian into our branch of the family is very cool. And it's outstanding that she still uses Parisi as part of her name, since it got married out of our family."

"It must be fascinating for you to find each other." Carolyn folded up Jillian's note page and tucked it in a pocket. "Enjoy your visit. I'll get Min's chocolates shipped off first thing next week."

"Thank you," Jillian said. "Next time I'll know to check with you and not go down to the ranch empty-handed."

Nolan walked Carolyn out.

"We need to sit down with a family tree," Jillian said to Cate. "I'm sure you can fill in a lot of blanks—considering all I have are empty leaves."

"My parents keep track. Sort of. My dad should know—it's his family—but my mom is the one who makes more effort."

"I've seen that happen," Jillian said. "Somebody becomes the keeper of information, in case someone might want it in the future."

"And now there's you." Cate grinned. "Someone who actually does want it. Somebody in my family has the letters from Uncle Sal."

Jillian's felt her heart rushed out of her chest, the heightened pulse clanging in her ears. "Letters? That Sal wrote?"

"I'd have to ask my dad where they are. Or maybe my mom stuck them away somewhere."

"But you're sure they exist."

"Like ninety-nine percent sure." Cate twiddled a cracker. "I guess we should be talking about when you're going to meet everybody. You could ask your own questions."

"Maybe." Jillian swallowed. She was curious, of course. But was she ready to enter a family with the conflict Cate described?

"You could come to dinner—at the restaurant. Or lunch. You could come next weekend. Just meet everybody casually. I could arrange a meet-up."

Nolan lifted his mug. "That sounds like a good idea. See the family business and the meet the family at the same time. Food always helps break the ice, don't you think, Jillian?"

Food? Sure. In Jillian's experience, it gave people something to fiddle with even if they didn't eat.

Cate picked up the last of the crackers. "That's nice your friend is sending Drew's aunt some candy."

"Carolyn makes all her own candy," Jillian said. "We'll make sure you have a couple of cherries. Right, Dad?"

Nolan cleared his throat. "You know how I feel about my chocolate-covered cherries."

"You can get them any day of the week."

"I don't really know Drew's aunt," Cate said. "More by reputation. Haven't seen her in years."

"Great-aunt, actually," Jillian said.

"They say she doesn't like to dilly-dally in town if she doesn't have to, so she doesn't come into the restaurants like she did in the old days. But I did hear a rumor from my mother who heard it from a customer that Min hasn't been feeling well lately."

"I just saw her," Jillian said.

"She was all right?" Nolan said.

"A bit tired from working on the church rummage sale." The truth was Jillian hadn't seen much of Min on her quick visit. Min had been weary Thursday evening and went to bed early, and on Friday morning Jillian didn't stay around too long after breakfast.

Now she wondered about Min as she gathered empty coffee mugs and snack plates. And of course, Cate's dilemma was hardly resolved. But Jillian couldn't simply spin her off now with the excuse that she wasn't a detective—not when Cate was the one who could lead her to letters from her own great-great-grandfather.

CHAPTER ELEVEN

"ARE YOU SURE YOU don't want to stay and come to church with us?" Jillian said the next morning. "My dad would love it."

"Her dad would very much love it." At the counter beside the refrigerator, Nolan snapped the lid on a plastic container and added it to a stack.

"I would if I could," Cate said, "but if I don't get home and work this shift, I may not make rent next month."

"We don't want that," Jillian said.

"But we do want you to be well fed." Nolan arranged food containers in an insulated sack to send home with Cate and added several frozen ice packs.

"You're so generous," Cate said. "I'll eat for a week on all this. Dinner was delicious last night."

"You've been initiated," Jillian said. "My dad cooks for everybody in town. But Dad, you know Cate's family owns two restaurants, right?"

"Not the same thing." Nolan snapped closed another container.

"And the singing Italian opera thing?" Cate asked.

"Yep. His favorite way to cook. He's been doing it since I was little."

"Sort of amusing. It might go over well at my family's restaurant if he needs a side gig."

"Did you hear that, Dad?" Jillian grinned at Nolan.

"Duly noted," Nolan said. "If my experiment with a legal career doesn't work out, perhaps I will explore the suggestion."

"I should get going." Cate arranged her overnight bag on one shoulder and checked her grip on the food bag.

"Let me give you the family blessing one more time for the road," Nolan said. "It's a Duffy blessing, but Parisis are allowed to use it."

"I'd be honored."

Nolan put his hands on Cate's shoulders. "May you always find nourishment for your body at the table. May sustenance for your spirit rise and fill you with each dawn. And may life always feed you with the light of joy along the way."

"That's lovely every time you say it."

"Seems relevant to the challenges you face right now."

Cate nodded.

"You have my card."

"In my purse."

"And you know the plan."

"You'll call the attorney and see about smoothing things over, and I promise to behave myself."

"Good. We are on the same wavelength. I'll be in touch as soon as I have something to report. Keep in mind it might take a couple of days."

"I can't thank you enough."

"That's step one—dial things down. As to who is actually behind the leak, we can't begin to sort that out until everyone's nerves are calmed."

"I understand."

They walked Cate to her car and got in Nolan's truck for the drive to church, trailing her out of the driveway.

"Dad, beyond getting Cate out of this legal snafu, I'm still not sure what we can do for her."

Nolan shrugged. "Maybe nothing."

"Why did you make it sound like we could?"

"In my experience, if the temperature gets turned down, a lot of things become possible."

"Your experience?"

Nolan glanced at her and wagged one eyebrow in that way Jillian could never master.

"Oh. You mean as a mediator."

"Ding, ding, ding."

"Dad, I would love for things to get better for Cate."

"I know you would, Jilly. Let's just start by turning the temperature down. Okay?"

"Thanks for your help, Dad."

Jillian was also grateful for a calming worship service filled with prayers and hymns and words of comfort and challenge. All of this reminded her of where she wanted to center her life after a week that felt like ping-ponging from one out-of-control moment to another. The stillness and opportunity to take deep breaths brought welcome hope.

Afterward, Kris gave her a quick wave and said, "Come by Ore the Mountain this afternoon. I'm trying out a new flavor and could use an honest opinion."

"You haven't had a new flavor in"—Jillian paused to calculate—"six years and four months."

"Well, I have an idea for one now. But I won't make a full batch until I have a few opinions I can trust."

"You got it. I'll have lunch and stroll on down for dessert."

At home, Nolan warmed creamy lentil soup and sliced Irish soda bread.

"Thanks for not giving away ninety-eight percent of our leftovers." Jillian's weakness for soda bread might require an extra long and vigorous afternoon walk around Canyon Mines, especially with ice cream in the picture. She picked up a second slice.

"I shall prepare you a veritable feast for our evening meal." Nolan swirled a hand in the air. "My child shall not go hungry."

"Dad, I'm twenty-nine and didn't starve before reaching adulthood or graduating college. I think you did your duty."

"I think I am capable of determining whether I have met that standard. I am a practicing attorney."

"I beg your pardon. I promise to do penance by doing my share of the cooking this week. And the cleaning. And the errands."

"And you are concerned about my tendency to overpromise."

"The apple does not fall far from the tree, or something like that." Jillian munched bread. "I'm going to call Drew. I'm worried about Min."

"Sounds like a good idea. I'll clean up."

"Oh great. I'll start the week in the hole on my penance."

"Go."

Jillian changed into jeans and a good pair of walking shoes, bound her hair in a red scrunchie, hooked her keys to a belt loop and called a final farewell to her father before heading out the front door of the house she'd lived in since she was two. It had started as a double cottage, two homes mirroring each other with a joining wall. Another owner in the home's history had opened up the center of the structure, and the

Duffys had undertaken the renovation that made it the home of a lifetime.

Jillian's lifetime. Until recently, she hadn't ever seriously considered living anywhere else.

She started down Main Street, earbuds transmitting the phone to her ears.

"Well, there's the voice I love to hear," Drew said.

And she was relieved. "I'm so glad you answered."

"I'll always take your call whenever I can. You know that."

"I do. Thank you." Jillian found a pair of sunglasses in her jacket pocket and adjusted them on her face. "Is Min unwell, Drew?"

"Why do you ask? Did she say something the other day?"

"Min? Admit she's unwell? Even I know her better than that."

Drew laughed. "Then what happened?"

"I heard a rumor."

"Uh oh. Now you have me worried. From who?"

"You won't believe it. From Cate. Rini. Whatever I'm supposed to call her when I talk to you."

"Rini? How would she know? She doesn't even really see Aunt Min these days."

"So she said. She heard from her mother who heard from a customer at the restaurant."

Drew was quiet.

"Drew?"

"I'm not sure who that would be," he said, "and I wish I did because I'd love to quash the rumor at the source. But it's not entirely untrue."

"What does that mean?"

"She had some tests because she's been run down. That's why she was too tired to stay up and visit much while you were there. She doesn't need to be working so hard on the rummage sale, but there's no talking to her."

"She had tests?" Jillian said.

"Nothing has come of it. Slightly anemic, that's all."

Jillian could tell Drew was slurping a beverage, probably some concoction he had created himself.

"Are you sure?"

"Her age is catching up with her," he said. "But she doesn't want to leave the ranch. We're trying to get her to go stay with her daughter Michelle in Wyoming for a few weeks and have a decent rest, like she did a few months ago. But so far no luck. Michelle may have to come down and do some convincing in person. So we'll see."

"You'd tell me if it was something serious, wouldn't you?"

"Of course I would. We talk every day, and you see right through me."

"I'm not sure that's true."

"Give yourself some credit."

"Okay then. Are you still working tonight at Mary Lou's?"

"On my way now. I'll be there until closing."

"Call me when you get off?"

"Maybe even on my dinner break."

Jillian smiled. "I'll always take your call whenever I can."

At the ice cream shop, Jillian was glad to see a line. Autumn in the Colorado mountains could be lovely—the Aspens spinning their golden confection while for the most part the days would still be awash in sun under heraldic azure skies. This weekend, in mid-October, might be the last chance for tourists to drive up from Denver and follow I-70 into the higher elevations and the old mining towns, including Canyon Mines, in search of an enchanting outing and stunning views of the Aspens. Temperatures and dazzling skies were still alluring enough to make ice cream appealing. Jillian's mouth salivated for her favorite chocolate chip cookie dough in a waffle cone with a hard chocolate coating, even as her brain reminded her that she'd promised to test a new flavor.

Kris looked up from behind the counter and signaled that Jillian should follow her through to the kitchen, leaving her weekend employees to face the lines for a few minutes. The kitchen is where the magic happened, where Kris churned the ice cream into silky perfection that melted on the tongue.

"Why all of a sudden a new flavor?" Jillian asked.

"The gelato shop." Kris's answer snapped right back.

"What gelato shop?"

"The one opening next to Leif's ski shop in a couple of weeks."

"We're getting a gelato shop?" Jillian's voice lilted. She did like a good gelato.

Kris sighed. "First of all, have you been living under a rock? And second, do you not see that gelato is a direct competition to ice cream and you are my friend, so you have no business being excited about gelato."

"You're right. I'm sorry." Jillian hung her head and kept to herself the question about why Kris had never chosen to sell gelato alongside her ice cream.

"Do you remember Mick Sanderson?"

"From when we were in school high school?"

"Yep. He's suddenly decided to open a gelato shop."

"I didn't know he was back in town. Didn't you used to have a crush on him?"

"I did not." Kris pointed to a gray metal stool for Jillian to sit on. "I'm starting to think you were the source of that rumor that plagued me for two solid years."

"I wasn't."

"Forget the gelato. And Mick. Close your eyes."

"What's the flavor?" Jillian complied.

"I want you to taste it first." Kris put a spoon in Jillian's right hand and a small bowl in her left. "Take a normal taste, please. Don't act like you're scared."

"Why would I be scared of ice cream?"

"Just do it."

Jillian rolled the frozen blend around on her tongue.

"Well?" Kris said.

"Buttery?"

"Anything else?"

Jillian took another bite. "I'm not sure. Salty aftertaste, but not like caramel. More like, I don't know, French bread. Is that weird?"

"I don't know. Is it?"

Jillian popped her eyes open. "Are you saying this is supposed to taste like buttered bread?"

"Buttered baguette. Who doesn't like a golden piece of bread slathered in butter?"

Jillian looked at what was left in the bowl.

"You hate it." Disappointment smeared Kris's voice.

"No, I don't hate it," Jillian said. "I thought the flavor was interesting. I confess I'm a little hung up on the name. Will people buy ice cream named after a baguette?"

"How about sweet butter baguette."

Jillian nodded. "Sounds more like a treat." The name might still need work. Sweet butter ... something.

"I'm going to send a pint home with you," Kris said. "Get your dad's opinion."

"My dad?"

"Sure. He has a classy palate."

"He might try to convince you it should taste like Irish soda bread, not a French baguette."

Kris smiled. "That's a risk I'm willing to take. I never mind talking to Nolan."

"Really?" Jillian scowled.

"He's an interesting man."

"Okay, but if he finds out I was here and didn't come home with pralines and cream or butter pecan or cherry chocolate chip chunk, I'll be in hot water."

"Fine. Pralines and cream for him and chocolate chip cookie dough for you. But don't let the fact that you get stuck in a rut close your mind to the possibility that something new could be beautiful."

Jillian cocked her head. "You think I get stuck in ruts?"

Kris laughed and snapped the lid on the container of her experimental flavor. "Have you met you? At least Nolan has three favorite flavors. You have one."

Jillian scowled. "I am not afraid of something new."

"Really? Then come dress shopping with me. Let's find some time this week."

Jillian made a face. "You know I'm not much of a shopper. And I hardly wear dresses."

"You look fabulous when you dress up."

"Are you giving me that ice cream or not?"

"Think about the shopping." Kris pushed the bundle toward Jillian. "I dare you."

"Doubtful."

Armed with three containers of ice cream, all packed in double tubs to keep them from melting before Jillian covered the fifteen-minute walk home—twelve if she hustled—she left the shop.

Coming around the nearest corner, she spotted Marilyn, director of Canyon Mine's Heritage Museum located a couple of short blocks off of Main Street.

"Have you been at the museum on a Sunday afternoon?" Jillian asked.

"Just tidying up," Marilyn said. "We have school groups coming in this week, and I want to be ready for them. Thought I would get myself a treat before I go home."

"It's a good day for it."

"Have you heard about the new gelato shop?"

Jillian made a face. "I wouldn't mention that here, if I were you."

"I suppose not. I heard about your cousin. Must be interesting for a genealogist to find her own distant relative."

The small-town chain of information was at work. Nia. Nia's husband, Leo. Veronica. Veronica's husband, Luke. Kris. Carolyn. The web of people who knew about Cate and all the people they knew grew rapidly, and Marilyn would have been among the earliest to hear.

"It is," Jillian said. "It wasn't sure what to expect when I sent off my DNA."

"I hear she's got a lot going on."

"She's facing some challenges." Jillian own instinct to defend Cate's reputation surprised her. "You would find her work interesting. She has a grant for studying and helping others learn about the southern Colorado coalfield strike in 1913 and 1914 in Las Animas County, especially how it impacted women and children."

"Then I'm sure she's familiar with the Ludlow Massacre."

"I'm only just learning the details myself."

"More people need to know more about it than they do."

"She's working on that."

"Good for her."

"She also might have some documents from my great-great grandfather," Jillian said. "If she can find them."

"Wouldn't that be remarkable!"

"I would give anything to see them. Cate's branch of the family is so big. I'm not sure she understands what it would mean to me."

"If she's the historian I think she is based on what you've said, I'm sure she knows the value of primary source documents," Marilyn said.

Jillian shifted the sack of ice cream in her arms. Marilyn was right. Maybe that's what niggled at her. Cate did know the value of primary source historical documents. She just might not know what they would mean to Jillian personally.

"Keep in mind," Marilyn said, "that if the documents do exist, they could be quite physically fragile by this time."

Jillian blinked twice at this truth. People stuffed things away in attics and basements all the time. Temperature, humidity, water, bugs—all sorts of things happened.

But she had to see them. She would stay on Team Cate as long as it took.

CHAPTER TWELVE

Friday, October 17, 1913
Outside Pueblo, Colorado

CATERINA RUBBED GIUSEPPE'S TINY HAND between both of hers. "Come on, Peppy. We must go see Zia Chiara."

"Dot," he said. "See Dot."

"Maybe. First we must go see Zia Chiara." She straightened the thick sweater that seemed to swallow her son and stuffed his arms into his jacket. Buttoning his shoes up over his ankles had tested her fortitude, and she would have to carry him anyway. Outside, snow had whitened the ground long ago. Mid-October was too early to be fighting the weather along with wrestling a toddler who hadn't been walking last winter. Caterina garbed herself against the elements as well before tying on Peppy's hat and hefting him to one hip.

They weren't walking far. Only the slick snow and frigid tempera-ture biting into her lungs made it seem farther than it was. The small outbuilding Ela had offered to Chiara was the nearest one to the little red house, and since temporary staff had stayed in it before for a few weeks here and there and the Parisis themselves had lived in it, Caterina knew it was water tight with an efficient stove for warmth. It was near enough that Chiara had privacy yet Caterina could bring food or provide company. Not all the fall days had been as miserable as the one on which Chiara had arrived and this one almost a month later. Many had been lovely enough to take a quilt and sit outside to soak up sun and vistas even if they wore jackets. When Chiara felt well enough, she came to the little red house or even the main house. Caterina prayed every day that the child in her friend's womb would thrive and the weeks of severe sickness pass. The doctor in Pueblo said it was the right decision to bring her to the ranch where she could be looked after.

Caterina slogged the few yards to the little hut, as the Kyps called it, and knocked. Geppetto said it was called a hut because it wasn't very big and because before she and Geppetto lived there, it was only used for temporary housing for people who worked on the ranch before the Kyps. Caterina thought there must be a better word, but she didn't know what it was in English.

"Chiara?"

"Come on in."

Chiara's face brightened at the sight of Giuseppe. "Peppito!"

Peppy wriggled down. At least he didn't demand to see Dot right that moment, and he thumped over to let Chiara kiss his cheek.

"How do you feel?" Caterina glanced around. Chiara was in bed, but the hut was tidy, the breakfast tray was empty, and the stove was still putting out heat. Chiara must have been out of bed at least for a little while.

"Better than this morning."

"You ate."

Chiara laughed softly. "You probably gave Peppito more breakfast than you put on my tray."

"The doctor said small meals are best. I thought you might like to come home with us. It's too wintry to think of you over here by yourself."

"I move so slowly."

"Then we will all move slowly."

"I will try. I want to write to Celestrino today."

"Good."

"Don't you have to go to the main house?"

"See Dot!" Peppy clapped twice.

The women laughed.

"Maybe later," Caterina said. "But if we go, I will make sure the fire is burning, and you have soup and tea and somebody can check on you."

Chiara gave a slight nod.

"Are you sure you don't want to just stay with us? Geppetto won't mind. We can set up a bed in the corner of the big room and then we will always be there."

"Not always. You both have jobs to do."

"I don't want you to feel alone."

"I miss Celestrino. But I don't feel alone."

"Okay, then. Let's find your coat and shoes."

An automobile's engine clattered outside the hut, and Caterina peeked out the only small window. "It's Ela."

"She probably thinks I need another blanket. I don't!"

Caterina chuckled and opened the door.

"Oh good," Ela said, "you're all here. Carrick insisted I learn to drive this automobile, but I wasn't at all sure how well it would do in the snow. It's a good thing the ranch is fairly flat. I am relieved to say I did not slide into a single canyon."

"We're glad!" Caterina said.

"I've come for you," Ela sad. "This day is turning too miserable for anyone not to be at the main house in my opinion. Carrick and Geppetto can't do much about the cattle spread around the ranch. That's the nature of ranching. It's not the worst storm ever. It will just be better if we're all together. Chiara, do you think you can manage that?"

Caterina recapped briefly in Italian.

Chiara nodded. "I will go."

"As you know, my davenport is quite comfortable," Ela said. "I've already put out a pillow and quilt for you. I was prepared to insist if necessary."

"Not necessary," Chiara said. "But I am a burden."

"Never." Ela took Chiara's coat off its hook and held it out for her.

"See Dot!" Peppy tugged at Ela's coat.

"Yes!" Ela scooped up Peppy and carried him to the car.

At the house, Carrick's gray eyes lit and his cheek dimpled. He was at the stove stirring a pot. "I have harmed neither the lunch nor the children."

"See Dot!"

"We really must teach him to say, 'See Carrick.'"

"Right after I teach him to button his own shoes." Caterina snatched Peppy back before he tracked dampness across Ela's good rugs and wrested his shoes off his feet. By then Dottie and Mina were squealing out of their bedroom as delighted to see him as he was to see them.

Ela quickly had Chiara situated on the davenport with a quilt, a pillow, and a second pillow nearby. "Caterina made some delicious bread yesterday, and I put some of every vegetable I had on hand into the soup. But if you'd rather just have broth, I'll strain it out."

"Where is Geppetto?" Caterina asked.

"He'll be along," Carrick said. "I sent him out with a hot lunch for the other hands stacking bales in the barn."

"The weather seems to be getting worse," Ela said. "A good day to stay inside and can, I guess!"

"If our little rascals will nap." Caterina laughed. "I will try to get them down as soon as we eat."

The back door opened and a blast of glacial air subsumed the warmth of the house. The children screamed in unison.

"Willie, what are you doing?" Carrick pointed a dripping spoon at his twin sister. "Close the door."

"Am I allowed to bring my husband in first?"

Charles crashed over the threshold and slammed the door. "I think the temperature has dropped ten degrees since we left our house in Pueblo. I'm a block of ice. I hope someday somebody invents a decent way to heat an automobile."

"I'll set two more places," Ela said. "Do you want coffee, Helmi?"

Carrick was the only one who called his sister Wilhelmina by her childhood nickname. To everyone else, she was Helmi.

"Yes, please," Helmi said.

"Where's my nephew?" Carrick asked.

"Home napping with Mrs. Meadows," Helmi said. "Too cold to bring him out."

"It's only going to get worse. So why have you come?"

Charles glanced toward Chiara dosing on the sofa. "We've had some news I thought you should hear in person. I know you have an interest in the mining situation."

The door opened again, and this time Geppetto blew in.

Chiara muttered in Italian.

"What did she say?" Ela asked.

"She said if she wanted to be this cold," Caterina said, "she could have stayed in the hut."

Carrick chuckled softly.

"So she didn't hear what Charles said?" Ela's voice was low and even.

"What did Charles say?" Geppetto's voice was not low and even.

Caterina glanced at Chiara, who now sat up to rearrange herself in an upright position and pull the quilt up.

"It's all right," Caterina said, "whatever it is, she might as well know."

"Do you want to know first?" Charles said. "You might have to translate."

"What is it?" Geppetto's whisper was hoarse now, but Chiara's dark eyes were wide and fixed on the huddle even from across the width of the house.

"There was a pretty bad shooting at the Forbes camp," Charles said. "I had a call from an old Pinkerton's connection who works for the sheriff's office down that way now. He doesn't have any idea I know someone connected to the strike."

"You know Geppetto and Caterina," Carrick said, "because he used to help me out when Willie and I were with Pinkerton's, and they know someone connected to the strike."

"Don't split hairs, Carrick," Charles said. "I know Chiara's English is limited, but this is going to be in the news. Forbes is practically just down the road from Ludlow."

"Ludlow?"

They all turned to see Chiara standing in the wide doorway to the kitchen. How had none of them noticed she'd left the sofa and inched toward their whispered conversation?

"Ludlow?" she repeated.

Geppetto pulled out a chair at the kitchen table for Chiara.

Mina, Dottie, and Peppy tumbled over each other, giggling, and Ela herded them out of the way and back into the other room.

Caterina swallowed and prepared to translate the facts as they came from Charles. They all knew there had already been an exchange of gunfire between strikers and guards hired by the mine operators ten days earlier. And Celestrino had written that the guards had been shining searchlights into tent colonies at night to taunt the striking miners.

Now, Charles explained somberly, they had attached a machine gun to an armored car. They called it the "Death Special." Earlier that day they sprayed it into the Forbes camp, which was only five miles south of Ludlow, and one miner was killed. A child was shot nine times in the leg. Gunfire raked the whole colony with dozens of holes shot into many of the tents.

"Celestrino." Chiara wept as Caterina finished translating.

"Celestrino is fine," Caterina said. "He hasn't said anything about going to Forbes, has he?"

Chiara shook her head.

"So he's fine."

"Today he is fine," Chiara said. "And tomorrow? When they take this Death Special to Ludlow?"

No one spoke. How could they? What promise could they make?

"I must see him," Chiara said. "You will take me? With an automobile? You will take me?"

"Chiara, no," Caterina said. "You are not strong enough. You can barely eat. You can hardly walk from one room to the next most of the time. Celestrino would not want you to come. You know this."

"I will try to find out what is happening in Ludlow," Geppetto said, "even if I have to go there on the train."

"Geppetto!" Caterina would not allow this. Geppetto was not even a miner. It was hard enough for them in Ludlow the first time they went. It was more dangerous now.

"They have a telephone," Carrick said. "We'll find a way to call them."

"What if they are cutting the line?" Chiara said.

"I'm sure the union will connect it again. We'll get a message to him. Remember, Charles and Willie and I all worked for Pinkerton's. And Geppetto used to help when he worked in the hotel in Denver. We know a few tricks."

Caterina translated in the most reassuring tone she could muster.

"This is all true?" Chiara sought confirmation in Caterina's eyes.

"All true."

"When you speak to him," Ela said, "ask him again if he will come to the ranch. Tell him I asked. Tell him I want him to come."

Chiara's eyes brimmed. "Then I will sit on the davenport and wait for Celestrino to call me." Chiara pushed her chair back.

"Eat," Caterina said. "The soup is ready."

"I will wait in there."

Caterina eased out her breath. "Then I will bring your soup in there."

The rest of them ate at the table.

Caterina put the children down for their naps. She had to rub

Peppy's back for a long time before his eyes stayed closed.

Helmi and Charles bundled up for the drive back to their home in Pueblo and their own little boy.

Ela set up the stove and jars and tomatoes to can.

Geppetto brought in more wood for the fire, and Carrick built the fire high and hot.

Caterina made tea for Chiara.

Geppetto and Carrick donned their boots and jackets for an afternoon round of chores before dark.

The children woke from their naps.

Caterina changed all their diapers and fed them a snack.

Ela and Caterina began preparing an evening meal. They took turns reading to the children to try to keep them calm while the other coaxed Chiara to take some fluid and a few bites of something.

When Chiara lost everything they had painstakingly fed her all afternoon, Caterina cleaned up the bucket and started over with trying to help Chiara keep down some sugared tea.

Finally the telephone rang.

Ela answered. "Yes, I accept the charges!" She handed the phone to Chiara.

Caterina listened to the rapid fire Italian Chiara shot into the mouthpiece and shook her head slowly at Ela.

Finally Chiara hung up the phone. "He doesn't come. Not now. The strikers fight back. He say he must fight."

"Chiara, I'm so sorry," Ela said.

"I want to go to the hut now."

CHAPTER THIRTEEN

NOLAN DECLINED THE NUMBER the first time it showed up on his cell phone on Tuesday, as he did most unidentified numbers he didn't recognize. Then two things happened in rapid sequence. First an icon showing the caller left a message appeared and, second, even before Nolan had a chance to listen to the message to ascertain its validity, the number appeared again. The spam filters he and Jillian had on their cell phones caught the vast majority of calls that were phishing or robotic, so this didn't happen often. It was a number in Pueblo.

He paused his review of case files in his home office and answered the call the second time.

"Nolan Duffy here."

"Nolan Duffy the attorney?"

"Yes, that's right."

"My sister had your card in her purse. My wife found it."

Nolan's stocking feet hit the floor flat and he sat up straight.

"I thought about calling your office," the man said, "but when I saw your cell number written on the back of the card, I figured that must be for a reason."

"You figured right," Nolan said. "You are Ms. Polombo's brother?"

"Yes. Marc."

"What can I help you with, Mr. Polombo?"

"It's my sister who needs help. Are you really her lawyer?"

Nolan hadn't phoned Cate since Sunday, two days earlier, because he hadn't yet been able to reach the satisfactory conclusion to discussions he'd begun yesterday with the attorney representing Epic EduKids. "Perhaps you'd better tell me what prompted your call beyond finding my card."

"It seems like you're kind of far away, but if Rini is in trouble, and if you're really her lawyer, then I guess we're asking if you can help. She doesn't listen to us."

Nolan reached for his pen and a legal pad. "Tell me what happened."

When the conversation ended, Nolan had less than a page of notes. Marc clearly was frustrated with his sister, but the legal facts were sparse. Nolan went downstairs to interrupt what otherwise had seemed like a quiet day for his daughter in her own office directly beneath his.

"Jillian, can I have a minute?"

She looked up at him, blinking a few times as her mind made the transition from what she'd been focused on.

"Someone from Cate's family just called me." Nolan pulled one of the side chairs close to Jillian's desk.

Jillian dropped the pen in her hand to the desktop. "Who?"

"Her brother, Marc."

Jillian was quiet. "You've talked to one of my other distant cousins before I even met any of them?"

"This was not a familial introduction, Jillian. It was a legal request."

"But didn't they know they were calling my father?"

"It didn't sound that way, actually. They found a lawyer's business card and phoned the number."

"But my name is Parisi-Duffy, and you're Duffy. Surely that should set off alerts."

His accomplished professional daughter was sinking in her desk chair, red-faced and beaten back by a call from a man she didn't know.

"Jillian, you know I would move heaven and earth for you," Nolan said softly.

"You're my father. It's in the parents' playbook that you have to say that." Jillian scratched the side of her head. "But I do know."

"I know Cate said something about having you meet her family next weekend, but we don't know that she has even said anything about you to them yet."

Jillian looked away. "I guess she has had her mind on other things."

"Marc's wife found my card in Cate's purse and he called."

"Marco."

"I'm sorry?"

"His name is Marco. She has two brothers, Marco and Rocco. Pretty Italian, right?"

"I guess he decided to be Marc."

Jillian cleared her throat. "Instead of having a meltdown about the fact that you got to talk to him before I did, I should have asked what he wanted. Why was somebody going through Cate's purse?"

Nolan raised his yellow legal page of notes. "There was an altercation. Cate had a short stay with the sheriff in Trinidad, requiring someone to come down and vouch for her. "

"She was arrested?"

"Think of it more like squabbling kids who had to be separated for their own good. In the end there were no charges—yet."

"Dad!"

"I know. This isn't what you thought you were signing on for."

"Not at all."

"Marc said he escorted her back to Pueblo."

"Probably a condition of no charges being filed."

"That's my daughter. Smart girl." Nolan stood. "Being in different counties might be the way to cool things off. If I'm her lawyer, which I guess I am, I need to talk to her. Since she's under house arrest for the rest of the day, I'm going to give her a video call right now."

"Can I listen?"

"That's up to Cate."

A few minutes later, Nolan opened his office door and signaled Jillian should come in. He had already pulled up a chair so they could both easily see Cate, whose face filled his computer monitor.

"I just want to tell my side of the story," Cate said. "It's not what you think."

"I don't think anything." Nolan turned to a fresh page in his legal pad. "Just tell me what happened, and we'll go from there."

"I was seriously minding my own business," Cate said. "I had some letters to mail. That's all. There's a mailbox down on the corner, and I knew there was a ten o'clock pickup, so I went running down to make sure I got there in time."

"That sounds harmless. So what happened?"

"The administrative assistant from Epic EduKids chased me, all full of drama. "

"Why would she do that?"

"She said some papers were missing from her desk, and she wanted them back. I said I certainly didn't have them. She didn't believe me and kept coming at me. Down the stairs behind the bookstore. Out the door. Halfway down the block. I was just trying to get to the mailbox."

"What kind of papers?" Nolan asked.

"I don't even know. I didn't ask. I was trying to do what you said and stay under the radar. Then I dropped my letters because I was walking too fast, and wow, her foot just happened to land smack on top of one of them. That ticked me off. I said I didn't have her stupid papers, but if anybody knew about stealing business documents, I was sure she probably had a few she'd like to return to me. We went a couple of rounds."

"Oh, Cate," Jillian said.

"I know. Not the best. People were staring, I was just trying to pick up my letters, and the mail carrier was driving away from the box and it was too late anyway, and she started saying she's going to report me for harassment again. I drove over to the post office to mail my letters, and by the time I got back to my office, someone from the sheriff's department was waiting for me, and the admin was gloating from the doorway of her office. Smirking."

Nolan finished making a few notes and then asked. "Can you remember who might have overheard any of this?"

Cate named the owners of several shops and a couple of townspeople she recognized.

"Did you give these names to the sheriff's department?"

"They didn't ask."

"Oh?"

"They just warned me about the whole harassment thing," Cate said. "But I didn't start this. She provoked me. I tried to just walk away and she wouldn't let me."

"Unfortunately, it doesn't really work that way," Nolan said. "You said you went a couple of rounds. Tell me exactly what you each said, as best you can remember."

Nolan and Jillian listened, Nolan writing key phrases.

"Maybe you should think about moving your office," Jillian said. "Some distance from Epic EduKids might help."

"I signed a lease," Cate said. "Penalties for breaking it are pretty stiff. My grant won't cover double rent. I'm barely making it right now."

"It was just an idea."

"I'll make some calls about the harassment question," Nolan said, "and be in touch."

They clicked off the call.

"What do you really think, Dad?" Jillian asked.

"She was baited, in my opinion, but of course that will be difficult to prove," Nolan said. "What will matter is what people heard and who they heard say it?"

"I'm sorry my quest for a cousin is turning into such a big time suck for you."

"Don't worry about it, Jillian. Go back to work. I can read cases later tonight, so I'll make some calls now, while I have the best chance to get hold of people. I'll let you know what I find out."

With the added motivation of this new event, Nolan leaned harder into reaching the authorities in the local office of the Las Animas County Sheriff's Department for the details of the previous harassment matter and the new information of today's occurrence. He wasn't settling for callbacks now, instead insisting on staying on hold until someone would come on the line and talk to him. Finally he called Cate back.

"It's a skirmish," he said. "I don't think there will be formal charges. You can assure your family you won't actually need the services of an attorney if you'll agree to make an apology and promise to stop making accusatory statements in public."

"But this was not my fault!" Cate's resistance was adamant. "They should be apologizing to me."

"I tend to agree they are not entirely without fault," Nolan said, "but the matter of the prior harassment does not stand in your favor."

"Can't you just tell them I won't do it again?"

"That's what I was trying to do after we talked on Sunday, but this escalation makes that argument unconvincing."

"I'm not the one who escalated!"

"There don't seem to be any witnesses who heard the admin accuse you of stealing documents, but there are witnesses who heard you accuse her."

Cate was quiet.

"Cate, this is a good solution."

"Not for me."

"I understand it doesn't feel that way in the moment, but from a legal perspective, it is. I'll talk to your brother, if you'd like."

"No. Don't call him."

"The sheriff's department is going to want to hear from you, or from me on your behalf."

"I'm not ready to say I'll apologize."

"Give it some thought and we'll circle back." Nolan could tell the opposing attorney Cate was thinking, and that would buy her some time. "In the meantime, you should probably stay in Pueblo."

He went downstairs to bring Jillian up to speed.

"She's going to need some persuading," he said after giving her the details.

"It's not family law," Jillian said, "but at least it's in the neighborhood of mediation, so it's up your alley."

"I suspect this is going to require a personal visit," he said. "Neither of us can keep driving back and forth between Canyon Mines and Trinidad. It takes half a day to get there. I had hoped bringing her here on the weekend would settle things down."

"I'll go."

Jillian's words shocked Nolan. Just a few minutes ago she'd been pushing the problem off on him. "I thought you were uncomfortable with all of this."

"Maybe that's not a reason not to do it."

"Maybe you feel a bit of a calling?" Nolan raised his eyebrow. "'Speak, for your servant is listening.' Isn't that what Samuel said when he finally figured out who was calling?"

"If Nia tells her children's sermons right, that would be it."

"'Here I am. Send me.'"

"That's Isaiah, and you know it."

"So you did pay attention in Sunday school all those years. Another memorable calling."

"I'll talk to Cate because it seems like the right thing to do. I want to see Min anyway and make sure she's all right." Jillian shuffled some papers together. "I'll go tomorrow, if Min and Drew will have me. I'll take my laptop and work from the ranch for a few days. Maybe it will still work out to meet Cate's family on the weekend, and I'd be going anyway."

Nolan nodded. "Maybe."

"If it does work out, you could come down—just for the weekend. It would be great to have you there."

Green eyes met green eyes. "Of course, Jilly. If you want me there, I would love to be there."

This wasn't supposed to be about the mess Cate was in. It was supposed to be about genealogy and findings her cousins. And maybe it still would be.

"I'll call Drew, then," Jillian said, "and see what he thinks about seeing me two weeks in a row."

Nolan quirked a half-smile. "I think we know the answer."

Jillian's phone rang. "That's Raúl."

"Talk to him."

Nolan dialed Drew's number on his way up the stairs. "Jillian's going to ask about coming down tomorrow for a few days. Maybe through the weekend. Tell her she can come."

"Of course she can," Drew said. "But I may have to take some hours at the restaurant."

"That's fine. She wants to see Min as well. I have a few personal matters to attend to, and it's better if she's gone for a couple of days, if you get my drift."

"Ah. Yes. You have my full support."

Nolan ended the call. He would go on Saturday if Jillian wanted him, or he'd stay out of the way if she wanted to meet her Italian cousins on her own. She was strong and independent. She'd made her own decision to spit in a tube and see if her DNA matched anyone's. But whoever she met were Bella's cousins too. And Bella would have insisted he come to see what her curiosity had uncovered.

He did have things to do between now and the weekend.

Nolan took a moment to pull up the photo on his phone that he looked at two or three times a day lately. Bella on their wedding day—not the formal portrait by the hired photographer but the picture his brother had captured after the ceremony when Bella turned with her wide smile and the sun backlit her radiant face. It had always been Nolan's favorite.

Of all the things you've missed, sweet Bella, this might be the worst.

CHAPTER FOURTEEN

Pueblo, Colorado

"YOU REALLY THINK I HAVE to do this?" Cate's brown eyes sagged, no luster shining from them.

"My dad is really good at what he does," Jillian said. "If he says this is the best thing, then I trust that."

They stood on a bridge along Pueblo's riverwalk overlooking Gateway Park and the water. Jillian had been here a couple of times with Drew. Once, at the height of summer, it had been beastly hot even on the river, but it was still a lovely memory.

"I got an email from my grant board." Cate leaned over the rail. "They're not happy."

"How did they find out?"

"I don't know. It doesn't matter. They said that if this matter is not satisfactorily cleared up, obviously the grant will be withdrawn, and if there is even another hint of impropriety, they will find it necessary to dissociate from my work."

"Wow. It doesn't sound like they asked you what happened."

"Nope. Just something else that's not fair." Cate kicked a rock, as if on behalf of every wrongly treated child who nevertheless was expected to apologize.

At least it seemed that way to Jillian. "I know. But there's no backing up the train otherwise, and you really need it to back up."

Cate sighed. "But I don't have to like it."

"No, you don't."

"Can I just leave them a note?"

"Whenever I messed up when I was a kid," Jillian said, "my mom would say that the sincerity factor would be a lot more convincing face to face."

"Your mom. She was the Parisi."

Jillian nodded. "She would have liked your Italian spitfire."

"But she would still have told me to apologize."

"Pretty sure."

"I guess if I agree, that means I could go home to my apartment in Trinidad instead of being under my brother's thumb and having my mother wondering why I'm here. I can't apologize in person if I'm not there."

Jillian chuckled. "If I were you, I'd go in to the office long enough to say sorry and gather what you need to work from home for the rest of the week. Just lie low."

"I'm paying rent and I can't even work in my office."

"Do you get along well with Patrice?"

Cate shrugged. "She only works for me part-time, usually only if I'm there or if I give her specific projects. She's not a researcher, but she does all right with organizing and errands. She seems to keep to herself."

"Then take a couple of days. Give Patrice a project or adjust her hours."

"You would never have to do that, because you would never get yourself in this mess in the first place."

"You'd be surprised how much I trip over my own good intentions." Jillian shifted her weight.

"Seems like your dad is in your corner, though."

"He is."

"I don't have that advantage."

Jillian didn't know what to say, so she said nothing.

"Well, I promised I would introduce you to the family. You can meet them all and decide for yourself. Before I leave today, I'll tell them about you."

Jillian's mouth went dry.

"You said you were going to stay a few days?" Cate asked.

"I think so."

"Then maybe lunch on Saturday. I'll email you if I can set it up."

"Maybe meeting one or two would be a start."

"Oh, they'll all want to be there," Cate said. "As soon as they find out there's another Parisi—one whose name is actually Parisi—they'll want to gawk. I guarantee you. If I don't at least invite them all, I'll just be in trouble."

"Then I hope to see you Saturday." Jillian gulped. "And you should probably give my dad a call and let him know what you decided about the other thing."

"I suppose he'll tell somebody to expect me. Hold my feet to the fire or something."

Jillian couldn't help but give a crooked smile. "That's my dad."

"And he did say if I get you, I get him."

Jillian had done her best. She could check in later to see if her father had heard from Cate and if the plan was proceeding. And she would have to sit on her hands and wait to see if Cate followed through on setting up a meeting with her family. Was Jillian even ready? All of them at once? To be gawked at? Curious, absolutely. But jittery nonetheless. For now, Jillian was ready to feast her eyes and spirit on the ranch—and some reassurance that Min really was all right and feel Drew's arms around her.

Her shoulders sank a little as she drove through the black iron gates and along the ranch road and didn't spot Drew's truck in front of the little red house or near the barns or up beside the main house. He'd said he might have to go into town. If she'd taken a moment to call him before she left the Riverwalk, she might have been able to meet him in town.

He'd be back. He knew she was coming.

Jillian pulled up to the main house and parked. Before going to the door she took a minute to check her phone and take it off silent.

Nothing from Drew.

But there was a voicemail from Nia. "My friend in Genesee says there's a fabulous new dress boutique in town with grand opening prices. How about I leave Leo in charge of the Inn and we go on a shopping spree?"

Jillian didn't need any new dresses, even if she weren't out of town, perhaps for the next four days. She tapped out a quick text and then went to the door to knock.

Min took just long enough to answer for a flush of anxiety to unsteady Jillian, but there Min was, nodding and gesturing that Jillian should come in.

"I've just made tea. I know you're a coffee person, but you can humor an old woman, can't you?"

"For you, anything." Jillian grinned.

"Drew says you've been to see the Polombo girl." Min led the way to the kitchen.

"It was a nice day for a stroll on the Riverwalk."

Min side-eyed her. "A stroll?"

"More than that." Jillian accepted the honey jar Min offered and dribbled some into her tea. "How much did Drew tell you?"

"Only that your father is advising her on a legal matter and you came down as sort of an emissary."

Jillian laughed. "I guess that's all true. She needs to apologize for something, but she doesn't believe it's her fault so she thinks it's unfair she has to apologize."

"What do you think?"

Jillian shrugged. "The bigger picture is not quite in focus, but she has a lot to lose if she doesn't do this." Mostly, Jillian thought, Cate needed to keep her head down and make sure there were no further incidents.

"The price of standing up for what's fair can be steep."

Min's words settled in as she poured her own tea. Cate must know this. Jillian had seen some of the photos Cate had from the coal strike. The simple sentence could caption her entire project.

"I might meet the Polombo family this weekend," Jillian said. "I'm not sure what I'm walking into."

"They're hardworking people. Drew knows them, of course. I don't see them much anymore. I see the friends I like to play cards with and people I've known all my life at church, but I don't feel much need to drive into town for a heavy dinner any more."

"It would be fun for me to see the restaurant where Drew used to be the chef and manager."

"It was a good job but a lot of hours." Min poured a dab more cream into her tea. "He seems to like the freedom he has to sing concerts and still cook but work fewer hours."

"He loves living and working here on the ranch."

"The Polombo girl's people started out working on the ranch—not her parents, of course. I mean when they were Parisis."

"Parisis? Right here on your ranch?" Jillian startled.

Min's gaze drifted out the kitchen window. "It was a long time ago, when the other little girl named Mina—short for Wilhelmina—was born on the ranch. And my mother, Dorothy. Dottie. You remember. You did our family tree."

Jillian nodded. The first Wilhelmina was Carrick Kyp's sister, the second was his daughter, and the third was sitting at the table having tea.

"My grandfather hired a Parisi couple to work on the ranch before they moved into town."

Jillian cradled her mug in both hands, flabbergasted. "Drew never said anything. Nor Cate."

"They might not know. It was so long ago. I don't know why I didn't think of it long before this, once I learned your name." Min's gray eyes fixed on Jillian's face. "I'm sorry. An old woman's mind can go missing so easily at my age. Forgive me."

"That was before your time," Jillian said. "Even your mother would have been a child."

"Of course. But there were always stories."

Wistful longing cast its spell over the silence of steaming tea, hunting for a nostalgic thread to tug. This house? Jillian wondered. This kitchen? Geppetto right here?

"Even when I was little and they didn't live here, we always knew them," Min said. "Family friends. There's a case somewhere. It might even be in that room I've been trying to sort out for the last few months. I've come across a few things I'm sure are from that time."

"A case?" Jillian asked. Tangible items. Sentimental reminders. Chosen and saved.

"The rummage sale has made me more aware how much stuff so many people have that no one is ever going to want." Min sighed. "I've been wrong to be one of those people. The house itself and the property of the ranch are one thing. They belong to a family trust. And I've finally agreed that important documents belong in the safe deposit box. But everything in the main house? And the little red house? No one will have the patience to go through everything."

"It's a shame when people discard history." Jillian guarded her comment.

"If anyone else wanted to live here full-time, they'd want to modernize. An updated kitchen. More bathrooms. Knock out a bedroom in order to have a walk-in closet. It would take quite an investment. The money would have to come from somewhere, and it's not hidden in any of the boxes in my spare room."

"I suppose not." Jillian sipped tea and wondered if Min would work her way back to the case that might or might not connect to Parisis on the ranch.

"The real value is the land. I know that." Min carried her half-empty mug to the sink. "They think I've been a stubborn old fool about so many things, but I'm not a complete dolt."

"No one thinks you're a fool or a dolt," Jillian said. Drew certainly didn't. And she'd met enough of his family to be certain that while Min did take some managing as she aged, she was well loved. "In my line of work, I've seen enough people overwhelmed by piles of old papers."

A few boxes was one thing. An entire house after someone passed away was another.

Min leaned toward the window over the kitchen sink. "Here comes Drew."

Jillian looked out now, too, and saw his truck. The question of a Parisi case would have to wait. He parked beside her car and began pulling groceries out of his vehicle. Jillian went out to help.

First she paused for a welcome kiss, stretching her face toward him over the bags he held in his arms and stroking one side of his face

"Mmm, hello," he said, barely breaking the kiss to greet her.

She finished a proper kiss before taking groceries from his arms, freeing him up to grab more.

"Min was watching all of that, wasn't she?" Jillian said.

"Right out the window."

"Well, she never goes to the movies. We can give her some PG entertainment."

Drew laughed. "How did it go with Rini?"

She gave him the day's report while they carried groceries inside and unloaded them into Min's cupboards and refrigerator.

"So we know what is supposed to happen," Jillian said, "and now we'll wait to see what actually happens."

"She'll come around," Drew said.

"You really think so?"

"I do. You've seen her at her worst. She isn't always like that. Rini is smart. Ambitious. Visionary."

"I told you I would get the groceries." Min stood in the doorway.

"I was in town anyway," Drew said. "It was no trouble. I got everything you would have gotten, plus a few actual fruits and vegetables."

"Don't get smart with me, young man."

"Too late, Aunt Min."

His phone rang. "It's the restaurant." Drew wandered into the living room while he took the call. When he returned he grimaced.

"That was Mary Lou."

Mary Lou Butler Polombo. Mary Lou's Kitchen. Cate's mother, the woman the restaurant was named for. Jillian took it all in.

"They're doing a big anniversary party tonight. The guest list just expanded and she's panicking that they won't have enough desserts. She's offering a premium price if I come in and whip up a batch of something."

"Oh." Wind went out of Jillian. She'd known he wouldn't be around every minute during this impromptu multi-day visit, but he'd just arrived.

"You could come along."

"To the restaurant? Where Cate's family is? I don't think so. I could never explain that to Cate later."

"We wouldn't have to say who you are. Just coming along to help. A chef's assistant."

It was tempting. Curiosity surged. But she might catch herself staring more than helping. And Cate might still feel double-crossed. Besides, what would she do about her Parisi hair and a face that looked so much like Cate's? Jillian wasn't interested in a role in a made-for-TV movie.

"I think I should stay here," Jillian said.

"Not an unreasonable decision. I'm sorry that I feel like I need to do this," Drew said. "I was hoping to cook for you both. But there's a lentil and spinach stew in the refrigerator that will warm nicely. And I bought plenty of things for a salad."

"I can handle that," Jillian said.

Drew pointed at Min. "You have to eat something."

"If I'm hungry, I'll eat. Don't get bossy with me."

Drew pointed at Jillian. "You have to kindly and gently persuade Aunt Min to eat."

"Um, I'll do my best?"

"I'm going to go put my feet up." Min shuffled out of the room again.

"Is she really not eating?" Jillian asked.

"Not enough, but she might with your company."

"I'll try."

He leaned in for a quick kiss. "I'll bring back dessert if you can wait up for me."

"Always."

CHAPTER FIFTEEN

Wednesday, December 24, 1913
Outside Pueblo, Colorado

CATERINA LEANED OVER THE SINK and peered out the window toward the hut.

"She is coming, yes?" Geppetto said.

"Yes." Caterina scrubbed harder on the pan where the remains of breakfast were overly stubborn.

"She just likes to be alone for a few minutes." Geppetto dapped a cloth under a weak stream of water and wiped Giuseppe's face.

"I know. She reads Celestrino's letters over there and writes to him."

"At least she stays here with us most of the time now."

"Down." Giuseppe slapped the side of his chair.

"Down, please, Papa" Geppetto said.

"Down, peez, Papa."

Geppetto set the boy on his feet and watched him race off.

"She's still so thin," Caterina said. "Six months gone, and no fat on her except the bambino bump."

"The doctor said she's doing all right, didn't he?"

Caterina scrubbed. "Yes. But she could be better. He thought she would be able to eat more by now."

"You're helping her as much as you can, Caterina."

"She's been here three months. I know she worries about Celestrino, but she still vomits every day, and I have to be so careful what food I prepare. If it smells just a little bit wrong to her, the next minute she is heaving over the pail."

"Caterina."

"I know. I cannot fix everything. You tell me this so many times."

"Because it is true."

Caterina cocked her head. "Peppy is not playing with the tree again, is he?"

"Probably." Geppetto pivoted to go around the corner into the main room.

Caterina listened to her husband's soothing tones explain—once again—why Giuseppe must not pull on the ornaments hanging from the tree branches and why he must not try to pull the paper off the packages underneath. But he was a boy close to two and curious about so many things. At the main house was another tree with more ornaments and more packages, and when they went into town to the shops in Pueblo, the windows full of lights and charm were nearly too much to keep any of the children in their own skin. Perhaps the wonder in their eyes was the best part of Christmas.

How lonely Chiara must be. Celestrino had promised to try to come, at least for a visit, after the shooting at Forbes. Ludlow was not so far, and the trains ran. But his letters only told Chiara why he had not come.

Caterina wanted to write him with a piece of her mind, but Geppetto threatened to hide all the paper and pencils in the little red house if she tried. Celestrino and Chiara wrote to each other often, he said. Caterina did not want Geppetto to go see Celestrino, and Geppetto did not want Caterina to write to him behind Chiara's back. Their separation was for the two of them to sort out.

"I have to go now." Geppetto was back, breaking into her thoughts.

"How long do you think you'll be?"

"A few hours, perhaps. We have to see to the animals even on Christmas Eve before Ela and Carrick go into town to have dinner with Charles and Wilhelmina. I said I would check on the barn animals again later so they don't have to hurry back."

"You are a good man, Geppetto Parisi." Caterina began drying dishes. "Ela insists we must come for Christmas dinner tomorrow, but she won't let me bring anything."

"Pandoro." Geppetto winked.

"Star cake! Your aunt gave me the mold for our wedding."

"Ela cannot be annoyed with someone who brings a star cake for Christmas."

"The bambinos will love it."

"Maybe even Chiara will eat a few bites of a traditional food." Geppetto kissed Caterina's cheek. "I will be back as soon as I can, and we'll have a nice day."

She nodded and put the clean plates back on the shelf before going to see what mischief Peppy might be getting into. He lay on his tummy on the floor, chin in his hands and feet kicking loosely in the air behind him as he gazed at the tree, obedient of the boundary Geppetto had established. Morning light spilling through the picture window brightened his dark brown eyes.

"My little Peppito," Caterina said.

He flipped onto his back, grinned at her, and giggled. She dove for him to tickle him and send him into spasms of laughter. His little arms grabbed her neck, and she smooched kisses all over his cheeks, making him squeal even more. Caterina's heart lightened. What had she done to deserve this perfect little boy who spilled so much light into her life?

Peppy's kiss on her nose was very wet, and Caterina shrieked in amusement. "Peppy, Peppy, Peppy, what are you doing?" She wrapped her arms around his form and rolled with him across the floor. He whooped in pleasure.

"Mama, cold!" he said.

Caterina looked up at the open front door as Chiara same in. "You're back! I'll make you some tea."

"I do not need anything."

"You need to stay warm."

"I need my Peppito." Chiara sat on the davenport and patted the cushion beside her. "Come sit with your Zia Chiara."

Giuseppe gladly hurled himself toward the sofa and climbed up to snuggle against Chiara. Slightly winded, Caterina got to her feet and returned to the kitchen to light the stove and put the kettle on. Chiara cooed to Peppy in Italian, reminding Caterina once again the she should make more effort to be sure he learned the language when he was already growing up with so much English around him on the ranch. Peppy spoke to Chiara in English, but Chiara answered in Italian, and the two of them seemed to have little trouble communicating.

When the water boiled, Caterina added a spoonful of sugar to one cup. She observed that if the tea was sweet, it was more likely to stay in Chiara's stomach and she might even agree to a piece of toast to go with it. With the cup in one hand and toast on a plate in the other, Caterina returned to the main room.

"*Neve!*" Giuseppe said.

"I teach him neve," Chiara said, "and he teach me snow."

"Snow at Christmas is beautiful," Caterina said. Snow made the work on the ranch harder for the men, but the sun was shining. No doubt the days would warm again soon and the snow would melt. Carrick said many times he was glad for the moisture going into the ground in the hay pastures. When they planted in the spring, it could make the difference in the crop's success.

"Celestrino says snow in the camp is deep. It is hard to move it, but they make snow balls."

"That sounds fun."

"They cannot throw snow balls at the Death Special."

"Drink your tea." Caterina took Peppy onto her lap to keep him away from the hot liquid. "You'll see Celestrino soon."

"Do you think so?"

Caterina gave the most sincere smile she could muster. It was Christmas. "Is the tea sweet enough? Not too hot?"

"Hot." Peppy reached out, and Caterina gently guided his hand down. He had understood the Italian word and translated it to English. Such a smart boy!

"Too hot for you, bambino." Chiara tentatively sipped. "But not for me."

Peppito grinned and Chiara beamed back.

"He loves having you here," Caterina said.

"He makes me want to be here. When I am in the hut, writing to Celestrino, I wonder if we will have a little boy. And I think it would be wonderful."

"A boy or a girl will be wonderful. But you must drink your tea and eat your toast."

"My toast." Peppy reached again.

"No, no, Peppito," Caterina said, "this is Chiara's toast."

"My toast."

Chiara smiled and tore off a bite to hand him. "We will share."

"You spoil him, Chiara."

"He likes to speak Italian with me."

Caterina laughed. "You speak Italian. He turns it into English."

"More, peez," Peppy said.

"Such nice manners." Chiara gave him more bread.

"Chiara," Caterina said, "do not give him all your toast. You must try to eat."

Chiara put a bite in her own mouth and chewed slowly.

"Papa!" Giuseppe slithered off the sofa and ran to the front window.

"What are you talking about?" Caterina said. "You know Papa went to work."

"Papa!" He banged his palm on the glass.

"Giuseppe, no. No banging." Caterina scampered across the room and scooped him up—and gasped at what she saw. She glanced at Chiara and moved toward the door with the boy in her arms.

Geppetto came through the door and stomped snow off his feet. "I have a present for Chiara."

Chiara set down her mug of tea and twisted around. "Celestrino!" She tried to get up, but her bulging abdomen kept her sunk in the cushions, and her husband reached her first and pulled her to her feet.

Caterina swatted Geppetto's arm. "You did not say!"

"I did not know! Celestrino telephoned Carrick. They arranged it all. He had already left for the train station by the time I got up to the barn."

"I think I should put on some coffee." Caterina handed Peppy to Geppetto.

"I think I should help you."

Caterina snickered as they took their son past the kissing couple in the front room.

"*Bacio, bacio,*" Giuseppe said.

"Now Peppy decides to speak Italian," Geppetto said.

"And kiss, kiss is what he says."

By the time they returned with coffee and warmed cake with a sweet drizzle, Chiara sat on the davenport again, and Celestrino had one big hand on her belly, fingers spread in wonderment.

"You have taken good care of her, Caterina," Celestrino said. "She is thin, but the bambino is growing."

"And you keep a very good secret." Caterina handed him a plate of cake while Geppetto stoked the fire.

"I wanted to be sure. We have had so much snow. I couldn't be sure the train would run. But coming here on Christmas Eve—I have been dreaming for weeks."

"Everything will be all right now that you have finally come," Chiara said. "We can move back to the hut. It is small, but it is not so bad. Caterina and Geppetto used to live there. And it won't be lonely at all with you there."

Celestrino swallowed a bite of cake and went back to rubbing his wife's belly.

"Celestrino?" Chiara ducked her head to capture her husband's falling glance.

"Let's just have a happy Christmas, Chiara."

"Are you only here for Christmas?" She stopped his hand on her midsection and gripped his fingers. "Celestrino?"

"I wrote to you that the Colorado National Guard came after what happened at Forbes."

"Yes. And Geppetto told me what the papers say. They are not keeping the peace. You are going to get hurt. They have taken the side of the owners."

"A strike is not just about one man, Chiara. It is not just about me. We are a union. One. You understand this."

"I understand we are a union." She pointed at her stomach. "One. Two. Soon to be three."

"Please understand, Chiara. We have to stop the strikebreakers from riding the trains to the camps above Ludlow. If they break the strike now, all these weeks are for nothing. All of us will lose our jobs, and the mines will never be any safer."

Geppetto poked the fire, which roared to higher heat instantly. Peppy leaned into Caterina's side, his thumb in his mouth.

"Shh, it's okay," she whispered.

"Zia Chia okay?" he said.

Caterina kissed his head.

"They are putting strikers in jail against the law," Celestrino said. "They don't follow the laws of the state or the country."

"You must stay here until this is settled, Celestrino." Chiara's voice broke. "I know others have left. We went to Ludlow colony because we did not think we had anywhere else to go."

"I know. I thank God every day that you are safe here. But there is work to do in Ludlow."

"What work? You cannot mine. You live in a tent with other men in three feet of snow."

"Chiara, twelve hundred people live in the colony. There are mothers and children there with nowhere else to go. We work together to stay safe. Digging trenches. Fighting back. Mother Jones is organizing protests. If it weren't for the bambino, I know you would want to be there too, for all the other bambinos."

"Celestrino, please."

Their dark eyes met. Caterina had to look away.

CHAPTER SIXTEEN

Outside Pueblo, Colorado

JILLIAN WARMED THE LENTIL AND SPINACH stew and tossed a salad with the mixed greens she found in the refrigerator along with slicing in some red and orange bell peppers for color. Four bottles of dressing lined a rack in the door of the fridge, and she put them all on the table hoping to entice Min with a favorite among them. When she had poured two glasses of ice water and set out plates for the salad and bowls for the stew, she went into the living room and spoke Min's name softly.

In her recliner, Min roused immediately. "I was only resting my eyes."

"I have supper ready."

"I've been making my own supper for over sixty-five years, you know."

"Then it's time someone else did it for you once in a while, wouldn't you say?"

"Are you this sassy with everyone?" Min lowered her footrest.

"Pretty much."

"I guess there's no hope of reforming you."

"My father would tell you I'm beyond hope."

"I've met your father. He is the source of your sassiness."

Laughter burst out of Jillian. "I am going to tell him you said that."

"You'll give him a big head."

They moved back into the kitchen and sat across from one another.

"Drew tells me your family has a special grace you say."

"That's right."

"Then let's say that one."

Jillian smiled. "May you always find nourishment for your body at the table. May sustenance for your spirit rise and fill you with each dawn. And may life always feed you with the light of joy along the way."

"It has the rhythm of an Irish blessing."

"From my Irish great-grandmother." Jillian began ladling stew into Min's bowl.

"And now you want to learn about your Italian side."

"I do."

"I hope you find what you're looking for."

"Thank you, Min." Jillian filled her own bowl and inhaled the fragrance of Drew's nourishment for the body.

Min put only a small amount of salad on her plate and said Jillian had given her too much stew—though Jillian had held back. Utensils clinking and dragging heightened the silence as Min seemed disinclined to much conversation. She ate, but not as much as Jillian would have liked to be able to report later to Drew. Was she tired because she didn't eat? Or did she not eat because she was too tired? It did seem like she had shed some weight since five or six weeks ago. Jillian found herself not at all artful at kindly and gently coaxing Min to eat more.

Finally, Min stopped pushing lentils around her bowl. "I'm tired. I think I'll just turn in early. Leave the dishes. I'll do them in the morning."

"That's all right," Jillian said. "I'll do them."

"Suit yourself." Min pushed her chair under the table and shuffled out of the kitchen and down the hall toward the wing of the house where the master bedroom was. If Jillian was remembering the history of the rambling house correctly, this had been the first addition.

Since Jillian had only warmed supper and not actually cooked, cleaning up was straightforward. She went to a guest room that had come later, as the original Kyp family expanded to their eventual four children and the ranch was enjoying prosperous days.

Certainly living at the far end of Main Street in a small mountain town like Canyon Mines was quiet, but the ranch unwound a bottomless silence. The creaks and groans of the house were unfamiliar to Jillian and still caused her to twitch and snap to alertness sometimes. If she was going to catch up on work, she needed some distraction. She found a playlist on her phone with just the right balance of relaxation and rhythm to work through the afternoon's emails and make a game plan for what she needed to accomplish during the next couple of days. A simple family tree for someone who didn't have the patience to work through basic genealogy sources available on a subscription website was the type of project that traveled fairly easily, at least at the broad initial stage. Finding some interesting original documents might mean digging into Jillian's network of genealogy colleagues in specific locations. Last winter Jillian had undertaken to help a new friend-turned-client whose foundation was looking for families of children who had been stolen and illegally adopted in the St. Louis area decades ago, and she had a team of other genealogists and researchers working with her now. She was the center of the brain hive of activity.

Jillian moved through the emails and a few voice mails on her phone, making decisions whenever she could to minimize transferring items to a task list for later. She had taken out her legal pad to make a realistic to-do list for two or three days on the ranch that allowed time to spend with Drew and Min while also keeping her business commitments.

A new email dinged in.

From Cate.

Reflexively, Jillian sucked in her breath as she opened it.

HI JILLIAN. JUST WANTED TO SAY THANKS FOR COMING ALL THE WAY DOWN AGAIN. I'M SURE THE DRIVING IS GETTING ANNOYING. I PROMISE TO DO MY ABSOLUTE BEST TO BEHAVE. I SUCKED IT UP AND APOLOGIZED. I ALMOST CONVINCED MYSELF I WAS CONTRITE. YOUR DAD SHOULD GET A GOOD REPORT OF IT ALL TOMORROW. NOW WE CAN GET ON WITH THINGS. ALSO, I FOUND THIS FAMILY TREE, SO I SCANNED IT FOR YOU. IT HAS NAMES AND DATES YOU MIGHT BE INTERESTED IN. LET'S PLAN ON SATURDAY TO MEET THE FAM. CATE.

Jillian shot back a quick acknowledgement and opened the attachment. It was handwritten, with some details marked out and corrections written in. Whoever had begun the project was making an effort for accuracy. Cate's generation was missing, but her parents appeared, and it went back from there with at least some entries for several generations.

This was gold.

Names and dates laid carefully in rectangles like bricks along a road called Jillian to the echoing past.

She heard a noise beneath the still-flowing melodies of her music and tilted her head as she paused the music. There it was again. Someone was moving around.

Taking only her phone, Jillian stuck her head into the hall. "Drew? Are you home already?"

The sound came again—clearly from a room across from the master bedroom in the old addition. No one slept there. Jillian was pretty sure it was a storage room of some sort. She padded down one hall, made a turn, and then down another toward the light of an open door and the sounds of scraping and grunting.

"Min? What are you doing up?"

"I thought of something." Min grunted against the weight of a box in an overstuffed closet. "That case with the things from the early days. It's in this closet. But there's so much in the way."

"Let me help you with that." Jillian moved toward the closet.

"I've got it." Min tugged on the box again.

"It looks heavy."

"I've moved it plenty of times on my own."

The box came free and toppled against Min's left wrist. Wincing, she jerked it back and let the box tumble to the floor, its contents spilling.

"Min!" Jillian reached her. Min was already cradling the injured wrist in the crook of her opposite arm. "That doesn't look good."

"Looks worse than it is." Min didn't meet Jillian's eyes, and she grimaced against her own breath.

"What it looks like is that you're in a lot of pain," Jillian said. "At least let me have a look."

They found a clear spot where Min could sit down in an empty chair, and Jillian gently lifted the wrist. Already it was swelling and turning colors.

"I'd feel better if we went to an urgent care clinic," Jillian said. "It's not that late. There must still be one open." If they had to, they'd go to the hospital's emergency room.

"I'm not going anywhere except back to bed."

"You need an X-ray. You might have broken your wrist."

"I didn't break anything except that box, which is now a big mess to clean up before we can get to anything else in the closet."

"Your wrist is what matters."

"I'm going back to my room, and you can find me an ace bandage. There should be a tub of first aid supplies in the big linen closet in the hall."

Jillian sighed. "How about some ibuprofen at least?"

"If you insist. There's some in my medicine cabinet. I don't know why I keep it. I never take it."

"Well, you need it tonight, so I'm glad it's there."

Jillian found the pain reliever and administered it before going in search of an ace bandage. On the way down the hall, she called Drew, hoping he could pick up. To her relief, he did.

"I broke your aunt," she said.

"I'll come as soon as I can," he said after her explanation, "but I'm mid-recipe at the moment. Wrap it and put some ice on it. If she won't go for an X-ray, we can't make her."

"Between the two of us," Jillian said, "we could pick her up and carry her to the car."

"And she still won't give consent when we get there. You're doing your best. We'll see what it's like in the morning."

"Are you still bringing me some dessert tonight?"

"I have to now. You're really earned it."

"Or really not earned it."

Jillian found the bandage in the first aid tub and an ice pack in the freezer and returned to Min.

"You're absolutely sure you won't go have this looked at?"

"Stop flapping on about that and get me a pillow to keep this elevated. You act like you've never seen a minor injury in your life. City people."

Jillian arranged a pillow to support Min's arm, wrapped the wrist the best she knew how based on her own experience of a strained wrist, and molded the ice pack around it.

"Twenty minutes before you throw this off," Jillian said.

"Turn off the light on your way out, please."

"I'll check on your later."

"No need."

Min's eyes were closed, whether in pain, rest, or simply to be left alone, Jillian wasn't sure. But she turned off the light and went back through the halls to the room where she was staying. It felt so far away now. She left the door open so she would have a better chance of hearing any sounds Min made. While she waited for Drew and the promised dessert, she dug into Cate's family tree and all the Parisi names she had never known.

Cosmo Polombo. Giuseppe.

Antenette. Carmella. Benedetta. Geppetto. Caterina. There she was, the first one.

Giuseppe—but not the first one. Salvatore—but not the first Salvatore, not Jillian's Salvatore. Valentina. Romana. C.C.

Geppetto. The young man Luciano in New Orleans had begged his brother Salvatore in Denver to receive. "At least take Geppetto," he'd written to Salvatore. "Save him. Think of Joe."

The first Sal, Lou, and Joe—Giuseppe, the third of the brothers from Sicily—who'd lost his life in mob violence because he picked the wrong side. But Sal had gotten out, and because of him, Lou's son had gotten out.

Luciano Parisi sent Geppetto to Denver, and Geppetto had brought his bride here to work on this ranch. Now it was a peculiar sensation, in the stillness of the creaking night and the acres of blackness wrapping the house under the wide, glittering sky, to feel the mingling of both her family and Drew's. Her mother's grandfather had stayed in Denver. His cousin had come to Pueblo to work on a ranch for Drew's ancestors.

CHAPTER SEVENTEEN

Outside Pueblo, Colorado

"Always good to see you." Nolan squeezed Min's uninjured right hand, his other hand on her shoulder to indicate she needn't get out of her recliner to see them off. Her feet were propped up, the television was on low, and Jillian had just refilled both Min's tea mug and her water glass.

"Likewise." Min adjusted the pillow propping up her left arm. "It's nice to have you here."

"Anything else you need, Min?" Jillian asked.

"Peace and quiet. You two scat," Min said. "Though I would not object if you came back with something in the neighborhood of dessert."

Nolan chuckled. "A daily habit?"

"Only the days Drew is making the desserts."

"How can I forget? I stopped by Carolyn's shop before I left town."

Min's eyes flickered with interest.

"I have a dozen of something or other for you."

"Don't just stand there."

Nolan produced the candies, a mix of marshmallow creams, peanut butter cups, and chocolate-covered cherries.

"We'll bring something for your supper," Jillian said. "You don't have to lift a finger until we get back."

"I will lift any fingers I choose to lift for any reasons I deem fit," Min said. "But I hope you have a good time."

Nolan and Jillian went out to his truck.

"Min needs a dog," Nolan said. "Don't people who live on ranches have dogs?"

"It's not a rule, Dad," Jillian said. "Besides, she's had lots of dogs. The last one died two years ago and she just hasn't been ready for another one."

Nolan turned the key in the ignition. "Somehow it doesn't seem right to leave her here alone."

"She insisted she didn't want to come to lunch with us, and she would have a fit if I canceled on account of her wrist. At least she finally let me take her to a doctor yesterday and get a proper brace. Drew and I have peace of mind that there's no fracture."

"But you said it's a very bad sprain."

"Yes. A small tear in the ligament, most likely. Six weeks to heal. Hopefully she won't get up and decide to move boxes. She's not much of a TV watcher, but she does like her recliner and a book."

Nolan turned out through the black iron gates onto the road leading toward Pueblo. "Big day for you, Jilly." He glanced over at her as she sucked in one cheek.

"What if the whole family is a bunch of Cates?" she said.

"You mean what if they all have your mother's wild curly black hair?"

"That could actually be kind of hilarious."

"Are you telling me you didn't stalk anybody on Facebook or Instagram after you found out the correct family name was Polombo, not Butler?"

Jillian's mouth turned up on one side, sheepish. "I might have. The men all manage the hair gene with short haircuts."

"In other words, Cate is the only one bold enough to embrace it full on—like you."

"I suppose that's one way of looking at it." Jillian fiddled with her phone, turning it around in her hands. "Cate makes her mother out to be so unreasonable. What if she's right? What if they're all that way?"

"First of all," Nolan said in his very best reassuring father voice, "you had the only reasonable mother on the planet. I'm sorry you didn't get to know that after your early adolescence, or you would know that the kind of complaint Cate has been making is hardly unheard of."

"And second?"

"Her brother didn't give me that impression. If anything, I got the idea that the family considers Cate to be the high strung one."

"Drew doesn't usually work so many hours," Jillian said. "Why all of a sudden does it have to happen now?"

"He's a man of his word. And I think in some ways he's a lot like you. He doesn't like to leave people in the lurch."

"I know, I know. I just wish he could simply be with me today at the restaurant, not working in the kitchen."

"He said he would take his meal break while you're there." Nolan pulled onto the short stretch of highway required to take them into downtown Pueblo. "And I'm here. You have your people."

"Cate never even said how many of her people to expect. Marc and Rocky? Her parents? Anyone else?"

"Like who?"

"Based on the family tree she sent me, there could be a lot of Parisis floating around under other names. She has aunt and uncles and first cousins, for instance. And her father had cousins."

"And you think they all still live in Pueblo?"

"I didn't get far enough to figure that out. It's only been a couple of days since I got the tree. Between trying to keep up with work and convincing Min to see a doctor—well, you get it."

"And you didn't ask Cate."

"Deciding what to discuss with Cate is still a fine line."

"I can understand that."

"Like you said a few days ago, keeping the temperature turned down for a while seemed smart."

"It is." Nolan nodded. "I doubt Cate is inviting all the cousins."

"I hope not. I do have questions."

"Of course."

"And I hope I get to ask some of them today."

"Specifically?"

"What Min said about Parisis living on the ranch a century ago."

"That is certainly an interesting question, considering where you and Drew are today, getting all lovey-dovey." He was making her blush, a deed for which he felt no repentance. "Parisis on the ranch that has been in Drew's family since 1909—of course that's fascinating, Jillian. What a chapter that would be to add to your 'how did you meet' story."

"Okay, yes, that's part of why it interests me. Of course I want to turn over every stone I can about Parisi history after I missed my chance to do that while Mom and Grandpa Steve were alive because I wasn't curious enough then to find out what they knew."

"Jillian."

"I know. Don't beat myself up about that."

"Also, I think you are on the cusp of finding out a great deal more than either of them ever knew."

"Do you really think so?"

"Absolutely I do. I don't ever recall your mom mentioning anything like this to me. Surely if she knew, she would have said something in our two decades together."

Nolan was certain she would have. One of the traits that first drew Nolan to Bella Parisi was the glow in her eyes as she explained the details of whatever had captivated her mind. Turning the old Victorian into the home it still was happened because Bella dug in and learned everything necessary to direct the renovation—and do much of it herself, one room at a time. Bella talked a lot. She had thoughts. Opinions. Suggestions. Wisdom. Her stunning self-confidence captivated Nolan's Irish heart every bit as her striking dark Italian appearance.

They were in town now, and Nolan was following directions Drew had given for finding both the restaurants the Polombo family operated.

"Drew Lawson Self-guided Tours," Nolan said as he eased the truck into a vacant parking spot across the street from an Italian restaurant under a sign brightly lit even in the middle of the day. "You will note from the brochure that the original restaurant location was four blocks to the south and had a small hotel attached. For three decades it featured clean, comfortable rooms at affordable prices for visitors to a growing, thriving community to enjoy hints of Italian ambiance and authentic, traditional Italian foods for all seasons of the year."

"Where are you getting this information?" Jillian asked.

"I told you," Nolan said, "Drew Lawson. Nice fellow. Have you met him?"

Jillian rolled her eyes. "Continue."

"Some years after the departure of one of the original owners, the remaining owner's son, who had taken over as general manager, decided to close the hotel and focus on an expanded restaurant with more space to serve its growing popularity. To this end, the restaurant was moved to its present location. To this day, the restaurant holds its own against chain competition as an enduring anchor in the history of Pueblo. Slightly off the main drag, the restaurant owns one of the oldest brick structures in the city and occupies the street level. It is well worth the deviation from the flow of traffic. Ample parking is available both on the street and in a rear lot."

"Is that it?"

"That is the extent of the brochure copy at this stop on the tour."

"Exactly when did you have this conversation with Drew."

"Mr. Lawson and I go way back." Nolan wiggled the lone eyebrow that aggravated Jillian. Perhaps it would distract her from the agitation written all over her face.

Jillian leaned forward for a better look. "Looks inviting enough. Sort of a charming building."

"Even in the brief time that our tour bus has been stopped here, we have seen robust foot traffic entering and leaving the establishment. This suggests that it remains a popular fixture in the city's culinary culture."

"Are you sure you didn't swallow another brochure?"

"Alas, we do not have time to go inside and have a look around. I'm sure that is a feature offered on the premium tour."

"An excursion for another day," Jillian said.

"Because there might be Parisis in there?"

Jillian shrugged. "They have two restaurants. They can't all be taking time off to be at the other one, can they?"

"They have staff, Jillian. People they pay to cook and serve the food and wash the dishes and set the tables and seat the guests."

"Well, we still don't have time," she said.

She was right. And Nolan wasn't going to test her last nerve by suggesting they go inside even for a quick peek. Maybe after meeting the Parisis at Mary Lou's Kitchen, where Cate would be waiting to make introductions and Drew was nearby for emotional reinforcement, they'd have time to duck into the Italian restaurant before driving back out to the ranch. They'd promised Min some supper. They hadn't promised it would be from Mary Lou's.

Nolan looked up at the lit sign one more time.

"Dad? You all right?"

He nodded. "Just thinking of your mom. Can you imagine telling her this was going to happen?"

"It would have blown her away."

They sat for a moment, both grief and love cycling around in that way emotions filled in moments that were never predictable.

"Here we go!" Nolan put the truck in gear and checked Drew's instructions for the three-quarter-mile drive to Mary Lou's Kitchen. In contrast to the historical red brick of the Italian restaurant, Mary Lou's was a modern, sleek, upscale combination of glass and white brick. Though there must be some lighting for the sign after dark, in the daylight, the lettering was a contemporary blend of bold and narrow navy strokes on an ivory background with a tasteful hint of a steaming icon.

"Quite different," Nolan said. "I'll bet antipasto is not on the menu here."

"Drew does a handmade butternut squash ravioli," Jillian said. "That's probably the only thing remotely Italian. Stuffed with spinach, water chestnuts, and parmesan cheese."

"Oh my heart," Nolan said. "What kind of sauce?"

Jillian squeezed her eyes, thinking. "Sage brown butter? I haven't actually had it. He just talks a lot about how he's tweaking the seasoning with this or that."

"Am I even going to have to read the menu?"

"You might. I haven't been here before either."

"I bet Drew has made some of his dishes for us and we didn't know they were from this menu."

"I wouldn't doubt it."

"We have been unwitting guinea pigs for the chef's daily special." At last he drew a soft half-smile from her.

Nolan reached over and stilled Jillian's nervous fiddling with her iPhone. She hadn't stopped flipping it over and over since they left the ranch.

"Are you ready?" he said.

"No. But I wish I were."

"Close enough."

They got out and walked together toward the restaurant's main entrance. Cate intentionally scheduled this meet-up after the worst of the Saturday lunch crowd and before the setup for the dinner crowd would begin in earnest, but the parking lot still seemed fairly full to Nolan.

Cate was there, right inside the front door. Nolan heard the rush of relief leave his daughter's lungs at the sight of her.

"I have a table for us right over here," Cate said. "I'm sorry it's busier in here than I thought it would be. Something about a baby shower group that didn't think eleven people should need a reservation for a party that is clearly tying up multiple tables for a long time."

"I see the balloons," Nolan said. A pile of gifts on the floor was right in the path of the wait staff, waiting to be opened until the group finished their leisurely meal.

"Come to the table," Cate said. "I'll get you some menus and let the fam know you are here."

"How are they taking the news of me?" Jillian asked.

"Curious! They had no idea I sent off my DNA. Why would I? We know who our cousins are on both sides."

"So why did you?"

Cate twisted her mouth. "A bunch of my friends were doing it. We were all together one night, and we decided to do it. So we all pulled out our phones and ordered the kits."

"I guess I have your friends to thank, then."

Jillian and Cate locked eyes. Jillian's hair hung loose, with only a small clip on one side, while Cate's was tied back. Their different eye colors didn't diminish the echoes of resemblance in their faces. Nolan had always seen Bella in his daughter's face and hair. What must it be like for Jillian now to look at someone else and see reverberation of the mother who had been gone for fifteen years, a face young enough to be her own sister's if she'd ever had one?

"I recommend the butternut squash ravioli," Cate said when she placed menus on the table. "It's on special today because Drew is working, and something about a secret ingredient, but we have a lot of other great things too."

Jillian buried her attention in the menu when Cate left.

"Jilly?" Across the table from her, Nolan reached out and tapped her hand.

"I'm okay, Dad."

"You sure?"

Jillian nodded, but she didn't look up until Cate returned.

"This is my brother Marc," she said. "Nolan, you talked to him on the phone."

"Mr. Duffy?" Marc said.

"That's right." Nolan offered his hand. "But Nolan will do."

"I didn't realize at the time. I'm sorry."

"No problem. The person you're really here to meet is Jillian."

"Of course. May I?"

Cate took a seat beside Jillian and Marc beside Nolan.

"Rocky will be here in a minute," Marc said. "Mom and Pop too."

The whole family had managed to be at the same restaurant after all. Soon the table was full. Vince Polombo and his wife, the Mary Lou for whom the restaurant was named. Marc. Marc's wife, Suzanne. Rocky. Rocky's wife, Beth. Vince's sister Cynthia—though it soon came out that her given name was the more traditional Italian Cinzia. Vince's name was also traditional, Vincenzo. They had a brother Mateo who went by Matt.

Behind the green glow of Jillian's eyes as she soaked all this up, Nolan knew she was linking images and details to the growing Parisi family tree in her mind. Her breath was still uneven, though, her nerves not quite settled. He knew his girl.

"My grandpa Steve was Stefano," Jillian said. "Not Stephen, as most people assumed. There's something beautiful about the Old World names."

Mary Lou nodded and smiled. "I think so. That's why I insisted we give our children good solid Italian names. Rocco could never say Caterina's name when she was born, and she became Rina and then Rini very quickly. It was sweet because it was her brother who gave her the nickname."

Nolan smiled at Cate, who was rolling her eyes at the repetition of the family story.

"My mother wanted to be here," Vince said, "but she wasn't feeling well today. I thought she should wait."

Jillian blinked a couple of times, something she'd always done in a moment of imbalance. Disappointment? Forming a thought? Reaching for the polite reply?

"Of course," Nolan said. "This is a wonderful beginning for Jillian to meet you all. It's a delight that she let me tag along."

"Your mother is Benedetta Parisi," Jillian finally said to Vince.

"She was, until she married Cosmo Polombo, which was a very long time ago." Vince laughed softly. "I guess this is the first time we've had someone named Parisi at our table in a very long time."

Nolan transferred his smile to Jillian. This was going well.

"Rini," Vince said, "can you pop up and get the order for table six? Drew should have it by now."

"Pop, I'm here with guests." Cate's low voice growled with resentment.

"I'm just asking for a little favor."

The temperature at the table spiked instantly. Cate didn't move.

"Rini, you can see we're incredibly busy," Vince said. "The baby shower. And Lisa has been out all week with her son. Just get the one order. Let me get to know my surprise cousin."

"Caterina, for once, just do as you're asked," Mary Lou snapped. "You haven't worked at all today."

Cate scraped her chair back, and Vince turned his attention back to Jillian. Vince asked Jillian a few questions about her work, and Nolan let his eyes trail Cate's movements to the kitchen, much of which was exposed behind a high, polished glass wall. He saw Drew's head bobbing under the chef's hat he enjoyed wearing when he cooked. Even in Nolan's kitchen he wore one—they both did. Cate emerged with a tray, delivered it with a smile to table six, returned the empty tray to a server stack, and came back to the table.

But the mood had shifted, and Vince paid no attention as Cate slumped back into her chair.

Jillian's eyes raised as Drew arrived a few steps behind her.

"Of all the remarkable coincidences." Marc looked from Drew to Jillian. "The two of you. I just don't know."

"I have come to see if anyone wants something to eat." Drew laid a hand on Jillian's shoulder and she tilted her head toward him with a smile. "I hear the chef is going on a meal break soon, but he wants to be sure our special guests are well taken care of."

Jillian's taut posture dropped slightly, eased by Drew's presence.

"Do you recommend the butternut squash ravioli?" Nolan said.

"Heartily."

Nolan looked at Jillian, who nodded. "Two orders for us, then. Cate?"

"Sure," she said.

"Make it three. Anyone else?"

The rest of the Polombos demurred, claiming they couldn't stay long enough for an entire meal, though they might pop back and forth one at a time. Cinzia was the first to excuse herself for a pressing prior commitment. Cate sank further in her chair.

"I'll be back," Drew said.

"So your great-great-grandfather was Sal."

Mary Lou turned to Jillian and again picked up the conversation as if there had been no disruption in mood, a habit Nolan found curious.

"Great-great-great," Jillian said. "Cate and I are around the same age but off a generation in the genealogy somehow."

"Probably because Geppetto was so much older than Aldo," Vince said.

"You know about Aldo?" Jillian's eyes widened.

"Sure. Sal's boy. Sal took in Geppetto when Lou sent him."

"I don't really know much about either Sal or Lou," Jillian said. "Geppetto is such a great name."

"My mother would tell you he was a wonderful man," Vince said. "He was her grandfather."

"Wow," Jillian. "This is all so much to take in. Your mother's grandfather was my mother's grandfather's cousin."

"I'm afraid you'll have to draw that out for me sometime." Vince pushed his chair back. "I have to go see if I can hurry that baby shower party along without jeopardizing anyone's tip."

"Why did Geppetto come, anyway?" Cate ignored her father's departure. "I've never understood that."

"Because something happened to Joe," Jillian said, "the third brother. I know that much. Somehow it ties together with the mob in New Orleans, right?"

"Joe got involved with the wrong people," Mary Lou said. "That's what Benedetta always said—what her grandfather said. They killed him. Lou was in too deep with the mob to get out, but he didn't want that life for Geppetto, so he begged Sal to take him in and sent him to Denver."

Jillian nodded. This information tracked what what she knew so far. "But why did he decide to come to Pueblo?"

"I think my father needs some help. You'll have to excuse me." Marco left the table, and his wife went with him.

"Somebody he knew helped him get a job." Mary Lou continued, unconcerned with the comings and goings of her family members. "I don't remember the particulars, or maybe I never knew them."

It didn't sound to Nolan like the Polombos of this generation knew Geppetto had ever worked on the Parisi ranch. He glanced at Jillian.

"Nonna might know the story," Cate said.

"She might," Mary Lou agreed. "You can ask her another time when she feels better. And there's a box of letters somewhere."

Nolan glanced at Jillian. The hot craving in her eyes slithered through yearning for what Bella had never known, never held, never felt. Sal's words. Pictures of Sal's life before there had been Stefano or Bella or Jillian.

"I mentioned the letters to Jillian a few days ago," Cate told her mother. "Primary source letters are gold in Jillian's line of work."

"Sal used to write to Geppetto after he moved to Pueblo," Mary Lou said. "As much as I love the Italian family I married into, reading Italian is not my strength. And I'm not sure spelling was Sal's strength. I've never tried to read them, but I know I should keep them."

"And you know where they are, right, Mom?" Cate's posture pleaded on Jillian's behalf.

Mary Lou lifted one shoulder in a small shrug. "I probably know where to look."

Drew was back with four orders of the ravioli and sat down to eat, without his chef's hat or jacket. "I have thirty straight minutes."

"If the chef is here," Mary Lou said, "it's my turn to go see what's happening in the kitchen."

"The busboys are getting a little behind." Rocky offered a hand to Jillian and then to Nolan. "I hope to drop by again before you leave. Enjoy your meal."

Nolan, Jillian, Drew, and Cate began to eat just as Vince cycled back and sat beside his daughter.

"Looks like you successfully nudged the baby shower along," Nolan said.

"I think so. It cost me a few free boxed desserts, but it will be worth it to have the tables back. Rocky and Beth can make sure they get reset before the ladies are out of the parking lot."

"This is exquisite, Drew!" Nolan hadn't had a meal that tantalized his salivary glands in this manner in weeks—perhaps since the last time Drew visited Canyon Mines. "Why have you kept this dish a secret? I might have come down here a lot sooner."

"I love seeing where you work." Jillian eyes settled on Drew. "I've heard you give concerts, and now I've tasted your chef food on duty."

Nolan wondered if he'd ever get used to seeing that shine on his daughter's face. He hoped she never tired of looking at Drew that way. Love had literally turned up looking for her in Canyon Mines last summer, and his girl was wholly and earnestly happy.

"Uh oh." Cate broke off a soft bite of ravioli as she glanced up an approaching pair.

"Caterina, be polite," Vince said.

"Hello, Caterina," a man said. "Not working today? Just here for the free meal?"

CHAPTER EIGHTEEN

Pueblo, Colorado

"Hello, mr. brotherton."

Nolan didn't like the way Cate's voice constricted at the sight of this forty-something man and the woman on his arm.

"I have a table for you right over here." The hostess who had been escorting them pointed away with a couple of menus.

The man ignored the young woman and eyed Cate. "I was hoping you would be my server tonight."

"I'm not working." Cate gestured around the table. "I'm here with friends."

"Surely you wouldn't mind taking care of us," Brotherton said. "You know I make it worth your while."

"You're always very generous," Cate said. "I'm sure André will look after you very well."

Vince cleared his throat. Cate refused to look at him, instead breaking off another bite of ravioli.

Nolan picked up his water glass. "Watch the aisle, Mr. Brotherton. I think someone is trying to get past."

Brotherton threw Nolan a glance, which Nolan met, but he moved on.

"Caterina," Vince said sharply.

"Pop, we discussed this."

Vince stood. "It was nice to meet you both."

He tucked his chair under the table and left. Nolan doubted he intended to return.

"I'm sorry," Cate said. "I should have figured out some other way for you to meet everyone. They're just stubborn about leaving the restaurants. But at least now you have."

"You're not the one who owes anyone an apology," Drew said.

Cate's eyes shone with the tears that sprang into them. "Thank you for that."

"Mr. Brotherton doesn't seem like the most likable person." Nolan offered his observation.

"He's despicable. But he always asks to be seated at my station. He'll even wait for a table in my station when there are others open. Apparently he's been complaining that I'm not working enough shifts here lately."

"That doesn't sound at all creepy," Jillian said. "Ick."

"His wife just overlooks it. And my family—they're all about the business. He orders a lot of expensive wines and sometimes brings guests."

"I'm getting a clearer picture of why you might want a different career path."

"If I fail at what I'm trying to do with my exhibit, if I fail to distinguish myself somehow, if I don't figure out a way to support myself better, I'll prove my father's low expectations of me and get sucked right back into the family restaurant business."

"And then everybody will be happy but you," Nolan said.

"Pretty much." Cate dropped her fork. "I'm sorry, Drew. Your food is wonderful, but I've lost my appetite."

"No offense taken," Drew said. "You inhale enough of my food that I know you love it."

"I do. I just … I just … tonight."

Vince was back after all. "Rini, I need you to grab an apron for a few minutes."

"You want me to actually work tables?"

"Just for a few minutes. Twenty minutes tops. I'll put your plate under a warmer."

Drew cleared his throat. "Vince, Rini's not on shift tonight. Brotherton coming in doesn't change that."

"I'm just trying to manage my restaurant, Drew."

"It's unfortunate you didn't have time to sit with us." Drew's tone was measured, deliberate. "But our plan is still to have a meal with Rini."

Drew refused to be stared down. Vince broke his gaze.

"You keep an eye on the clock, Drew." Vince pivoted and left.

"Whoa, Drew," Cate said. "Thank you."

"Does he often speak to you that way?" Nolan asked.

"Rarely." Drew forked a bite of his dinner. "He knows there are half a dozen other restaurants in town that would love to hear my services are available, and he'd be in hot water with Mary Lou."

"He really would." Cate moved food around on her plate but still didn't eat. "Thank you, Drew. Somebody sticking up for me like that to Pop—it means a lot."

Nolan launched into an analysis of the spices in the ravioli, and for a few minutes the mood at the table lightened. Then Vince returned, hovering but not engaging with Cate's guests.

A timer went off in Drew's pocket. "Sadly, that's my five-minute warning," he said.

"Good," Vince said. "Mary Lou says the kitchen is getting backed up without you."

Drew put the last round ravioli on his plate in his mouth whole and chewed only briefly before swallowing. "I'll see you again before you go." He looked around, as if deciding whether to kiss Jillian and picked up his plate without kissing her and carried it toward the kitchen.

"You're not even eating, Rini." Vince pointed at the plate she'd pushed away. "I'll send out some nice dessert and coffee for Jillian and Nolan. By the time they're ready to start on that, you'll be back. Maybe your mother will even be able to sit down with you again."

"Pop, I brought Jillian here to meet the Parisi side of the family tree." Cate was not budging. "I'm not here to work a shift."

"Because we're not good enough for you."

"Pop, don't start."

"You're mother's right. We're never good enough." Vince switched to Italian and fired a barrage.

Nolan knew a fairly large repertoire of Italian opera lyrics, but none of that equipped him to keep up with what followed.

"You're my family," Cate shot back in English. "Of course I care about you."

More rapid Italian. Rocco was in on it now.

"I know how many generations have been working in the family business," Cate said. "Does every person in every generation have to work here? Not every person has."

More Italian. Not louder, because they were in the restaurant and people were starting to stare, but faster, more insistent. Vince and Rocco played a tag-team game.

Cate put a hand to her head and squeezed. "Why do you always say these things? Don't you want me to be just as sure I'm doing the thing I'm supposed to be doing as you are in your work?"

Cate seemed to have no interest in speaking Italian but there was no doubt she absorbed every word spoken to her.

Then she left. Gone from the table. Out the door of the restaurant.

Vince and Rocky muttered at each other in Italian but smiled amiably to the guests.

Nolan and Jillian stared at each other over their nearly-eaten lunch plates and salads.

Nolan pushed his chair back. "I'm sorry for the position I'm about to put you in, Jillian, but I'll be back as soon as I can."

Jillian blanched but nodded.

Nolan's long legs caught up with Cate quickly enough. She'd left without a purse or bag, so he was fairly certain she wouldn't be trying to get in a car and leave without returning to the restaurant. He found her around the side of the building, one foot and her back pressed flat up against the white brick while her fists balled at her hips.

"If I stayed any longer, I was going to need a lawyer," she said.

"Lucky for you, I'm also experienced with family mediation." Nolan leaned against the wall beside Cate.

"What my father did was unreasonable and embarrassing."

"I can see that."

"And why can't my brother mind his own business?"

"Valid question."

"You don't know the half of what they were saying."

"But I did make the happy discovery that you are fluent in Italian."

She laughed. "You'll never catch me speaking Italian. And those Old World names that Jillian thinks are so charming—to me they're just another generation unwilling to admit that the modern world has arrived and not everyone wants to go into the family business."

"Jillian assures me that what you're trying to do with your work is very worthwhile."

Cate turned her head to look at him. "Do you think she really means that?"

"I do."

"She tells me that, but I don't know her well enough to know if she's just trying to be nice."

"Jillian does like to be nice to people, but she also tries to say things that she means."

"I have to succeed. I just have to."

"You have a strong idea, great research, a grant, a board to advise you."

"I need Jillian. I didn't mean to need a lawyer. I really didn't. But someone like Jillian can help me figure out what's going wrong with my project, help me hone it, help me make it really stand out."

"Caterina Polombo, you are a remarkable young woman. You wouldn't have stuck with it this long if you weren't sure this was your path."

"I don't know you well enough, either, to know if you're just trying to be nice."

"Oh, I don't have to try to be nice. I'm genetically incredibly nice. Anybody will tell you that. Affable to the point of annoyance."

Cate scuffed the ground with one foot, toying with a rough stone.

"But as someone who has considerable experience with people who are trying very hard to get what they want, I feel I must point out that you might be in the realm of trying so hard to prove something that you are cutting off your own nose."

"I can't help it!" Cate banged her fists against her thighs. "I cannot get stuck in the restaurant. To me they're as bad as the mine operators who used to want to control everything about the miners' lives. I don't want to live like that. And I can't let whoever is messing with my work jeopardize everything. I thought Jillian would care about history."

"I'm on your side, Cate, but I have to stop you right there." Nolan moved now so that he was looking at Cate straight on. "You're disappointed about a lot of things, but you can't make Jillian one of them. Of course Jillian cares about history. And Jillian understands a big, complicated emotional family—she has one on her Irish side. It hasn't been rosy perfection, but we're family and we keep working at it."

Cate exhaled.

"Jillian spat in a tube because she wanted to see what might be out there on her Italian side," Nolan said. "She found you. You're the connection, even if you are a fourth cousin."

"Fourth cousin once removed."

"I stand corrected. Now you have to decide if you're looking for a cousin or a magic bullet to solve your problems."

Cate swung her foot and hurtled the stone down the side of the building.

CHAPTER NINETEEN

Wednesday, March 11, 1913
Outside Pueblo, Colorado

"CHIARA?" CATERINA LEANED ON HER HOE. "You don't need to be out here. No one expects you to help get the garden ready."

"I want to. I can't bend over, but I can still pull a rake through dirt." Chiara grimaced as she said this.

"Chiara, why are you making that face?"

"It is nothing." She sounded winded. "I have become a sloth sitting around all winter. Now I'm not fit. That is all."

"It's too early to plant. We will have several more frosts. We're just turning up the earth a bit while we decide what we want to plant this year."

"I know that. You have told me four times."

"I wish you would sit down."

"You have told me that at least seven times." Chiara managed to swing her rake with enough force to break ground this time.

Caterina raised her hoe again. She shouldn't have come outside at all. If she hadn't said she was going to, Chiara wouldn't have followed her out. Most of the snow had melted, but persistent patches lingered here and there in the yard. When they bundled the children up for some fresh air, they always found the snow. Giuseppe was the first to smash his hands in it and chase the squealing girls around. Caterina thought coming out to stand where the garden would be, and perhaps chop at the earth if she felt like it, might help her think about planning it. If Ela wanted to order any seeds, the time to decide was now. Caterina would put in another smaller garden beside the little red house. Lonely, restless, and uncomfortable—Caterina knew she was all those things—Chiara had insisted on coming outside as well.

Chiara had been stubborn for as long as Caterina had known her. When she had made up her mind, it was not easy to persuade her otherwise. If she hadn't been so ill during her pregnancy, she would never have agreed to leave the Ludlow colony without Celestrino, and she had only reluctantly agreed to remain apart because her morning sickness was so severe and lasted well into her seventh month. By the time she was well enough to recover her appetite only a few weeks ago, she was far enough along to find many other reasons to be uncomfortable. And Celestrino would not hear of her returning to the colony. She must have the baby on the ranch, he said, where they would both be safe. Ludlow had a better doctor than the Berwind company town, but he was glad she was under the care of the doctor in Pueblo and closer to a hospital if she needed one.

"Ela likes tomatoes, cucumbers, lettuce, beans, peas, zucchini, and corn," Caterina said. "For the fall, pumpkin and squashes."

Chiara nodded, but she was grimacing again and leaning on her wobbling rake.

Caterina dropped her hoe. "Chiara, you must go inside."

"It is nothing. It will pass."

"Are you having pains?"

"Indigestion. I have to get used to eating normally again, now that I am not so sick. I should not have eaten lunch when already breakfast was not sitting well."

Caterina startled. "You've been feeling unwell all day?"

"It comes and goes."

"This may be your time, Chiara."

Chiara shook her head. "Two more weeks. Celestrino said he would come next week. He promised to be here."

Caterina slipped an arm around Chiara for support and knocked the rake aside. "We are going inside. We'll see what happens after you sit down and rest." This was a first baby. Chiara might labor many more hours. They could try to telephone the Ludlow colony, but no one could tell how long it would take a message to reach Celestrino and whether he could get a train to Pueblo.

"It's gone now."

"We're going inside."

Chiara did not protest further, and her steps were the slowest Caterina had seen in days.

Ela was in the front room with a mending basket in her lap and one of Dottie's favorite little dresses with a tear Caterina had assured her could be repaired. She pushed everything into the chair and stood.

"What's wrong?"

"I think Chiara's baby might come," Caterina said.

"Two more weeks," Chiara insisted. After six months on the ranch, Chiara's English had come a long way. She required little translation in the near-daily interactions with Ela.

"These dates are not exact." Ela helped guide Chiara to a seat. "Shall I call the doctor?"

"No!" Chiara said.

"Yes, please," Caterina said. "I believe she has been in a slow labor all day. If there was someone to stay with the girls, I would wake Peppy and ask you to drive us down to the little red house. I can look after her there. Perhaps when the men come in before supper."

"Nonsense. If Chiara is about to have her first baby, she should be in a place that has a telephone. This is not the Dark Ages. First I am going to put the doctor on alert, and then we are going to make Chiara comfortable in the new guest room." Ela spun and left the room.

The addition to the Kyp house was barely finished in the late fall, before winter set in, expanding the home from two bedrooms to four. Carrick and Ela had moved into one of the new larger rooms. Now perhaps the other would welcome Chiara's child.

Chiara picked up the discarded mending. "I can do this."

"Another day," Caterina said.

"These stitches are not tight enough."

"Ela did not grow up doing her own mending. She has learned to do many things these last few years. She will learn to mend."

"Why can't this bambino wait for his papa?"

"So many things we cannot control, Chiara, but we trust God as always. Yes?"

Chiara nodded.

Ela returned. "Dr. Madison wants to know as labor progresses. He will plan to come out to attend the birth when the time is closer. You have become a special case to him, Chiara. Let's get you set up."

"You are so kind," Caterina said.

"Between the two of us," Ela said, "we've birthed three children. It's time to come together for Chiara."

The fight had gone out of Chiara now that the pains were not as spread out as they had been all day. She followed Ela to the bedroom and obediently changed into a loose nightdress that would be comfortable whether she wanted to pace the room, lean over the bed gripping the sheets, or lie in it. She did all three in rotation as her time drew nearer. Ela phoned the doctor two more times and the Ludlow colony once, and Caterina and Ela traded between attending Chiara and caring for three small children now awake and clamoring for attention. Change them. Feed them. Wipe their hands and faces. Change them again. Read to them. Let them chase each other but only in the front room. Get out the set of small wooden blocks. Wince at the intensifying sounds in the guest room. Watch out the window for signs of Geppetto or Carrick, who finally arrived with Dr. Madison not far behind.

"Did you hear back from Celestrino?" Geppetto asked once Caterina had told the men the story of the day.

"No. I don't know if Ela's message even reached him." Caterina drew the heel of one hand across the hairline of her forehead. "All Chiara does is ask for him."

"I'll try calling again."

"Thank you, Geppetto."

A wail rose from the guest room.

"It's getting worse," Caterina said. "I'm glad the doctor is here now, but I should go back in there."

"I will take charge of the children," Carrick said.

Caterina looked from one man to the other.

"Well, between the two of us we can manage them," Carrick said. "Two of them are mine, after all. Go to Chiara."

She hustled to the wing that the new addition had created and found Ela grasping one of Chiara's hands between both of hers and Dr. Madison at the foot of the bed.

"It won't be long now," he said. "Your baby has a lot of black curly hair. Just another push or two."

Chiara grunted and bore down. Caterina remembered the sensation of one wave of pain on top of another with so little time to rest in between. But then she had little Giuseppe in her arms, a squalling slippery ball of life born of love.

"We have the head," Dr. Madison said. "The shoulders are almost there. One more."

Caterina paced to the bed now, putting a firm hand behind Chiara's back and spreading her strong fingers to help hold up her friend to bear down one last time.

And then the baby's cry.

And Chiara's tears.

And counting fingers and toes.

And quick fuss to clean him up and diaper him and wrap him in the blanket Chiara insisted must be the first soft swaddling he knew.

Yes, a boy!

"Everything looks good," Dr. Madison said after he had finished tending to both mother and son. "He looks very healthy, and I'm relieved that you do too. I think you will quickly regain your strength now that the difficulties of your pregnancy are over. I am confident you are a person of great spirit and determination."

"Thank you, doctor," Chiara said. But she had eyes only for the child in her arms. After the doctor had gone, Chiara said, "Celestrino must see his son."

"Geppetto is calling the colony again," Caterina said. "The minute we know something, we will tell you."

"If he cannot come to the ranch, then we must go to Ludlow."

"I'm sure he will find a way to come to you," Ela said. "We need to be sure he got the message."

"I'll see if they heard anything," Caterina offered, though she hadn't heard the telephone ring.

Geppetto and Carrick had the children on the screened-in back porch now, playing under the light of one bare bulb. Everyone was layered up against the extra chill that frosted the air as soon as the sun set. Evening encased the house, and bedtime for the little ones had already passed. Peppito would get cranky if they waited too much longer.

Both men looked up when Caterina stepped out onto the porch.

"The doctor said a boy!" Geppetto said. "Celestrino will like that."

"He hasn't called back?"

Geppetto shook his head. "Not yet."

"Mama!" Giuseppe hurtled himself at her and she braced to received him.

"Should we call again?"

"Caterina, there is some news."

She felt her own face blanch beneath Peppy's sloppy kisses.

"The man I spoke to at the colony said there was more violence in Forbes today. This is why it is hard to find Celestrino. Everyone is upset."

"What happened?"

"The Colorado National Guard burned down all the tents—all but one."

"Geppetto!"

"Down, please, Mama." His greeting over, Peppy was ready to return to play with Dottie and the blocks.

"No one was hurt." Carrick fastened Mina's shoe more securely and she slid off his lap. "Apparently the entire colony had gone to Trinidad for the funeral of stillborn twins of a pit boss's wife, Emma Zanetell. I'm not sure the Guard knew they would be gone. The only one left in the camp was Emma, because she was still too ill to go to the service. One of the guardsmen had enough humanity left in him to insist that they spare her tent."

"Whether they thought anyone would be there or not," Caterina said, "the message is clear. And what happens in Forbes can happen next in Ludlow."

"I don't disagree." Carrick stood up and rubbed one temple. "We have to remember that originally guardsmen were regular citizens whose tours lasted ninety days. They started out thinking they were keeping the peace. When they mustered out to go back to their real lives, it was someone else's turn. The state couldn't keep that up. The strike wasn't supposed to last this long—six months and not showing any end in sight. Now the soldiers all are mercenaries employed by the coal companies. They have no reason to feel sympathy for the miners."

"Even at Christmas Celestrino said they were arresting strikers," Geppetto said. "They keep them in jail without ever charging them. Beating them. Torturing them. The law seems to mean nothing."

"Daddy," Mina whined and banged on Carrick's leg. "Dottie won't share."

"Ask nicely," Dottie said.

"Girls, please," Carrick said.

Peppy flopped on the floor, turned on his back, and balanced a block on his forehead. He hadn't asked at all.

"Peppy, that's mine!" Dottie shrieked and snatched at the block.

The children all needed to go to bed.

"What am I supposed to tell Chiara?" Caterina said. "She just had a baby. A beautiful boy! All she wants is her husband."

Geppetto shrugged. "Let's wait and see what Celestrino says when he calls."

CHAPTER TWENTY

THE CALLER ID SAID DREW, so Jillian answered.

"You doing okay?" he said.

Jillian tapped her thumb against the edge of her desk, a nervous gesture Drew would recognize if he could see it. She made herself stop.

"I guess. I still wish everything hadn't fallen apart on Saturday."

"It's been two days. Nothing from Rini? I mean, Cate? I'm still not clear whether she hates if I call her Rini away from Trinidad."

"It's confusing," Jillian said. "She's confusing. And the silence is eerie."

"At least she came back into the restaurant on Saturday."

"No telling how hard my dad twisted her arm."

"In his genial way."

"It was still incredibly awkward." Jillian picked up a pen and started tapping it against a yellow legal pad. "Her parents never came anywhere near the table again."

"I know. Mary Lou never left the kitchen, even though I told her I had everything under control."

"Marc and Rocky came by only to say goodbye when we hadn't even had dessert yet. I was afraid they were going to box it up, like they did for the baby shower women, to hurry us along."

"They don't trot that trick out too often."

"They might as well have. Cate hardly said another word to Dad or me. She just smashed her cheesecake around like she was waiting for us to finish ours so we would go."

"She stayed to work the dinner shift that night."

"I'm sure that was a lot of fun for everyone."

"To be honest, Vince and Mary Lou acted like nothing had happened."

"Swell. I made a terrific impression." Jillian stabbed her pad with the pen.

"It wasn't you, Jillian."

"I'd sure like to think it wasn't."

"Someday I'll tell you more about why I gave up managing the kitchen full-time at Mary Lou's."

Jillian sank back in her desk chair. "I thought it was because you wanted more freedom to take singing opportunities."

"I did. I do. But as you can see, the restaurant is a driven environment."

"I admit I have little more sympathy for Cate now," Jillian said. "At least I understand why her anxiety is so high about flopping in what she's trying to do. But she has a good degrees and she's smart. She'd have other options even if her exhibit didn't work out—and I'm not saying it won't."

"I agree."

"Maybe it's all over, Drew. My having Italian cousins, I mean. If my dad drew a line about Cate depending on me for solving her success, especially if she keeps shooting herself in the foot, maybe she doesn't need a distant cousin. She has plenty of real ones."

"I hate hearing you think that way. Feel that way."

"I don't know what else to think or feel."

"I wish I could do something. Do you want me to talk to Rini?"

Jillian hesitated. "No. She's your friend, and I don't want to muck that up. Plus you work for her family. I know it's not all the time, but it's still income you rely on."

"I can get another job any day of the week. For you I would do it in a heartbeat."

Jillian melted in the middle. "Maybe not one that is as understanding as the Polombos are about the flexibility agreement you've worked out—for your music and for Min." She wasn't going to ask him to take sides in a mess with someone he'd known all his life and she'd only met a few days ago.

"Aunt Min liked having you around last week," Drew said.

Jillian laughed. "Sometimes it was hard to tell."

"She's that way. But she's smitten with you."

"She does seem like she's slowing down."

"Michelle is working on getting her to come up to Wyoming for a while. I think it's going to happen. But she won't go until the church rummage sale is over."

"Even after hurting her wrist?"

"The church ladies still let her come down there and boss them around. They even volunteered to pick her up for the privilege so she won't get any ideas about driving."

Jillian's laughter was full-throttled now. "When is the rummage sale?"

"Second weekend in November. Speaking of Min," Drew said, "I've got to go. Time to pretend I'm just happening by the main house because I got thirsty on my way down the road from the barns."

"You are a sneaky one."

They ended the call, and Jillian sighed. Whatever Cate decided, Jillian still had the family tree Cate had emailed her. Already Jillian had put the names and whatever dates the scan offered into her own software to leaf out the generations and branches of the Parisis descending from Lou, and Sal. Joe had no one, not even a wife as far as Jillian knew, but he deserved to be remembered. Lou and Sal each had only one son, but the branches on Lou's side were so much fuller than Sal's. Then there was that old photo of the little girls with the Parisi hair standing in front of the grocery story sign in New Orleans. They must have belonged to Lou. Geppetto's sisters? Jillian would have to look for her scan of the photo to see what clues it offered. Filling in the gaps that interested Jillian most was difficult because they were so long ago, and she'd only been at it for a few days with one very distracting weekend.

She'd really wanted to find someone when she spit in that tube. Cate was intelligent, passionate, determined, motivated. Jillian admired all of that. And now that she saw the family tree, and could see her own leaf one branch over, it saddened her to think the story would end there.

Salvatore's letters. Cate's family had them, but they were Jillian's great-great-grandfather's letters. Mary Lou even thought she knew where they were.

Jillian was so close, and now she might never see them because Cate's parents couldn't give her space to forge her own future.

Jillian clicked open her calendar on her computer. The next few hours were clear of any meetings, and the truth was her concentration for the day had never kicked in the way a Monday deserved. What she needed was a good run. A few minutes later, changed into sweatpants with a pocket to hold her phone and a mismatched sweatshirt that didn't matter because no one would see her, she tied her hair up off her neck and went out the front door. After being sure to pull the front door closed and tug it again to double-check it, the way her mother always had when Jillian was little, she headed off into the hills above where the Parisi-Duffy home sat in a neighborhood at the end of Main Street aimed away from downtown and curving toward the mountain vistas. A favorite trail was perfect for a mid-October day that was neither too hot nor too cold to get up a good speed and maintain it for a few miles.

Her father was right. If the only reason Cate responded to Jillian's message about being a DNA match was to get something that Jillian can't give, then Jillian would have to accept the limitation of where her quest led.

She pushed her speed, surrendering to the run.

Cate would have to see that her frenzy was about her family expectations as much as it was about the future of her exhibit, which would probably take care of itself if she assembled a truly excellent exhibit that told the truth of the Southern Colorado coalfield strike and lived up to the goals of the grant.

Jillian pushed her speed up another notch even as she faced an incline. This was the best way she knew to let go of whatever troubled her.

When the phone in her pocket started sounding text messages, she slowed just enough to take it out and make sure it wasn't Cate. Anyone else could wait a few more minutes.

Not Cate. Kris.

Jillian shoved the phone back in her pocket and resumed her speed.

One message after another sounded in, practically in rhythm with every hundred yards she covered. Finally she slowed enough again to look at her phone a second time. Nine texts were stacked on top of each other.

The top one said, PLEASE CALL ME. NOW!

Using a boxer bounce to keep her feet moving and her heart rate up, Jillian glanced through the other messages and then pushed Kris's name in her favorites list.

"What's up?" she said when Kris answered.

"You need to come to the shop," Kris said.

"Do you have another breakfast option ice cream flavor to try out on me?"

"Don't mock me. And this is serious. There's someone waiting for you."

"Who?"

"Your cousin."

Jillian's feet stilled and her breath pressed out in three labored pulses. "Cate is there?"

"That's who she says she is, and she looks just enough like you for me to believe her."

Jillian gulped air. "I'm up in the hills, running."

"Good thing it's all downhill from there."

"I'm at least four miles away—maybe three if I find a shortcut home and grab my car."

"I guess I'll see how many flavors I can get her to sample."

"Put it on my tab." Jillian pivoted, filled her lungs, and began her descent.

Probably half an hour to get down the trail, a couple of more minutes on the flat stretch of Main Street to the house, inside to grab car keys, a quick drive to Ore the Mountain. Even parking in the alley and coming in through the kitchen to avoid parking headaches in town, Jillian was at least forty minutes from reaching Cate.

Every ten minutes, she stopped to text Kris and make sure Cate was still there gorging on the best ice cream of her life. At home, assured that Cate seemed to be going nowhere, she took an extra three minutes to splash water on her face and a couple of key places before changing into a dry set of sweats. No time for a shower.

Parked in the alley.

In through the back door, which Kris only allowed a few elite friends to do.

Through the kitchen.

Into the ice cream parlor.

"Oh good." Cate wiped her face with a paper napkin. "I wasn't sure how much more ice cream I could eat."

Jillian wanted to laugh in relief, but Cate looked so sincere—and not at all as if she was joking.

"When no one was at your house," Cate said, "I remembered the day the lady from the candy shop came by."

"Carolyn."

"Right. So I found her, and she pointed me over here, and your friend Kris practically held me hostage."

"Carolyn knows Kris usually knows how to reach me."

"I was afraid you wouldn't take my calls." Cate really wasn't joking.

"You drove all the way up here without even trying to call me." Jillian dropped into a chair across from Cate and the remains of all her ice cream tasting.

"I do want a cousin." Cate's voice went hoarse. "That's what I want, and I felt like I should tell you in person."

"You probably burned a whole shift of tips getting up here," Jillian said.

"I don't care. I mean it."

If Jillian were pressed to described the features of a penitential face, this would be it—what Cate looked like in this moment framed by the shop's window behind her and the sun sliding in at an angle past the awning to make her sincerity shimmer.

"Well, I want a cousin too," Jillian said. "Usually I celebrate the big moments of my life with ice cream, but you got a head start on me."

Cate's dark eyes glimmered. "I'll watch you eat. I'm in no hurry."

"Chocolate chip cookie dough, double chocolate dip, in a waffle cone coming right up," Kris said.

Jillian hadn't even realized Kris was lurking within earshot.

By the time Kris put the ice cream in front of her, Jillian's heart had finally stopped pounding—not from the run, she realized, but from the anxiety she'd felt that Cate might have left or that she'd have something different to say than four simple words. *"I do want a cousin."* At least a dozen questions whirled in Jillian's mind, but she didn't have the least idea where to start.

The shop's door opened, and Marilyn came in. "Oh my goodness. This can only be your Italian cousin."

The cousins both giggled.

"It's true," Jillian said. "Cate, this is Marilyn, who runs our local heritage museum. I was telling her a bit about your work, actually."

Cate's eyes lit. "You were?"

Marilyn said, "We didn't get into the details, but I understand your work is about the strike in 1913 and 1914."

"That's right."

"And you are working on the Ludlow Massacre?"

"As part of the larger study of how the Las Animas County experience affected women and children, yes." Clearly Cate was tickled to meet someone knowledgable about her field of interest.

"Most people have little or no understanding of how defining that strike was for labor standards in general," Marilyn said. "Its historical context is significant, and its importance was not only about the men who worked in mines but about the standard of living and agency of their families, who often had almost no independence from company towns."

"Yes!" Cate said. "And the children. The boys started working in the mines so young despite the extreme risks that they might not survive because it seemed like the only employment available to them. The girls expected to marry boys who somehow survived their teenage years doing that dangerous work. The strike was about changing their future as much as changing the present for their fathers."

"And of course the girls and women during the strike bore the brunt of the extra work," Marilyn said. "The men stopped working because they were on strike, but the women were expected to keep house in tents during a wretched winter, all the while wondering if there was going to be enough food to go around or clothing to keep everybody warm."

Jillian had stopped biting into her cone. In this rapid-fire conversation, she was soaking up all the truths she had seen glimmers of in Cate's research.

"Have you noticed the old photos?" Cate said. "The families stand in the snow? How many of them are out there in sweaters? Sweaters! Are we supposed to think they left their parkas in the tents or something?"

"Very astute observation," Marilyn said.

"Cate is working on a traveling exhibit for school children." Jillian realized the moment of opportunity lit like a miner's lamp in front of her. "Something to help kids understand what it was really like."

"A brilliant idea!" Marilyn said. "You should come by our heritage museum and see a real example of how your exhibit could work in the small-town settings that are all over this state, not just in the south. I would love to book your exhibit when it's ready."

Cate looked at Jillian, questioning.

Jillian nodded. "We'll come by."

"Good. That's quite a calling you have undertaken. I'd better order my treat and get back to work."

"That was unbelievable," Cate said after Marilyn had moved to the counter.

"Marilyn is fabulous," Jillian said. "And she knows lots of other small museum directors."

"This could really help turn me around. Help me break into networks who won't take my cold calls."

"Marilyn does a lot of school field trips. She knows the drill."

"I can't thank you enough."

"Cate, you're the one who talked strike history with her. That wasn't me. Don't sell yourself short." Jillian licked her cone. "There's something else I was hoping I would get to tell you," Jillian said. "About the Parisis."

"Oh?"

"Drew's great-aunt told me there were Parisis out on their ranch in the early twentieth century—probably around the time of the strike, now that I think about it."

"Before they came to Pueblo?"

"Must have been. I've only had time to dig around a little bit on that family tree you sent me. I want to be sure I'm looking for the right people. Giuseppe Luciano Parisi would be Benedetta's father, right?"

"Yes. He was Peppy to people who knew him well."

"Like the restaurant!" Jillian and Nolan had stopped and looked at the outside of the family's Italian restaurant on Saturday, with the brightly lit letters spelling Peppy's.

"Yes, that's right. Peppy's. He was a child when it opened, and it was named for him."

"It's an adorable nickname and fun family trivia." Jillian tilted her head. "Peppy. You have his wife's name down as Julia on the family tree."

"That's what it looks like in the notes I have."

"Ricco?"

"To the best of my knowledge. You're a genealogist. You know how the old spellings change."

Jillian did indeed know.

Kris had removed her apron and picked up her purse and was headed for the shop's door.

"Where are you going?" Jillian asked.

"I have to see a man about ... some things." Kris pressed her lips together and avoided Jillian's eyes.

"A man?"

"Just eat your ice cream, Jillian." Kris pushed out the door.

"What was that about?" Cate asked.

"Not sure. But I'm going to find out."

CHAPTER TWENTY-ONE

NIA HANDED JILLIAN A DOUBLE caramel latte with white cream at the Canary Cage two days after Cate's compunctious declaration that she did in fact want a cousin.

"Clark promises me you'll like this," Nia said. "Drink it and tell us all about Dreamy Drew."

Jillian took hold of the beverage. "Clark usurped my order?"

"He muttered something about being out of syrup. I said something about what kind of coffee shop was he running, which he didn't seem to appreciate."

"Nia, Nia, Nia." It was late in the day for a loaded caffeinated drink, but Nolan was the one who had to switch to decaf by noon, not Jillian. She leaned forward to inspect the late afternoon plate of pastries Nia had set on the coffee table, sure to spoil everyone's appetite for supper. The price was worth it. As usual, Veronica and Kris completed the foursome.

"Kris tells me she stuffed your cousin full of enough free ice cream to wipe out her day's profit margin," Veronica said.

"I told her to put it on my tab." Jillian sipped her latte.

"Would that be the imaginary one or the nonexistent one?" Veronica said.

"I'm good for it any day of the week," Jillian said.

"The main thing," Veronica said, "is that things are going well with Cate."

"They were hugging when they left my shop," Kris said. "I have a secret miracle family reconciliation ingredient. No extra charge."

"Maybe you can work a deal with my dad," Jillian said, "for his worst family mediation situations."

"I will mention it the next time we speak."

"We should celebrate with a shopping expedition!" Veronica batted her eyes at Jillian. "My cousin is getting married. I need a new dress.

Why don't you come along? Give yourself a breather from all this complexity and just give me simple answers about whether the dresses are pretty or not?"

"I don't know," Jillian said. "I'm not much in the mood for shopping."

"We'll zip into Denver. When we're finished, we can have gelato at that place you like."

"That part is tempting."

"I am sitting right here." Kris's admonition was instant.

"So we're not allowed to enjoy gelato anywhere in the state because Canyon Mines might get a gelato shop and you don't approve?" Jillian asked.

"I haven't determined the rules yet," Kris said.

"All nonsense aside," Veronica said, "it's true? Things are good with Cate?"

"I think so," Jillian said. "She ended up staying the night on Monday because the day got away from us just getting to know each other for the first time. She asked about my mom and Grandpa Steve. Dad got protective and didn't want her leaving when she would get home after midnight, so she left before dawn yesterday. She had work to get back to, but she left me the sweetest note. She even signed it Caterina. It was as if she wanted to be in the family tree together and nothing else."

"That's great, Jills," Kate said. "I know it's what you wanted."

Jillian selected a cream pastry and bit into it. The last two days had been the calmest of the last couple of weeks. She and Cate had parted on a genuinely affectionate status. Cate hadn't barraged her for help with her professional woes a single time during her visit, and while Jillian hadn't heard from Cate since she left Canyon Mines, she no longer feared the silence meant she was cut off from the family tree for good.

She had an Italian cousin. It felt good.

"Your phone is glowing," Nia said. "I can see it in your pocket."

"It's on silent," Jillian said.

"Well, it's lighting up. Isn't it buzzing?"

It was buzzing. Lost in her cream pastry, latte, and three best friends, Jillian had chosen to ignore it for the moment.

"Jillian, your phone is blowing up." Nia handed her two napkins.

Jillian did the best she could with her sticky fingers before handling her phone. Her throat tightened.

"I think I have to take back that nice little speech I just made."

"Cate?" Kris said.

Jillian nodded as she scrolled the messages. "Photos. Lots of photos."

Her friends huddled around her phone.

"Clearly someone broke into a truck," Veronica said. "Do you think it was Cate?"

"She says it wasn't." Jillian scrolled further. They saw an open box and strewn photos.

"That looks like a journal. Something old," Veronica said. "People who come into my store looking for antiques would eat that up."

"The photos are large," Jillian said. "Enlargements of what life was like, Cate says."

"Whose truck was this?" Nia asked.

"She doesn't say," Jillian said. "She just says she had nothing to do with it, even though everyone will think she did."

"Based on what you've told us," Kris said, "she probably has a point."

"You should call her," Nia said. "Or Nolan should."

The stone of disappointment in Jillian's gut sank deeper.

"I guess I will step over there into my remote corner office and see if I can reach my remote cousin." Jillian took her latte with her as she left her friends enjoying their pastries and found a quiet spot in the coffee shop to dial Cate's number.

"Oh, thank goodness." Relief gushed from Cate's core. "I just want you to know I absolutely did not have anything to do with this, but now I don't know what to do. Should I just ignore it? Do I need a lawyer? Should I call Nolan?"

"Slow down, Cate," Jillian said. "Tell me what happened."

"I got these photos on my phone. That's what happened. The same ones I sent to you. I don't know what that truck is. I can't even tell where it is. But it looks broken into, and the stuff is part of what Epic EduKids is planning to put up at the museum."

"Are you sure? Have you seen drawings or something?"

"It's the only thing that makes sense. Enlargements of what life was like in a company town? Journal pages? It's not mine. Where would they even get something like that?" Cate's words rushed at a dizzying speed. "Maybe they made it all up. I wouldn't put that past them. Nothing they do is authentic or original work. But I didn't do this! I don't need to steal their stupid journal, which probably isn't even real. I have my own journal which I know is real, if I wanted to use a journal."

"All right, Cate, let's focus," Jillian said. "Someone sent you the photos. Did you recognize the number?"

"No. I already tried using reverse white pages, but all it said was that the number was a low spam risk. It wouldn't tell me who the number belonged to unless I paid a fee."

"Don't do that." It was probably a prepaid cell phone that couldn't be traced through the white pages anyway, but Jillian had paid accounts that she used in her work. "Give me the number and I'll try tracing it for you. If I get any information, I'll let you know."

"Jillian, I did not do this. You have to believe me."

"I didn't say I didn't," Jillian said. But did she? Doubt flickered and dispelled the cheer of only a few minutes ago.

"I can't unsee what I saw. Those photos are a travesty of history. Your friend Marilyn would agree."

Oh please don't pull Marilyn into this mess.

"I guess I should just delete them and forget the whole thing. Try to put it out of my mind. I promised Nolan I would behave, and I will."

"Don't do that." Jillian's words surprised even her, especially how quickly they came out.

"Why not?"

"If someone is setting you up, you'd be erasing the evidence. Or trying. It's all in the cloud somewhere. That's my guess. Even taking it out of your own cloud doesn't delete them everywhere."

"Grrr. Jillian! What am I supposed to do?"

"Let me talk to my dad."

"The sheriff is going to be knocking on my door. I just know it. I'm already on thin ice with them. I'll be at the top of their list when they find that truck. I'm going to be in so much trouble with my parents. And my brothers. I don't even want to think about it."

"Obviously if that happens, whip out my dad's card again. Otherwise we'll call you later."

Jillian rejoined her group, which was breaking up. Nia was stacking plates and empty mugs.

"So?"

Jillian shrugged. "She says she has nothing to do with it. But she's terrified the sheriff is going to come looking for her as soon as somebody reports the break-in."

"She's not wrong," Kris said.

"I know," Jillian said. "And if they find a reason to look at her phone or if she blurts out that she has pictures, it won't go well."

"Evidence," Veronica said. "Contrived, but somebody will try to make it evidence. And now it's on your phone too."

"Gee thanks, cuz," Jillian said.

"What are you going to do?" Nia added a wadded paper napkin to her stack of dishes.

"Text my dad, order his favorite Chinese food for dinner, and await his wise legal counsel."

"That's the best plan."

"And hope and pray Cate doesn't fly off the handle at somebody in the meantime."

"Sorry for the complications," Kris said. "I've got to shoot to another commitment, but catch me up later, okay?"

Jillian was still nodding when Kris was out the door. "What's going on with her?"

Nia grinned. "A man. But she says she wants to take it slow."

Jillian scowled through the glass at Kris on the sidewalk. Kris was seeing someone and hadn't told her? How was that possible? She and Kris confided everything.

Cate. That's how. Kris saw how much Cate had consumed Jillian energy recently. So she told Nia instead. And now this.

Alas, more Cate drama, her first text message to Nolan said. But i think this time she is the innocent party.

I'm almost home. order chinese. Nolan was adept at dictating texts while he drove, a skill he acted like he alone had mastered.

One step ahead of you.

As she walked, Jillian pulled up the app of the Chinese restaurant and with a few clicks had ordered their usual beef and snow peas, cashew chicken, egg rolls, and fried rice. She hadn't eaten enough of her pastry to dull her appetite, but the conversation with Cate had done the job. After closing the mile between the Cage and home in an easy fifteen minutes, Jillian had time to set out a couple of plates and pour two glasses of raspberry lemonade before Nolan came in the back door and a few minutes later the bell rang at the front with the food's arrival.

Nolan listened and munched.

"Technically," he said, "possessing forwarded photos is no kind of proof that she had anything to do with breaking into the truck. She knows that and you know that."

"We do." Jillian picked at an egg roll. "But you can see how the whole thing is going to look."

"She absolutely cannot take action on the basis of anything she obtained from an anonymous source. It might be illegal. She doesn't know the motive of the person who sent her the photos."

"So she should send them to the sheriff? Just get ahead of it?"

"My guess is the sheriff's office also got a set."

Jillian's throat thickened. "They couldn't use them either, then."

"No, but they could use them to locate the truck and go from there."

"And it would still point to Cate."

"So is somebody trying to warn her or implicate her?"

"Interesting question, isn't it?"

"Dad! Cate is scared."

"Being warned would make a good defense."

"So you think she's going to need a defense?"

"I didn't say that."

"What exactly are you saying?"

"Would you like me to call Cate?"

"Very much so. And don't mess with her the way you mess with me." Jillian jumped when her own phone rang. "It's Drew."

"Then you'd better take it."

She picked up her phone from the table and wandered into the other room.

"I need a favor," Drew said.

"Anything."

"I know you've been burning up the highway lately, but can you come and stay again? I need to be away for a few days. I don't want to leave Aunt Min on her own right now."

CHAPTER TWENTY-TWO

Monday, April 20, 1914
Ludlow, Colorado

GEPPETTO'S WARM ARM, LADEN with sleep, stretched heavy across Caterina's hip under the two quilts that insulated them from the still-cold nights. Slowly she shifted and eased out of the bed. Soon the day would break. For now, only the barest hint of pink stretched across the horizon outside the bedroom window, but Caterina was already restless. If she was careful, she could leave her husband and son undisturbed, pass by Chiara and the bambino sleeping in front of what was left of last night's fire in the front room, and sneak into the kitchen for what were likely to be the only moments of the day she would have to herself. Wrapped in the thick robe Ela had given her for Christmas—a gift so extravagant Caterina had tried to refuse it—and her feet in Geppetto's shoes because their large size meant she could slide into them without stopping to fasten them, she shuffled out of the bedroom and silently closed the door behind her.

In the front room, little was left of the fire, and the space was chilly. If Caterina stopped to stoke embers or lay on more logs, she might rouse Chiara and lose her moments alone. Instead she would just be sure Chiara was covered well as she passed by. She needed to put something in her empty stomach before her discomfort mounted.

The bed in the corner was vacant, as well as the cradle Giuseppe had used before he outgrew it.

But the kitchen was unlit and unoccupied.

If the bambino was fussing, perhaps Chiara had taken him outside to walk and soothe him, dark and cold though it was. Caterina would tell her once again that she did not have to worry about keeping him quiet for the sake of the Parisis. They understood that babies cried. Swallowing against the gurgle in her gut, Caterina took Geppetto's barn jacket off a hook next to the back door and went outside, now craving light.

"Chiara? Are you out here?"

No answer.

"Chiara?"

Wishing she had lit a lamp but not wanting to take the time to go back for one now, Caterina circled the little red house. Surely if Chiara were out trying to soothe the baby she wouldn't go far.

But she was not there. Not sitting on the back porch. Not sitting on one of the wooden chairs Geppetto left sitting out year-round in front. Not pacing along the side of the house.

Caterina picked her way through the dark toward the hut but found it dark and cold and empty as well.

"Chiara?" She lifted her voice now, calling toward the line of rising pink.

Caterina returned to the house and looked around. Of course she expected Chiara's coat would be gone if she was outside with the baby trying to get him to sleep, but Caterina was looking deeper now. What else was not as it should be?

The bag—the one they used when they packed the baby's things for a visit to the main house—was gone.

Chiara's good dress, the one she hadn't worn the whole time since coming to the ranch, even though her illness meant her weight gain was slight and she'd gotten her waistline back easily. Gone.

The good scarf Celestrino gave her for Christmas, made by one of the women at the colony. Not folded on top of the cabinet where Chiara always left it.

And the baby's dearest blanket, the one that had been Chiara's blanket when she was a baby and saved all these years for her own firstborn.

"Geppetto!" Caterina shouted. "Geppetto!"

By the time she reached the bedroom, he was sitting up in bed, startled. Peppy was rubbing his sleepy eyes.

"Chiara left with the baby."

"Left? Where?"

"We'll have to find her and ask her that question."

"The sun is not even up." Geppetto shoved one leg and then the other into his trousers.

"She can't have gone far." Caterina kicked off Geppetto's shoes and shirked off his jacket. He would need them.

"Mama," Peppy whimpered.

"I know, baby, Mama and Papa are being so noisy."

"I'll find her," Geppetto said, "and bring her back."

"I'm going with you. We'll all go. She may be hurt. The baby may need something. It may take both of us to convince her not to …" What was Chiara trying to do?

"I'll be back as soon as I can with a horse and cart." Geppetto sped out of the house.

"Mama?" Peppito looked up at Caterina in the still-dim room.

"Let's get you changed and into something warm." Caterina almost had Peppy dressed before she had to run out the back door and give in to her stomach's objections.

But her mouth was rinsed and her face splashed and they were ready when Geppetto was back with the cart. Peppy was bundled in a blanket, and Caterina held him close.

"I assume we are not searching the ranch first," Geppetto said.

Caterina shook her head. "She is trying to leave."

The little red house was one of the nearest buildings to the ranch's entrance. Geppetto guided the cart to the road and turned left on the road that would lead them to Pueblo.

"This makes no sense," he said. "Has Celestrino sent her any of his union pay? He has so little. Does she even know how many miles the ranch is from Pueblo?"

"She has been to the doctor's office many times," Caterina said. "It is close to the depot. She knows the way."

"It's a long way to walk with a newborn."

"He never came, Geppetto. Five weeks, and Celestrino never came to see the baby. She is out of her mind."

"At least it is light now."

"I've been thinking about when I last heard the baby cry. Maybe two hours? She can't be far, Geppetto."

"Unless she already persuaded someone to give her a ride to the depot."

Panic sprayed through Caterina. "When do the trains start running for the day?"

Geppetto urged the horse faster. The light was in their favor now, and up ahead Chiara's small figure, clothed in her dark coat and her head wrapped in the knit scarf, came into view. Geppetto passed her and then reined in the horse. Caterina handed him their sleepy son and climbed out of the cart.

Chiara met them with defiance carved into her face. "I belong with my husband. It was all arranged and he never came. Five weeks. His son is five weeks old and he has not met his father."

"This distresses you greatly." Caterina put an arm around Chiara, and Chiara flinched.

"The guards see everything they do. He writes this. Now two weeks go by and I have no letter. What if he has been arrested? What if it is Celestrino's turn to be in jail when he does nothing wrong? So I will go to him. He will see his son, and he will understand that he must come to the ranch and not go back. If he is in jail and he makes this promise, they will let him go."

"Chiara."

"I will go. I do not ask your help. I do not ask your permission. I am a grown woman."

"Of course you are."

"I am a wife. I belong with my husband. I belong with my Celestrino. I get on the train and I go to Celestrino."

"How about if we call the colony again," Caterina said. "I'm sure Ela would let us. We'll find out for sure that he's not in jail. Then we'll wait for him to call back. We'll find out why the letters stopped."

"I have decided this thing."

"Please let us help you, Chiara."

"Zia Chia okay?" Peppy's small voice cracked Chiara's stone face. Caterina would remember to cover him in kisses later.

"I must go to him." Chiara words broke into a sob. "I must. Can you help me with this?"

Caterina and Geppetto met glances.

"Where Zia Chia go?" Peppy asked.

"We would have to go back and let the Kyps know where we are going," Geppetto said.

"And ask them to keep Peppy," Caterina added. "They don't even know we took one of their horses. Can you imagine what they might think if we don't show up for work and they find all of us gone?"

Slowly Chiara nodded. "And then we go together, or I go again alone."

Caterina eased out her breath. This would take some explaining to Ela—and so early in the morning. She and Carrick were sure to object to the plan because of the danger of going into the strike zone with an infant. The only defense was to let them see for themselves Chiara's determination. At least they wouldn't be taking Giuseppe.

They spoke little after leaving the ranch again, nor on the the early train ride between Pueblo and Ludlow. Ela and Carrick had no more success reasoning with Chiara than the Parisis had, so they had sent them off with embraces and prayers and a bit of extra cash. Chiara clutched her baby, discretely feeding him with the added cover that Caterina's presence provided while Geppetto turned his eyes away.

They got off the train in Ludlow and gained their bearings. Just to the north was the tent colony, which they passed on their way down. Across the tracks from the depot and post office, the military detachment had not been there six months ago when Caterina and Geppetto came to fetch Chiara. They were hardly more than a stone's throw from the strikers' colony. Caterina took a deep breath.

"What is that?" Chiara pointed to the south.

"Water Tank Hill," a voice behind them said.

The three of them turned toward the man, dressed in shabby wool trousers and a jacket that could not begin to keep him warm.

"Are those machine guns?" Chiara asked.

"They shoot from there sometimes, if they can't be bothered with the Death Special."

Chiara paled.

"They will never kill our spirit."

At this Chiara perked up. "You are a miner? Do you know my Celestrino?"

He cocked his head. "Sounds Italian."

"Yes, Italian."

"I don't know him. But someone will."

Caterina interrupted to ask, "Is it usual to have so much activity going on at Water Tank Hill?"

"The militia want us to give up a certain miner they think is here. We don't have him. But if they don't believe us—which they won't—they'll try to search the camp. When that happens, we always lose our weapons and cash, and they disabuse our women."

Caterina's stomach roiled. "But two machine guns and all those soldiers?"

"If they are fixin' for a fight, they are going to get one."

"I must find my Celestrino!" Chiara said.

"I hope you do." The man, whose name they never learned, took a long jump off the depot platform and dashed into into a low-lying area alongside a spur that angled northeast.

"What are those other men doing?" Caterina asked.

"We are not safe here," Geppetto said. "We have to find out when the next train leaves, whether it is going north or south. We can't stay. We should never have come."

"I will not leave!" Chiara said. "Not without Celestrino!"

"We have no way to contact him from here," Geppetto said. "You are in danger. Your baby is in danger. Is that what Celestrino would want?"

"Do not tell me what Celestrino would want." Chiara's voice snapped, a taut wire cut without warning.

"What are those men doing?" Caterina repeated her question. Miners dashing from the tent colony ran along the railway cut. "Why are they exposing themselves?"

"Get inside the depot right now." Geppetto's large hands pushed on the women. "They are trying to draw fire away from the colony."

"By getting themselves shot?"

"If that's what it takes to give others time to get away, yes."

"Others," Caterina muttered. "You mean women and children."

"No! No!" Chiara screamed. "I cannot go. Celestrino is there!"

"Chiara," Caterina said, "be reasonable. This is far more dangerous than we realized."

"I saw him. He is one of those men. He is just over there. We are so close." Chiara pushed the bundle of her child into Caterina's arms. "Keep him safe. I will bring his father back. This I will do."

She was gone in a flash, gone from the depot, off the platform, scrambling across the ground straight into the maze of men putting themselves into the line of fire.

Caterina and Geppetto stared at each other wide-eyed.

"Pray for me, and I will pray for you," Caterina said. And she put the bambino in Geppetto's arms.

"I can't stay here," Geppetto said. "Not with a bambino. Even the depot is in the direct line if they start firing at the colony with that machine gun."

"Then you'll have to go somewhere safer." Caterina began trotting after Chiara. Running. She trusted Geppetto to make a sensible decision, but not Chiara.

Chiara had lost her mind! This would not help anything, but losing sight of her now would only make things worse. Caterina's chest was about to explode with fear, but she could not let that five-week-old bambino become an orphan. Not on that day because of men who could not see answers beyond guns.

When the machine guns blasted behind her, she was desperate to look back, to see if Geppetto had stayed inside with the baby, to be sure he too had not lost his mind and chased her. Would it be the last sight she ever had of this man who loved her, sacrificed for her, gave her the joy of a child, made her heart sing? She would hold his face in her heart forever, but in this moment she could not lose sight of Chiara. And he should be gone, finding his own place to hide now, where she would have to find him later. When, she did not know. But he would be safe with that child. This she knew.

The guns blasted again, and Caterina pumped her legs harder until she caught up with Chiara.

Tackled her.

Knocked her to the ground.

Covered her there.

Held her there.

"You will not run into that camp!" Caterina screamed. "You will not chase those men."

They stared at each other, breathing hard. Caterina kept Chiara's shoulders pinned to the ground. Never in her life had she done something like this.

"The bambino?" Chiara asked.

"With Geppetto."

Then came the horror that made the machine guns sound like a child's drum. The bomb's blast was deafening, one followed by another.

The canyon, a warren of mines and rocks, trembled.

Chiara screamed for Celestrino.

Caterina wanted to insist that they must return to Geppetto and pray that there would be a train, but the canyon shuddered with the unlikelihood of escape. She clamped a hand down on Chiara's mouth. In a moment of quiet between bomb blasts, her screams would only make them a target of the machine gun. Caterina was no soldier, but she did want to see her husband and son again.

And then Chiara's name came back to them on the wind. They stared at each other again with their matching dark Italian eyes until a moment later when they were both overcome by a force they did not see coming and rolled into a foxhole alongside the railroad cut.

"Celestrino!" This time the whispered name was on Caterina's lips.

CHAPTER TWENTY-THREE

DREW OFFERED HIS HAND, and Jillian took it, feeling the fresh callous he had developed since the last time she'd held his hand six days ago. Rebuilding that stall in the barn must have been getting the best of him. They left Nolan at the kitchen table either amusing or annoying Min, depending on the interpretation of her facial responses, and walked outside toward Drew's truck. He'd already loaded his things.

It's a good thing I came back," Jillian said. "I left my favorite pen here last weekend. I've missed it all week."

Drew eyed her. "If that's what you missed all week, I'm doing something wrong."

Drawing her out of line of sight from the window, where Min might look out if she tired of her dad's entertainment, Drew took her face in both his hands.

"Oh this," Jillian said. "There is definitely something to be said for this." She leaned into his kiss, giving her mouth to his warmth, deepening along with his eagerness, standing there in a moment she would happily make a forever moment.

"There," Drew finally said. "Can your favorite pen do that?"

"What pen?"

He put his lips to her ear. "Blue. Fine tip. Rolling."

His breath tickled, and she pushed him away, but not very hard. "You think you know me so well.

"Thank you for coming on short notice."

"You didn't have much notice for the singing gig in Albuquerque."

"People can't help when they get sick. And the whole concert program is built around opera music. They know I know the solo pieces they're using."

"You're going to be great."

They resumed their progress toward Drew's truck.

Drew's parents were out of town for a couple of weeks, and his sister Josie's kids had a soccer tournament all weekend. Min refused to stay with a friend in town even though her injured wrist still limited her movements.

"If she would just sit in her chair and watch TV for three days, that would be one thing," Drew said. "But she thinks her wrist is better and keeps taking off the brace. She's not supposed to do that. And once she gets it off, I can always tell, because she doesn't get it fastened back on right."

"I'll keep an eye on it."

"She's determined to clean out that room for the rummage sale, and I can't stop her."

"I've got that covered. I've already offered to help as much as she wants all weekend."

"Perfect."

"And my Dad has a way of keeping people trapped with his stories. He's never had a whole weekend at the ranch before."

Drew grinned. "That should be interesting."

"He'll have to check in with Cate—drive down to Trinidad or see if she has a shift at one of the restaurants up here. But we won't leave Min on her own."

"You are the best."

Standing behind the open door of his truck, Drew pulled her into another embrace. Jillian buried her head against his shoulder for a moment. She wanted to remember this scent, his freshly laundered plaid flannel shirt swirling with his understated aftershave and the earthy October day in the sun. Sometimes it was hard to believe she didn't even know Drew Lawson six months ago, and now her heart was his.

"Your phone is buzzing," Drew said.

"What phone?" Jillian said. "I don't have a phone." Out here on the ranch, gazing at the far-flung acres and the mountain views beyond, what did she want with a phone?

"If you don't have a phone," Drew said, "how am I going to call you four times a day all weekend?"

"To ask about Min?"

"To remind you that I am better than your favorite pen?"

Jillian smiled and pulled the buzzing phone out of her pocket. "It's Cate."

"Then you'd better answer." Drew kissed her cheek and closed the truck door.

"Hi Cate."

"They came," Cate said. "Someone from the sheriff's department."

Oddly, Cate was not hysterical. Drew waved as he pulled away, and Jillian yearned for that last kiss they didn't get.

"What happened?" Jillian pulled herself to the moment.

"They showed up at my office yesterday asking me questions about where I was on Tuesday night between seven and nine." Cate's words tumbled out in a victorious rush. "But I had an alibi."

"Did somebody back you up?" Jillian walked slowly back toward the house.

"They say the break-in happened between seven and nine. Don't ask me how they know. I don't even care. But that truck was in Trinidad all night, and I was in Pueblo. That's the point."

"You were working at a restaurant?"

"Peppy's! We were open till nine. I helped wipe down tables and didn't leave until nine thirty."

"So a lot of people would have seen you."

"Only about a hundred, if the police actually wanted to track everyone down." Cate's voice gushed with the relief of uncontested innocence. "I never thought I would be saying I was glad to have my family vouching for me because they made me work, but both my brothers were at Peppy's that night, and they said absolutely I was there and never so much as went to the bathroom during the dinner shift."

"You must not have been back to Trinidad until at least ten thirty."

"Even the sheriff's deputy did that math pretty quickly."

"Well, that's great, Cate! I'm so happy for you."

"It's such a relief."

"I can only imagine." Jillian glanced through the kitchen window. Nolan still had Min captive at the table. "With that crisis averted, can I ask you a question?"

"Sure."

"The other day you said something about how you didn't need to steal somebody's fake journal when you had a real one of your own."

"Because that's the truth."

"But what did you mean? I don't remember your mentioning a

journal to me before."

"I must have. It's the inspiration for everything I'm doing."

"That sounds pretty important." Jillian paused outside the back door, one foot on the low step. "I would have remembered."

"I can't believe I haven't told you," Cate said. "Maybe because I keep it under lock and key. Even Patrice hasn't seen it. It's what made me so interested in the children of Ludlow and all the mining families in the first place."

"How did you come to have a journal like that? It sounds like an incredibly rare find."

"My grandmother had it."

"Benedetta? Peppy's daughter?"

"Yes. But it wasn't hers. It was in her parents' things and somehow she ended up with it. Her sisters didn't want it, and she always thought it was interesting, so she saved it."

"Where did her parents get it?"

"I don't know the provenance. Neither does Nonna. That's why I'm being extremely careful about how I use it. How do I know it's not made up?"

"If your great-grandparents had it, what makes you think it's made up?"

"They weren't at Ludlow. They never lived in a mining town. Why would they have something like that? I just want to be careful."

"That makes sense. What's in the journal?"

The back door swung open and nearly knocked Jillian over.

"Dad! Watch it!"

"There you are," Nolan said.

"Yes, here I am. Ow."

"Sorry. I honestly didn't see you."

Jillian rubbed the spot on her head that was sure to grow a lump. "Did you need something?"

"Min is getting antsy. She's asking for you," Nolan said. "And you'd better get some ice on that."

"Here." Jillian held out her phone. "Cate's on the line. There's good news on the legal front."

Min was waiting for her in the kitchen with ice cubes wrapped in a dish cloth. "Saw the whole thing. That screen door has been swinging open too fast for at least ten years. You aren't the first person to get clobbered like that."

"It's a wallop, all right."

"It wasn't so bad in the days when we had a porch out here. But it rotted out and my husband tore it off. He always said he was going to build a better one and never did."

Jillian eased out her breath as the ice numbed her pain. "My dad said you were looking for me."

"You did say you would help me with that room."

"Of course. I'm happy to."

Jillian rounded up some empty boxes and strapping tape Min directed her to, and they went to the store room together.

"You can tell me what to do," Jillian said, "but you have to let me do it if it's anything more than moving papers."

Min huffed. "I see you have your marching orders from that nephew of mine."

"I do."

"It's a good thing I'm fond of both of you."

Jillian let her mouth quirk up on one side.

"On the other hand, you might have some explaining to do about the knot on your head, and I will not take responsibility."

Jillian laughed. "Maybe Drew will finally fix the door."

"When we were so rudely interrupted a week ago," Min said, "I had just about decided I knew where that old case was."

Jillian pulled out the one unencumbered chair in the room. "Sit here. I'll start by picking up the box that fell apart."

"Yes, we'll have to get the mess out of the way, and make space to pull out some of the other things in the closet. But I don't want to get too distracted by all of that. It's that case I'm after."

Jillian sealed the bottom of a fresh box with tape and scooped up the scattered detritus of Min's determination last week. No wonder the box had been too heavy for Min that night. It had contained old *Life* magazines.

"Wow." Jillian picked one up from the 1960s. "These are in mint condition."

"No, no. We're not going there right now." Min wagged a crooked finger. "Keep your eye on the prize. Just put them in the box and set it aside. Leave all of that for another time."

At Min's direction, Jillian removed boxes from the closet and stacked them in a tower. Some were heavy, some light, some labeled, some unmarked. Finishing the job of clearing out this room was not a weekend task.

"There," Min said finally. "Black leather. I was thinking it was brown, but now I remember. Black, just very worn."

Jillian saw it. Displacing a bag of yarns and one of children's clothings gave her access, and she took it out.

"We won't be able to open it in here," Min said. "We might as well take it back to the kitchen table."

"This is old." Jillian held the suitcase with both hands, hesitant of its fragility and not trusting the handle.

"I'm an old lady," Min said, "and I have a lot of old memories."

"In my line of work, those are the best kind."

"I haven't looked inside that case for decades, but it might interest you."

As they passed down the hall and into the kitchen, Nolan spied them. "What have you got there?"

"We're going to find out." Jillian said.

Nolan followed them into the kitchen. Jillian set the suitcase on the table and fiddled with the stubborn latches until they gave. She raised the lid. Blue ribbon tied together bundles of yellowed papers, and an old flour sack was wrapped around a few black and white photos. Jillian set these on the table. What remained in the case were various other household items—more flour sacks, which Jillian knew many women used as towels or even pillow cases, a carved wooden cross, a aluminum coffee pot, an English primer, a small canvas drawstring sack holding a dozen marbles, two tin cups, a small white baptismal gown, three more baby gowns in varying sizes, a Christmas tablecloth folded around four sturdy pottery plates. Finally, a soft, well-worn, faded yellow blanket cushioned the bottom of the case.

"Who did this belong to?" Jillian asked.

Min shook her head. "It was just always in the house. For years it was in the attic. A lot of stuff was. But my husband and I had to reinsulate up there, so it came down. This was after it was just the two of us in the house, so there wasn't a lot of point in dragging it all back up."

"So you left it in that room."

"That's right."

"May I?" Nolan gestured toward the photos.

Min turned a hand up.

Nolan laid open the protective towel and lined up the photos. All were couples standing in front of the same small structure, some with a child or two, labeled with a surname and a date.

"What is this building?" Jillian asked.

"The old hut," Min said.

"Hut?"

"It wasn't really a hut. A small outbuilding near the little red house. It was gone before I was born. I've only ever seen it in photos from the early days."

"Why would all these people be standing front of it?" Nolan asked.

Jillian leaned in to look closely. "The dates are all 1914 and 1915. That must mean something. But what?"

"The papers might tell us."

"I can see without pulling the ribbon that they are all in Italian."

"Pull the ribbon," Min said. "You can at least look for names. Isn't that what a genealogist does?"

CHAPTER TWENTY-FOUR

Monday, April 20, 1914
Ludlow, Colorado

CATERINA, CELESTRINO, AND CHIARA HUDDLED against the frigid, hardpacked winter earth. How long had the miners been scraping out these foxholes along the railroad spur with axes and shovels? How long had guards at the militia detachment on the other side of the north-south tracks watched them do it? How long had this day been brewing? Weeks. Months, if Celestrino's letters and the newspapers were accurate.

They should never have broken their resolve and bartered with Chiara on the road outside the ranch. They should have heeded Carrick's stern caution and abided by Ela's silent concern as she took charge of Peppy. They should have given up their bedroom, boarded up the window, and locked the door if that's what it took to keep Chiara in the house. And then Geppetto should have called Celestrino so often on the telephone that the colony leaders would personally put him on a train to Pueblo to make the nuisance stop.

But they hadn't done any of that. So here they were.

When the three of them tumbled into the foxhole, a pair of men had leaped out.

"What is happening?" Chiara cried.

"They are taking their turn," Celestrino said. "We jump up, run like madmen, and dive for cover again. They cannot shoot at all of us."

Chiara clutched her husband. "I came to take you to meet your son. You are no madman. You are a father now."

"You should not have come, Chiara. You can see that, can't you?"

"I'm sorry," Caterina said. "We couldn't convince her. She would have come with or without us. When we saw what was happening, Geppetto wanted to get on the next train, no matter where it was going, but Chiara ..."

"I am not leaving without you, Celestrino," Chiara said.

"Geppetto is here?" Celestrino lifted his head toward the daylight above them.

"He is with the bambino," Chiara said.

Shock split Celestrino's face. "The bambino is here?"

"At the depot. Waiting for you. Waiting to meet his papa."

Caterina did not know where Geppetto was. Wherever he was, he was keeping the baby save, and that was enough for any of them to believe in this moment.

Gripping Chiara's hand, Celestrino features melted to silly. "Our bambino is here? Will he smile at me?"

Chiara giggled. "Only if he has gas."

"You wrote that he has very big eyes."

"Your eyes. Big and dark. With long lashes. And chubby cheeks."

Celestrino brushed Chiara's cheek. "I hope he has your dimple."

A bullet whizzed above them.

"Where is your gun, Celestrino?" Caterina nudged his leg with her knuckles. "I thought you had a Winchester."

"The militia took it the last time they raided the camp," he said. "I cannot fight with a gun, but I am very nimble. I have run across the field twice already today."

"You will not run anymore," Chiara said. "No more."

They lay there flat to the ground, speaking little, while gunfire flew above them in both directions.

"The bambino," Chiara whispered. "He will be hungry soon."

"You know Geppetto will take good care of him," Caterina said.

"But I am the only one who can feed him." Chiara started to push herself up.

Celestrino shoved her back down. "Chiara! We cannot leave now."

"The bambino. He does not cry much, but he cries when he is hungry. What can Geppetto do for him?"

Caterina eased out a silent sigh. Hadn't Chiara thought of that question when she left her baby to run along a railroad track in sight of a machine gun?

"How long will this last?" Chiara asked.

"Chiara, how can I know?" Celestrino said. "They are shooting a machine gun and throwing bombs in the canyon."

"I can't believe you left the ranch to come back to this."

"Well, I did. I can't believe you came to find me here when I have written to you about how unsafe it is."

"But many women and children are living here. You say this all the time."

"Not because I think it is a good thing! I tell you because I think it is a frightful thing, Chiara."

The sweet reunion of parents still learning the wonders of their new son had evaporated.

Caterina squeezed Chiara's arm. "You have had your bambino with you every moment until now. Of course you are worried. But you know Geppetto is a good papa. You see him with Peppito all the time. He takes very good care of Peppito, doesn't he?"

Tearful, Chiara nodded.

"He will find a way to take very good care of your son too. You can believe this. He is a good man. You have seen this for yourself."

"He takes good care of you." Chiara choked out the words. "He takes good care of the land. He has shown me it is beautiful to live there, away from the mines, away from big cities."

"Yes, yes."

A burly man hurtled into the crowded foxhole.

"I cannot take a turn running," Celestrino said.

Caterina breathed relief.

"This is my wife and our friend." Celestrino wiped tears from Chiara's eyes with one thumb. "I must stay with them."

"Just let me catch my breath," the man said. "It's chaos in the camp. Families are leaving everything behind. They're just trying to get out with their lives."

"But they are getting out?" Celestrino said. "That is why we are running like madmen, after all. To give them time."

"Many are. The creek bed north of the camp is dry, and people know where the friendly ranches are. And into the Black Hills. I also heard some are hiding in the well."

"The water must be freezing," Celestrino said. "How long can they last there?"

"There's no time to think things through. The militia means business this time. You can't keep womenfolk here all day either."

"Celestrino!" The cry was back in Chiara's hushed tone.

He put a finger to her lips.

The man gulped air for a few more minutes and took off again.

"Celestrino," Caterina said, "how many of these protected positions for the men are there along this rail cut?"

"I'm not sure," he said. "Only a few of us volunteered to run between them as a distraction. The other positions have men with guns. Not always very good ones, just what we can get from sympathetic ranchers if the militia don't get to them first."

"Do you know where they are?"

"Most of them."

"We can't just lie here and wait to get shot. If the gunfire shifts toward the colony, can we run? And where would we run?"

"If gunfire shifts toward the colony, then we have failed to do our job."

"Celestrino," Caterina said, "the gunfire will shift. The goal is to destroy the colony, just as they did at Forbes. They won't shoot at these foxholes all day."

He was silent as her logic set in.

"Your job was to give people time to get out," she said.

"Celestrino," Chiara said, "when will it be our turn to get out? Your turn?"

He closed his eyes. "Let me listen."

"It's time to feed the baby," Chiara said.

Caterina said nothing. Chiara's milk was probably letting down, and in her discomfort she would think of nothing but the bambino.

They lay there for a few minutes before Celestrino said, "It's shifting. I can't decide if that's good or bad, but I do think it's shifting."

"We can't change whether it's good or bad," Caterina said, "but if it's our chance we have to take it."

Two miners tumbled into the foxhole. This time they carried Winchesters.

"What's happening?" Celestrino asked.

"They're definitely getting ready to gun the camp directly. They're finished playing with our little trick of drawing fire away. There are more of them all the time. They are making sure to have more men, more guns, more ammunition than we have."

Caterina's heart pounded. "Is everybody out?"

"Whoever is left now is probably trapped."

"Are they using the cellars?" Celestrino asked.

The man nodded.

"Cellars?" Caterina asked.

"A lot of the tents have cellars dug underneath," Celestrino said. "For situations like this. The women and children go there when the militia start firing."

"Like the Death Special?"

He nodded.

"What about Mary Petrucci?" Chiara asked. "She was my friend. She has so many children."

"She has a good cellar," Celestrino said. "She knows how to use it."

"Is she there now?"

The miners shrugged.

"No one is sure where anyone is," one of them said. "I guess we'll find out later where everyone was."

"Do you have families?" Caterina asked.

They both nodded.

"We told them to get out. To run to one of the ranches. But we don't know."

The uncertainty thrust a jagged edge through Caterina's heart.

"We have the best guns we could find. We're on our way to Water Tank Hill to see what damage we can do closer up."

"Against a machine gun?" Caterina was shocked.

"Our plan is not to let them see us."

The men left on their bellies, rifles in position.

"How can we get out of here?" Caterina said. "I don't care how big a detour we have to take, how wide the circle is. The fight is shifting. Celestrino, take us out of here."

"To the depot, Celestrino," Chiara said.

"No!" Caterina said. "That's right in the middle of the battle. Geppetto won't be there anymore."

"Where is he? Where is my bambino?"

"I don't know. But I'm sure he would have the sense to get himself to the other side of Water Tank Hill, to the other side of the main tracks, away from all of this."

"Maybe the Section House," Celestrino said. "It would provide some shelter. If not there, then the underpass where the tracks go through the arroyo."

"How do we get there?"

He glanced up out of the foxhole. "If we stay down low, we can get to the highlands and hike down the arroyo from there."

"How far will that be?"

"We have to go far out of our way. Three miles? It won't be a summer stroll."

Caterina gripped his shoulder and gritted her teeth. "Celestrino, take us to your son, and don't get us shot."

Celestrino turned to his bride. "Chiara, you will do what I say, yes? And only what I say, yes?"

Thank you, Celestrino.

Chiara nodded solemnly.

"Tie up your good dress, because we will be crawling to start."

"I don't care about the dress. Only about you and our bambino."

"No shouting. No crying. No questions."

"I promise." Two circles of leaking milk dampened Chiara's dress.

"I go first, and you follow only when I signal that it is safe."

"I promise."

Celestrino glanced at Caterina, and she nodded as well. Then she turned away and let her stomach heave.

"Caterina," Chiara said, "you are ill!"

"It's nerves. It is not every day I find myself running across a field of gunfire."

"It's my fault."

"Let's just get ourselves out of here."

The battle—and unquestionably that is what it had become—had fully shifted in direction, which bolstered Caterina's confidence that if their movements were noticed they would be of little consequence to the guardsmen behind the machine gun. But she followed Celestrino and made sure to keep Chiara tightly between them as they crawled out of their dirt hollow, scuttled between foxholes, dashed across the tracks, and ducked low while they crept along alarmingly exposed land before reaching what Celestrino called the "highlands," which did not seem high to Caterina at all. Circling wide to come well behind Water Tank Hill, and above the arroyo that flowed out of the underpass, they were sweaty and exhausted although they had only come a few miles in cold spring air. They were clear of the gunfire, but the reverberations thundering across the canyon raised sickening images of what the bullets might have done. Climbing down from the height they had gained still remained. Caterina's breath grew heavy as her stomach prepared another revolt. She'd had nothing to eat all day, yet it heaved. She slowed enough to let Chiara get a few yards ahead before turning her head and spitting up what little she had left to lose.

"Caterina?" Chiara had looked back.

"It's nerves." Caterina wiped a hand across her mouth.

They pushed on. Following the path of the tracks that joined Trinidad and Walsenburg might have been easiest, but trying to get out of sight as efficiently as possible had the women following Celestrino's lead to descend the structure of the underpass as soon as they were over the arroyo. Chiara balked for a moment at the height, but Celestrino held onto her as much as he could as they climbed down. Geppetto was not sheltering there under the bridge, so Caterina prayed to find him when they crossed the two stretches of track where the Berwind branch joined the main path at the Section House. Chiara was remarkably silent through all of this. Caterina was remarkably confident that Celestrino had done something like this before—perhaps not guiding two women to safety but certainly trying to evade the danger of the militia with a circuitous route through the exposed landscape. She shuddered to think what Chiara would say if the same thought occurred to her. Three simple miles must have taken them at least two hours.

As they approached the Section House, a baby's cry came.

Chiara's steps quickened, but Celestrino held her back with a finger to his lips.

"But it is the bambino," she whispered. "Ours."

"Stay." His eyes abided no argument.

Caterina reached for Chiara's hand and gripped it.

Celestrino crept toward the cry while Chiara pressed a fist into her mouth. Even Caterina recognized the desperate sound of the bambino's hunger. It had been hours! Celestrino looked in the corner of one window after another before allowing his shoulders to relax and waving them forward.

CHAPTER TWENTY-FIVE

Outside Pueblo, Colorado

"DID YOU SLEEP AT ALL?" From behind her, Nolan put s hand on Jillian's shoulder and leaned forward to see what she saw. Her coffee mug was empty, and the fingers of one hand were tangled in the blue ribbon from last night. The entire contents of the black suitcase had been moved to the living room and spread out for closer examination. Right in the midst of them was a narrow-ruled yellow legal pad, the kind he had always used and she had first asked him for when she was eleven years old.

"I tried, but I couldn't sleep," Jillian said. "So I got up. What does all this mean?"

"What does it ever mean?" Nolan shrugged. "It's somebody's story."

"But whose? Min said it was a case from the days when there were Parisis here, but even without trying to read Italian, I can look for names, and I don't see any mention of a Parisi."

"That's what you have on your pad? Names?"

"And a few phrases that I could make out and put through a Google translator." Jillian stretched. "I need coffee."

"How many cups have you already had?"

"Dad, it's seven in the morning. Way too early for you to be policing my caffeine intake."

"Fine. I'll see if I can manage making fresh coffee."

"I'll do it." Jillian stood up. "You don't know your way around Min's kitchen, and you'll bring me some straight black nonsense."

"I suppose you brought your own fancy creamers down here."

"Might have. Want to make something of it?"

"What I want," Nolan said firmly, "is to make a cup of morning coffee, but you are trying to be the boss."

"Not so loud. You'll wake Min."

"Too late. You two are quite a pair."

They both turned their heads toward the voice in the hall.

Min, guarding her wrist, advanced toward them. "I will make the coffee. And before you start protesting, I can make a pot of coffee in my own kitchen with one hand tied and both eyes closed."

"I'll keep you company, then." Jillian picked up her empty mug. "Maybe rustle up something for my father to eat."

"You don't have to say words like *rustle* just because you are on the ranch," Min said. "I usually have oatmeal on Saturdays."

"Oatmeal it is." Jillian followed Min into the kitchen.

Alone with the contents of the case, Nolan picked up Jillian's yellow pad. She'd filled two-thirds of a page with phrases in Italian in one column and translations in another. At the bottom of a page was a list of names—Italian surnames, from what Nolan could make out.

Esposito. Conti. DeLuca. Rillo. Giordano. Moretti. Romano. Marchesi. Berese. Pedregone. Bartolotti.

"You're snooping." Jillian was back and handed him a mug of black coffee.

"Collaborating."

"Oatmeal will be ready in a few minutes."

"What have you got going here?"

"Not much." Jillian took the pad from Nolan and tossed it aside. "Handwriting is hard to read, old ink dried in smudges, some of the letters are creased in bad places, I have a feeling not everybody was a great speller. I guess I'll try putting more of this through an online translator, but it will take some time and guessing."

"Come and get your breakfast," Min called from the kitchen.

Nolan rubbed his hands together. "I'm hungry."

The kitchen table offered steaming oatmeal, blueberries, yogurt, and orange juice. They said grace and dug in. When Jillian's phone rang and it was a FaceTime call from Drew, Nolan wouldn't let her leave the room.

"You sit down in your chair, and you put him where we can all see him."

"Dad."

"Don't Dad me."

"What's going on?" Drew asked.

Nolan leaned into the camera's view. "We all want to see you."

"I should have known." Drew laughed. "I wasn't sure what schedule you'd all be on."

"Jillian is on a schedule where she is not sleeping because she has a project her brain won't let go of," Nolan said. "She's rolling her eyes at me."

"I see that." Drew leaned forward toward his camera, as if to be closer to them all. "What project has you working so early on a Saturday?"

He really was a lovely young man, perfect for Jillian, if a father was allowed to have such an opinion. Nolan's insides were grinning.

"We dug that old suitcase out of the closet last night." Min scraped oatmeal around in her bowl. "I think we all knew what Jillian would do with that."

"In my defense," Jillian said, "I am a genealogist. You cannot just plop old things in front of me and expect me not to be interested."

"What did you find?" Drew said.

"Letters. In Italian. From assorted people."

"To whom?"

"Some to Chia. Or Chiara. I figure those are the same person. Some to Amica. Some to Celestrino. I started trying to type some of them into a Google translator, but it's slow sledding with the dubious legibility of the handwriting and my lack of any instinct of what the words are supposed to be."

"What you need is someone who reads Italian." Drew sipped his own mug of coffee in Albuquerque.

"I suppose so."

"Have you called Rini? I mean Cate?"

Nolan looked at Jillian, who returned his glance. "We are utter dolts."

"I could tell last weekend she understands everything her family says in Italian," Jillian said, "but reading it might be a different skill."

Drew leaned back in his hotel chair. "It's worth a shot, isn't it?"

Nolan certainly thought it was. He was planning to speak to her before the day was over anyway.

"Hold on." Drew held up a finger. "I can call her right now."

"Do you really think she'll come?" Nolan raised one eyebrow.

"I'm not sure she's ever been to the ranch, but there's a first time for everything. Look what you've done for her. Why not call in a favor?"

Jillian sipped juice. "Someone from the Polombo family would make sense."

"And she's the one who owes you. I'm calling her now."

Drew muted their end of the video call, but they could see him speaking to Cate.

"More coffee?" Min raised the coffee pot in her good arm and Nolan grabbed it immediately. They were on "watch Min" duty, after all.

"I'll pour." He refilled Jillian's cup without asking. She did not object.

Min started clearing dishes.

Drew's voice popped back on. "She's coming to the ranch. In fact, it won't be long. She was on late at Mary Lou's last night and has the lunch shift at Peppy's today, so she sucked it up and stayed in Pueblo last night instead of driving back and forth to Trinidad."

"From what I've heard, she hates that." With her parting observation, Min made her way out of the room.

From what Nolan heard, Min was right. But on this morning, it was fortuitous to have Cate so handy.

"She also said she has a surprise for Jillian," Drew said.

Jillian's chin raised. "What is it?"

Nolan laughed. "It's a surprise!"

"I have to go." Drew was waving. "First rehearsal of the day in an hour."

"If I leave now, I could be there to hear your splendid performance."

"All sold out, my friend." Drew wiggled some fingers and then he was gone.

Jillian pouted as she pushed her phone back in a pocket. "I didn't even get to ask how the first performance went last night."

"He'll call again." Nolan took the last of the dishes to the sink. "Tonight's concert is not for another twelve hours."

"How do you know the concert time?"

"Speaking in generalities." Nolan waved a hand. "Am I at least allowed to help with the dishes in someone else's kitchen?"

Jillian looked overly thoughtful for the question. No doubt she was thinking either about Drew or the Italian letters. "I suppose. You're the one who taught me how to load a dishwasher."

"That's quite an endorsement. I shall rinse and load and then go for a walk."

"Again? That's your fourth walk since we got here yesterday afternoon?"

"Fresh air. Open views. Country life."

"Well, I'm going to have a shower and get properly dressed. Keep an eye out for Cate while you are enjoying a life of leisure."

"Young lady, you are getting sassy."

"Whatever."

The dishes were few, and Nolan dispatched the responsibility efficiently. Outside, he was on the phone swiftly.

"I came along on this weekend because she thinks I'm not paying enough attention to what's going on in her life."

"If only she knew. As far as I can tell, you're doing a fabulous job."

"Things were easier in Canyon Mines while she has jaunted down here so much lately. I could do what I wanted, and she wasn't there to ask questions."

"You're entitled to a personal life."

"An interesting concept." Nolan hadn't had much of a personal life since Bella died fifteen years ago. But that could change—or the opportunity for it could change.

"I hope you're going to have some time to explore that in a more personally satisfying way."

"Stop reading my mind. Let's not get ahead of ourselves."

"I think we're going at just the right speed."

"Okay then." Nolan glanced back toward the house. He hadn't actually wandered too far from it. His goal was only to be out of earshot. "She's suspicious of how many walks I'm taking."

"I guess we'll have to do better. Any loose ends in Canyon Mines?"

"I have to make a call. I'll get back to you." Nolan dialed another number. "How are things there?"

"I aim to please."

"So everything will be waiting when I get home?"

"Ready for inspection. The dress is still a dilemma, but we're working on it."

"You're a good friend, Kris. This would all be so hard without you."

"Dad?"

Nolan wheeled around. How long had Jillian been there?

"Why are you talking to Kris?"

Nolan snapped off the call.

CHAPTER TWENTY-SIX

Monday, April 20,1914
Ludlow, Colorado

TEARFUL MOTHER. BEAMING FATHER. Ravenous suckling infant. Looking on, Caterina could not help thinking of the holy family. Christmas was months ago, but Easter just a week ago—and Greek Easter only yesterday. The violence of today starkly reminded her of why the world needed the holy infant who had grown up to endure his own violent death.

When would it all end? How long, O Lord?

The five of them found shelter in the Section House tucked between rows of equipment workers used to keep trains running. They weren't alone. A smattering of others who were neither miners nor militia found themselves in the crosshairs of the battle by virtue of being at the Ludlow depot or post office when shooting began. Some had wagons or cars nearby and raced to get out of the way. Others, like Geppetto, had fewer options, and once the battle ratcheted up, the likelihood of a train diminished.

Geppetto would not have gotten on a train. He would not have left Caterina behind with no way to tell her where he had gone. This she knew. The Section House harbored a dozen souls now.

"Oh bambino," Chiara cooed, "you have met your papa at last."

Finally sated, he smacked his tiny lips and stared at the strange man with unblinking wide eyes.

"We cannot call him 'bambino' forever, Chiara," Celestrino said. "Our son needs a name."

"We didn't decide," she said, "before he came early. Then you didn't come, and your letters stopped."

"Shh," he said. "That is all over. We are together now. He is beautiful and strong like his mother. We should call him Gianni, because God has been gracious to us."

"Gianni." Chiara kissed her son's head as he drifted into the slumber of satisfied hunger.

"I need some air," Caterina said. The smell of the oil barrels around them suddenly crushed against her nostrils and agitated her stomach.

"Caterina!" Geppetto moved with her toward the door.

"Just some air, Geppetto."

"There's a broken window over here. You don't have to go outside."

"Has there been any shooting over here at all?" Caterina needed more than a hole in a window if she was going to fill her lungs. She got to the door before Geppetto. It was a small door, facing west, into Berwind canyon, into the mountains, away from the tracks and Water Tank Hill and the railroad cut full of foxholes and the striker's tent colony being torn to shreds. Every blast from the machine gun echoed through the canyon as every one before it all day had done. It was the approaching late afternoon now. The sun would set.

How long, O Lord?

"However did you manage the bambino for so long?" Caterina asked.

"I guess he likes the taste of my knuckle," Geppetto said. "One of the other stranded passengers had a bit of goat milk."

"Did it make him spit up?" The baby had never had anything but Chiara's milk.

"All of it. But for a while it calmed him."

Caterina leaned her head back against the structure that had kept Geppetto and the bambino—Gianni—safe and inhaled deeply. Even the canyon and the mountains, though, did not obscure the nearness of the industrial supplies.

"You are making that face," Geppetto said.

"What face? I have only one face."

"I love your faces—all of them. But you have a face for when you feel queasy."

"It has been a long day, Geppetto, and it is not over. I would like to get home to our own bambino."

"You have a strong stomach for just about anything, Caterina."

"I have never run from gunfire before."

"Are you sure it is nothing else?"

"What else would it be?"

He knew. At least he suspected. If he had suspected yesterday or this morning he would never have let Caterina chase after Chiara.

"You are unwell."

"I will be all right. I am better now that I am with you again. But we must decide what we do next."

"Some of the others inside were talking about making a run for it."

"Run for where?" Caterina was dubious. "Down into the canyon? Straight into the line of fire? Where, Geppetto?"

"We could wave a white flag. We are all civilians caught in the crossfire."

"Have you forgotten so quickly that Celestrino is with us now? A striking miner puts us all at risk."

"Yet you risked everything because of him."

Caterina pressed the heels of her hands into her eyes. "Please, Geppetto, I don't want to quarrel. We must think what is safe for everyone."

"Do you feel well enough to come back inside?"

"I told you, I'm fine." Caterina hadn't eaten all day. How could her stomach keep betraying her this way?

Inside, it was tempting to look for an electrical light switch or an oil lamp, but drawing attention to their presence as dusk fell seemed unwise. Caterina imagined the frantic state Ela and Carrick would be in. By now news of the day-long battle at Ludlow would have reached Pueblo.

Slouched on the ground against a wall, Celestrino held Gianni in one arm and kept Chiara tucked against his chest with the other. All three were asleep.

"We have to wake them," Geppetto said. "Celestrino is the one who might know a way out."

Caterina nodded, though she craved the opportunity to lean against her own husband and give into sleep—if she could. Exhausted as she was, and masking the intermittent waves of sickness, still she doubted she could sleep in the circumstances.

Geppetto slumped down beside Celestrino, stroked the baby's head and whispered. "We need a plan."

Drawing a long breath, Celestrino opened his eyes. "It will be dark soon."

"Will they stop shooting?"

"They may just turn on the search lights and keep going. It has never been this bad here before, so I cannot predict. Two machine guns. They must have two hundred men on Water Tank Hill. I don't even know where they've all come from."

"How long will the strikers hold out?"

"I'm sure they are in retreat. Worried about their families. Out of ammunition. No way for reinforcements to come."

"We should be among those who retreat," Geppetto said. "But there is nothing on this side of the tracks but the militia detachment's camp, and only bullets flying on the other. I haven't heard a train in hours, and the ones that have come through go at high speed right past the depot."

"Even the mine owner wouldn't try to get strikebreakers through today, and no one else would stop in the middle of this."

"What should we do, Celestrino?"

Celestrino scratched his head. "We could hike back the way we came from the foxholes and around up to one of the ranches."

Caterina's heart sank. "That was miles, and it will be dark and cold."

"Dark will be safer," Celestrino pointed out.

"Not for breaking a leg."

"We can stay here all night. As long as the bambino has something to eat, the rest of us can get by."

The huddle of travelers at the other end of the Section House jumped to their feet and ran to windows.

"What is it?" Geppetto asked.

"A train! Do you hear it?"

"It won't stop."

"This one sounds different."

Geppetto cocked his head. "Slower." He got up.

"Geppetto?" Caterina allowed herself fleeting hope. If the train stopped, and they could get to it from this side of the tracks, they would get on it no matter where it was going and debate the need for tickets later. She might even run out and wave it down herself.

"It's on the Colorado and Southeastern tracks," someone declared.

"A freight train."

"It's really slowing down."

Even a freight train could take them somewhere.

"Chiara, wake up." Caterina wiggled her friend's shoulder. "We're leaving. Gather the baby's things."

"Where are we going?"

"This could be our chance." Celestrino pulled Chiara to her feet. "That train is going to stop."

They all ran outside in the fading dusk light. The train was in fact a freighter and its presence fenced in the machine guns on Water Tank Hill, separating them from their target and stilling their violence.

"Celestrino," Geppetto said, "how far to the colony from here? A mile?"

"Approximately."

"And if we get there, you know where the hiding places are?"

"I cannot guarantee they are safe, Geppetto. It's been hours since I have spoken to anyone who has news of the colony."

"But something about a steel bridge? Safe ranches?"

"Yes, yes. All our people knew to go to those places."

"Look, Celestrino. It's a freight train. A long train. A slow train. And it has stopped between Water Tank Hill and the colony. Stopped."

"That's perfect. People can get away while the militia cannot see them."

"We can get away," Caterina said. "Chiara, do you need help with anything? We are going to run up the tracks because we know the terrain is clear. If we can't get on the train, we can hop between cars and keep running north. This is right, yes, Geppetto?"

"Yes, my sweet Caterina."

Celestrino tucked the bambino in his jacket and gripped Chiara's hand, and they took off with Geppetto and Caterina right behind. The freighter was one sealed boxed car after another, so they didn't waste time trying to gain entry but pressed north. They guzzled air and ran. Militiamen shouted at railroad men about getting the train started again and off the tracks, and railroad men shouted back. Caterina gripped Geppetto's hand and they pummeled the ground behind Celestrino. She gave thanks for the stopped train and all it was carrying and prayed for time. Time to run. Time to hide. Time to believe they would find the way home.

"Don't look back." Geppetto pulled Caterina forward. "They will do whatever they will do. It is dark now. Safer for us to be moving."

As long as the search lights don't come on, Caterina thought.

Past the depot. Past the militia detachment. Approaching the striker's camp. Forward. Forward.

Angry threats echoed around the train. Furious retorts flew through the air. Demands. Answers. More demands. But finally the sounds of the train starting up began. The engine firing, the brakes releasing, the slow, massive tug of weight. A freighter that has come to a standstill does not easily regain momentum.

Still they ran.

And then they were behind the protection of the steel bridge catching their breath.

"Where to now?" Caterina's breath heaved.

"A safe ranch or the Black Hills." Celestrino's eyes scanned the options.

"Or home," Geppetto said.

The others fixed their eyes on him.

"We keep following the tracks north. The miners are going to those other places because they have nowhere else to go. But we have a home and people who are wondering if we are all right and a little boy who is asking about us."

Caterina nodded. "Home. Yes. But we can't walk all the way to Pueblo."

"We'll look for someone with a wagon who can take us to Walsenburg," Celestrino said. "Maybe some trains have been running at least that far."

"And perhaps a generous person will let us use a telephone to call Carrick," Geppetto said. "I left one of his horses in town, after all."

"Geppetto, his horse is not what he will be worried about and you know that." Caterina put one arm through his and leaned on his shoulder. His weight against her in response was everything she needed to push on.

They trudged north and heard the freighter's whistle finally blow behind them. Only then, from a distance that felt safe, did they turn and look back.

"It's burning." Chiara's grievous pronouncement was hoarse with dismay. The colony was ablaze, orange flames lighting the darkness as they roared through the canvas and wood dwellings.

"No one left to shoot," Celestrino said. "So they'll make sure we have nothing to come back to."

He pivoted and stomped up the tracks. Caterina enfolded his weeping wife.

CHAPTER TWENTY-SEVEN

Outside Pueblo, Colorado

"Dad, you just said Kris. My Kris?"

Nolan pushed his phone into a pocket. "Silly Jilly, you look refreshed."

"Dad, all I did was shower. Were you talking to my Kris?" Jillian persisted.

"Nobody owns a friend, do they, Jillian? Your mother and I didn't raise you to think like that."

"Don't scold me. You're trying to change the subject." Why was her dad always acting so weird lately?

Nolan turned toward the vista. "You know, I can understand why you don't mind driving three hours to get down here—apart from Drew, of course. This is a beautiful place."

Jillian huffed.

"You should take a walk today too, Jillian. I can stay with Min. I'm sure I could be useful moving boxes."

"Maybe later. You're not answering my question."

"Someone's coming down the road."

This at least was the truth.

Jillian shaded her eyes to peer. "That's Cate's car. She got here fast."

"Drew said she was in town." Nolan spread his feet and put his hands in his pockets. "It's great she came right away."

"She's driving awfully fast, don't you think?"

"A bit of a lead foot."

Jillian and Nolan stepped back a couple of yards as Cate stirred up the dust around them and slammed out of her car.

"What now?" Jillian muttered.

"Cate, good to see you." Nolan tried to put on a more positive front. "We're excited you could come so quickly."

"I thought I was too." Cate's tone was as agitated as Jillian had heard so far in the weeks since she'd met her. "When will it ever end?"

"What happened?"

"I thought when the sheriff's department checked my alibi, everything was fine. But no. My family won't let it go. They want me to resign the grant and settle down to the more sensible family business where I don't have to resort to things like that."

"What?" Jillian lurched a little. "But they vouched for you."

"Because I was working during those hours. Somehow they think the sheriff's office has the time frame wrong and I actually did it."

"It would be highly unusual for the time frame to be off," Nolan said.

"Never mind that it would be highly unusual for their daughter to break into a truck!" Cate exhaled heavily. "When they started in on me about that, I couldn't get out of there fast enough. I traded my lunch shift for dinner. Then I'm going home to my own bed in my own place."

"Your parents will both be at Peppy's today?" Nolan was wagging that eyebrow again.

Cate nodded.

"Suddenly I'm in the mood for Italian food."

"Better you than me."

"Just a little friendly chat over a friendly meal to talk about how things are."

"Sounds like a mafia meeting, if you ask me." Cate shifted her bag from one shoulder to the other. "Are we going to stand outside all day or are we ready to get down to business?"

"I am if you are." Jillian pivoted and headed back into the house, leading Cate into the living room where the artifacts were laid out.

Behind them, Nolan's phone sang a tune, and he nabbed it, delaying his own entrance into the house.

What? Another "walk"? But Jillian had more important things to think about at the moment than her father's curious phone and exercise habits. And whatever he was doing with Kris.

"I confess I came partly out of curiosity." Cate fingered the edge of the yellow blanket. "Drew said you found letters. He didn't say anything about the rest of this."

"We didn't get around to telling him everything before he wanted to call you."

"What can I do to help?"

"I haven't gotten too far. I started with some phrases before I realized it was going to be a bigger job. Most of what I accomplished was pulling out names." Jillian handed her yellow legal pad to Cate.

"These were all miners at Ludlow." Cate's announcement was immediate and certain.

"All of them?"

"I've seen these names in my research. Most of them came from the Berwind company town a few miles away. They lost their housing when they went on strike."

"So they ended up in the tents at Ludlow."

Cate nodded.

Jillian reached for the bundle of photos. "Some of them are the same names as in these photos."

Cate's eyebrows furrowed. "That's not a strike tent. Where is this?"

"Min says it's right here on the ranch. The building is gone, but she knows where it was."

"Ludlow strikers? Here?"

Jillian nodded. "It seems so."

"And the letters are from them?"

"Or about them. A combination, I suspect. If you can read them, that will be a huge help."

"All right, we've got to get to the bottom of this," Cate said. "Let me try to read the letters."

Nolan came into the room. "I found Min in the rummage room and thought she might be interested to see Cate."

"The Polombo girl," Min said. "Yes, I can see that. I always thought you favored Benedetta."

Cate cocked her head. "A lot of people say that."

"We were children together. I haven't seen her in many years. But I saw you from time to time at Peppy's when you were little and I felt more like going into town.

"I'm very glad to meet you again now."

Jillian's heart surged.

Cate cleared her throat. "Let me see if I can get anywhere with these letters."

They gathered at the dining room table, where Jillian set up her laptop so she could transcribe as Cate translated.

"They don't all have dates on them." Cate handled the letters with the reverence they deserved as she ordered them. "What's this envelope?"

"Oh, I can't believe I didn't open that," Jillian said. "Please go ahead."

Cate slid a folded sheet out of the stiff envelope. "It's in English!"

"No way! What does it say?"

"Dear Miss Ela. I try to write in English. Caterina she help. I say many many thanks. You very good to me. Many kindness for me, for my Celestrino, for my baby Gianni. Many many thanks. Now I give back. These things someone else can use also. Now that I know you, I say to everyone you have biggest heart. We see you at Peppy's, yes?"

"Who is it from?"

Cate turned the card over. "It's not signed." Her hand trembled. "Caterina. Caterina Parisi? Am I holding something handwritten by someone who knew the first Caterina?"

Jillian held her breath. There was no telling what gold the Italian letters held if these few lines gave them this much already.

Cate blew out a long slow breath. "This day is just mountains and valleys and mountains all over again, and it's not even lunch time."

"Do you feel up to trying to translate?" Jillian asked.

"Of course! We can't stop now. And these pictures are Ludlow miners. They're connected to my project somehow. What were they doing on this ranch?"

"Then let's dig in."

Cate's reading Italian turned out to be quite good. She could sound out enough of the misspelled words that had tripped up Jillian and read past the smudges to make out the meaning of a sentence and find the purpose and sense of each letter.

News that the Bartolottis had made a smooth train journey to New Jersey where they had cousins and the children were in school, but that they would never forget their time in the hut to get a fresh perspective.

The Contis and Bereses were in Wyoming, working on another ranch. Even the few weeks working on the Kyp ranch gave the men the skills to be hired, and they would always be grateful that Chiara persuaded them to come.

The Marchesis gave credit to the Rillos. Their bravery was the example they needed to break away and believe mining was not the only life in their future because the Rillos did it first.

Cate set down the letters. "They were all miners who came to the ranch at some point in the months after the Ludlow Massacre."

"Because of Chiara and the Rillos?" Min said.

"I think Chiara was a Rillo." Jillian reached for a faded letter, one with the most uneven lines. "And she was sometimes just Chia."

"Rillo is a very common Italian name—many of these are," Cate said. "There were several Rillo families at Ludlow."

"Was Celestrino one of them?" Jillian asked.

"I'll have to get back to Trinidad to my research to know for sure. Now I really don't want to go back and work a shift at Peppy's tonight."

"Peppy's." Jillian echoed the word. "That first note you read mentioned Peppy's. Chiara knew the restaurant, or saw Caterina there. And the Kyps."

"They all came here even when I was a girl," Min said.

Jillian turned toward Min. She'd been so quiet.

Min scratched an itch under the edge of her wrist brace. "I don't remember anyone named Chiara, but I knew the rest of the Peppys."

Nolan's phone buzzed, and with a smile and a nod, he left the table—again. Jillian's gaze followed him as his time he went out the front door. Another of his "walks"?

"What do you mean, the Peppys?"

Cate's question pulled Jillian back to the table conversation.

"That's what we called the Italian families who came to the ranch at holidays until everyone grew up and had their own families. The Kyps and the Peppys. I guess that included the Parisis. There were others who were closely involved in the restaurant and hotel in those days." Min tilted her head, thinking. "I guess I never thought of the Parisis separately, or anyone's last name, because we just called them the Peppys since we knew them all from the restaurant. Whether they were actually related or not, the children called the adults Zia and Zio—aunt and uncle—and we did it too. The crowd got too big even for the main house, and the Peppys were got so busy at the restaurant—and the hotel until Giuseppe decided to close it. Our family was getting bigger, too, as we grew up. The large gatherings faded, and we would just see each other in town."

"That's how you knew my grandmother," Cate said.

"Antenette, Carmella, and the youngest, Benedetta. Also the daughters of some of the people who worked in the restaurant for many years. The Peppys. With my sister Gretchen, we were all girls together. Giuseppe and my mother had known each other all their lives."

"What was your mother's name?" Cate asked.

"Dorothy Kyp, when she was born."

Jillian shook her head. "I still can't get over it. All those years ago, Giuseppe Parisi knew Dottie Kyp. Here. In this space."

"And now, you and Drew." Cate gestured around. "Here. In this space."

"And you're here."

Min chuckled. "The Peppys are back. Next time, Caterina, bring your grandmother."

Jillian saw the lump pass through Cate's throat.

"She would love that." Cate looked around. "What happened to Nolan?"

"I'll go find him." Jillian left her chair and slipped out the front door, almost afraid to find out if her father was talking to one of her best friends again. Before she had a chance to overhear anything, he pocketed his phone and turned to her with a glum face.

"Dad, what is it?"

"Do you know a Patrice in Trinidad?"

"Cate's assistant? I met her once in passing."

"She's trouble."

Jillian blinked twice, studying her father's face. He wasn't joking. "She's the leak?"

"Friends since high school with one of the exhibit planners at Epic EduKids."

"What do we tell Cate?"

"Nothing yet," Nolan said. "We can't afford to have her fly off the handle."

"You're missing some great stuff in there, Dad."

"You'll have to catch me up. But I'm coming back in now."

Cate's face brightened when they returned to the living room. "I almost forgot your surprise. I was so mad at my parents about the truck break-in business. I forgot that before they brought that up, my mom gave me the letters from Uncle Sal. She actually remembered to look for them."

Jillian sucked in her breath. "You have my great-great-grandfather's letters?"

"This is turning into kind of a bonanza day, isn't it?" Nolan rubbed Jillian's back.

Cate handed Jillian a manila envelope.

Jillian opened the clasp. "Have you read them?"

"I didn't really have time. I just wanted to get out of there."

There were eight letters, none of them long. Jillian would call them notes, rather than letters, but they were in Italian so she handed them back to Cate and she sat at her laptop once again to type what she heard coming from the mouth of her fourth cousin once removed.

Salvatore appreciated Geppetto's invitation for his cousin Aldo to join him in Pueblo and help him open a small hotel, but Aldo had decided to remain in Denver.

Whispers of what might have been glided through Jillian's mind, wispy thoughts of her own great-grandfather Aldo here on the ranch or in Pueblo, crossing paths directly with Drew's family line instead of being one family limb over from the main action. Denver wasn't so far even a hundred years ago. He must have visited.

Sal sent some money for the miners.

"But that note is dated after the Ludlow colony was burned," Jillian said.

Cate nodded. "The union brought in more tents. They didn't give up. Not for months."

"And Sal sent money for the union?"

"Not for the union. For the miners. He was very clear that Geppetto should not give it to the union for the strike. It was for the miners."

"On the ranch." Jillian glanced at Min. "In the hut that's not there anymore."

"I suppose so," Min said. "That was all over and done with long before I was born. I never knew there were miners here. Just people in old photos."

"Some of the ranchers near the strike colonies sided with the strikers," Cate said. "They provided weapons, food, even safe harbor after the Ludlow battle. But all the way up here?"

"It had to be something different." Jillian picked up Sal's letters again. "Here. Doesn't this say Celestrino and Chiara?"

Cate leaned over. "It does. He's talking about the good work Chiara and Caterina are doing to help the miners get a new start. He wants to help."

The four of them around the table looked at each other. Cate reached for the first card they'd read when she first arrived.

"'My Celestrino.' This note to Ela Kyp is from Chiara Rillo. Celestrino, Chiara, and their baby Gianni."

"It sure seems that way." Jillian was tracking right along with Cate. "And they knew Caterina and Giuseppe Parisi quite well."

"I wonder."

"I'm sure I'm right."

Nolan's phone rang.

"Are you going for another walk?" Jillian added air quotes to her question.

Nolan silenced his phone. "No, I'm not. But I do need to talk business with Cate before it gets much later."

"I'll fetch some refreshments." Min pushed herself out of her chair.

"I'm going to cut to the chase." Nolan had his serious lawyer face on. "I've been putting some eyes and ears on your situation."

"What does that mean?" Cate's features tangled in confusion.

"Just trust me. The upshot is I think your assistant does not always have your best interest at heart."

"Patrice?" Cate's olive complexion faded a shade lighter as she listened to what Nolan had learned. "I guess I was naive not to suspect the obvious, but it all makes sense."

"We need to set out some bait. You'll calmly leave some enticing and insecure information in an email, and we'll see what happens to it over the next few days."

"I can't have anything more coming back on me."

"I've already spoken to the sheriff. In this particular circumstance, you have zero risk——as long as we choose wisely what to dangle in front of Patrice. It has to be something that seems neutral, but also something that you can prove only you would have."

"Does it have to be real?"

"Real is better, but something you're willing to risk losing."

"Why should I have to lose anything?" Cate's tone heated in protest.

"It's up to you, Cate."

Her shoulders sank. "This day. I don't know whether to love it or hate it."

"Use Chiara's note." Jillian slid it toward her. "It's not signed. There's no date. Ela's last name is not in it. You could send a picture and a couple of excited lines about a great new find of primary source documents. That would all be true, but Chiara's note doesn't contain enough to give anything away about the miners or what went on here at the ranch."

Cate looked at Nolan, hope in her eyes.

He nodded. "That would do. We'll work on the wording together."

CHAPTER TWENTY-EIGHT

IN OCTOBER, TWO OR THREE WEEKS could slip by with incremental autumnal changes until one day Jillian's feet would be cold in her office and she wished she had put on fuzzy socks and a thicker sweater. This final Tuesday of October was that day. The furnace her parents installed when she was two, and the family moved into the Victorian home, had been updated five years ago with a newer high-efficiency model that was cleaned and serviced every fall. Still, it seemed every winter Jillian and Nolan discussed what more they could do to keep heat from leaking out of the old house. Better windows. New insulation. More insulation in the attic. This and that to stop the gaps on the exterior doors. Only a few days ago, Jillian had been running the trails in sweats. Now it felt as if they might get their first mountain snow of the season any day.

Jillian trundled up the rear stairs in search of added warmth for her feet and torso and back down again into the kitchen for a stop at her elaborate barista quality coffee station to refill her favorite mug, the one that also had been her mother's favorite all those years ago. It was large enough to accommodate the generous portions Jillian preferred with the enhancements she required no matter how much her father mocked them. The taupe—not beige—mug's maroon swirl around the lower portion always felt like an energetic signal to Jillian that seemed to amplify the effect of caffeine.

Jillian was barely back to her desk when her phone rang with a number and ID showing the Las Animas County Sheriff's Department. Her stomach tightened as she answered.

"This is Deputy Pesko in Las Animas County Sheriff's Department." The bass voice on the other end was all business. "Mr. Nolan Duffy left you as an alternate contact person in the event we were unable to reach him in connection to a matter we have been jointly investigating."

This was news to Jillian. "Yes?"

"You are his daughter, correct?"

"Yes, that's right."

"And he is not available at your location currently?"

"No. This is my cell number, and he's not home." Tuesday was a work-from-home day for Nolan, but he'd left a couple of hours ago, saying nothing more than that he had errands and meetings in town. "Is it Cate Butler? Is she all right?"

"More than all right. I haven't spoken to her yet. Mr. Duffy might like to do that as her legal representation, but I can forward to you the relevant document."

"What document?"

"I think you'll find it self-explanatory. If you wouldn't mind passing it along to Mr. Duffy and having him contact me, I'd appreciate it."

"Of course."

"I'll send it right now. Your email, please?"

Jillian rattled it off and then hung up and stared at her inbox.

The message dinged in. She could hardly believe her eyes. That hadn't taken long, barely seventy-two hours from when they hatched the plan at the ranch.

Wherever Nolan was, if he was just in town, surely he'd take her call even if he hadn't taken the deputy's.

The call rang four times and rolled to Nolan's voice mail.

"Dad, call me. The sheriff's office called. They sent me a document you're going to want to see."

Jillian drummed her fingers on her desk. Where could he be? He hadn't said anything to her lately about having local clients. It was rare for anyone in Canyon Mines to need his expertise in family law or mediation, but occasionally he did a legal favor for someone in town who needed help with a simple will or property transfer. What kind of errands would he have? He had just picked up the dry cleaning last Thursday, and Jillian did the grocery shopping. If Nolan was let loose in a grocery store, he was too haphazard about what he came home with, overlooking staples in favor of exotic vegetables. Besides, since he did the lion's share of the cooking, it seemed fair to Jillian for her to keep the cupboards and fridge stocked.

She dialed the Canary Cage. Clark Addison answered. "Haven't seen him all day."

The hardware store? He might have decided he needed something for a fix-it project. One of the benefits of living in a small town was being able to call and say, "Have you seen my dad?"

No, not at the hardware store.

Diggers Delight. It would be like Nolan to decide that picking up chocolate-covered cherries was a necessary errands.

"He was here earlier," Carolyn said. "He had quite the conversation with Kris next door."

Jillian sat up straighter. "About what?"

"Oh, you know. Whatever it is they talk about when he stops in lately. But he's gone now."

"*Whatever it is they talk about when he stops in lately.*" What did that mean?

"You didn't happen to hear him say anything about where he might be going, didn't you?" Jillian asked.

"Sorry. I had a bit of a rush this afternoon. Strange for a weekday, but the sales were nice. A big party."

"I'm glad for you."

Jillian's thumb hovered over Kris's number. "Whatever it is they talk about these days" might have included where else he was headed. In the moment, though, Jillian wasn't sure she could keep from asking Kris what she and Nolan had to talk about so often.

Instead she texted Nolan. We have some news in Cate's case. Call when you can.

She called Veronica at the Victorium Emporium. "Have you seen my dad? Has he dropped by to see Luke?"

"Not today," Veronica said. "If I see him, I'll let him know you're looking for him."

"Thanks."

He hadn't been in Motherlode Books, where he sometimes went to browse or shoot the breeze with Dave Rossi if the store was quiet. Marilyn at the Heritage Society said she hadn't seen him since last week, although Jillian found her emphasis of the word *seen* odd. No one picked up the phone at the Inn at Hidden Run, and Nia didn't answer the text Jillian sent to her cell. Any number of things could be happening at a bed and breakfast. Theoretically Nolan could be in any store on Main Street or a block over on Second Street, though most of them didn't generally interest Nolan, and Jillian didn't see the point of calling every single one.

Jillian stared again at the document on her screen and decided to print it and tuck it into a folder she'd started yesterday after they returned from their weekend at the ranch. When she still hadn't heard from Nolan an hour—and two more messages—later, Jillian had made up her mind to speak to Cate herself. She had the information. Cate was entitled to it before it got to her some other way.

But Cate didn't answer her phone either, and three text messages went unreturned.

And that was extremely weird for Cate. They had cleared the air between them and kept it that way. Why wouldn't Cate respond?

Nolan, Kris, Nia, Cate. Where was everybody?

Jillian dialed one more number.

"Butler Education Exhibits, Patrice speaking."

"Hi Patrice. This is Jillian Parisi-Duffy, Cate's friend. Is she in?"

"I'm sorry. She's not."

"Will she be back soon?"

"She just said not to expect her back today."

"Was she headed to Pueblo?"

"I didn't have that impression, no."

"Perhaps some field research?"

"Maybe."

Jillian eyed the document in her open folder. "Hopefully she left you with some interesting work to do."

"The work always has interesting aspects," Patrice said. "I'm fortunate to be involved with creating such a fascinating exhibit for the children to learn such important perspectives."

Oh puleeze. The words might be vaguely right, but Patrice was making little effort toward an uncontrived tone.

"Nice chatting with you," Jillian said. "Maybe I'll see you again."

She was too distracted to bear down on her own projects for the rest of the afternoon. Even her coffee had gone cold. Jillian dumped it out and made a fresh concoction, even treating herself to extra whipped cream on top to try to keep herself interested in the here-and-now. Then she decided to call Drew. If she could just tell someone what she was putting together in her brain, maybe she'd get it out of her system and could be patient until Nolan got home or Cate called her back.

But Drew didn't answer either. So much for always taking her calls.

"*If I can.*" That was his qualifier. His caveat. His way out.

"Drew, where are you?" Jillian said aloud to her own ears. She tried to remember if he'd said he had taken a shift at Mary Lou's, or if Min had a doctor's appointment. He could be doing who knows what somewhere on the ranch, something that required two gloved hands and he couldn't get to a cell phone stuck in a barn jacket pocket.

Still, she wished she could talk to him. She left him a message.

Opening her to-do list was another attempt at focusing, even if Jillian could find just one simple task to accomplish while awaiting a response from her father or her cousin or Drew. Music might help, so she turned some on.

Nothing made a difference. By the time Jillian finished her latte, she had made up her mind, about ninety percent, that she would just start driving south. She could keep trying to get hold of Cate and maybe they could meet in Colorado Springs. She might end up all the way at the ranch, but that wouldn't be the worst thing in the world. A just-in-case overnight bag would take five minutes to pack. She sent Nolan one last text and got ready to leave the house.

When her phone finally rang, she was on the short path between the house and the garage, bags over her shoulders, keys in hand. It wasn't Nolan or Cate or Drew. Jillian tried not to be disappointed it was only Nia, one of her best friends.

"Hey girlfriend." Nia was munching something crunchy. "Sorry. I had guests checking in. Your dad hasn't been by here today, but I'd love it if you would come by."

Jillian hesitated. "I was just heading out."

"Great. Then you'll be right over."

"I'm not sure I have time to hang out today." Jillian raised the garage door.

"I really could use your help."

"What's up?"

"Just stop by. It's on your way wherever you're going."

"All right." Jillian stowed her things on the back seat and slid behind the steering wheel of her small SUV.

Nia's bed and breakfast was only half a mile down the street. Maybe she'd hear from her dad, Cate, or Drew before she hit the road. At the Inn, she used the front entrance. It was fast, and she could have that moment she loved of standing in the wide, always-polished hallway on the main floor and letting the breathtaking curve of the stairs sweep her gaze upward.

"Good, you're here." Nia came in from the parlor breaking the fleeting enchantment, with an armful of fabric and paint swatches.

"What's all this?" Jillian was supposed to be stopping by, not digging in.

"Leo thinks the room at the top of the stairs needs updating."

Jillian tilted her head. "Leo cares about how you decorate?"

"He notices things. Ever since he had to do some repairs on the drywall around the closet in that room, he's been unhappy with matching the paint and thinks we should just do it over properly."

"Sounds great. I was thinking of driving down to see Cate. Maybe I could help you pick out colors another time."

Nia shook her head. "Leo wants to start on the painting tomorrow. I have to make up my mind. He's putting his foot down."

Jillian laughed. "Leo? Putting his foot down?"

"He can be firm when he chooses to be."

"I've just never actually seen him be firm with you."

Nia rolled her eyes. "Come upstairs. The room is vacant so we can look at some combinations."

"I'm sure whatever you choose will be fine." Jillian glanced at the time on her phone as she trailed Nia up the stairs.

"Now you sound just like a man."

"I don't understand what's going on," Jillian muttered. "No one is answering any of my messages."

"What do you mean?" Nia opened the room under scrutiny.

"My dad. Cate. Drew. Don't you think it's funny that none of them have responded to me?"

"I thought you said you were going down to see Cate? Doesn't she know you're coming?"

"Not exactly."

"As in not at all?"

"But she'll be glad when she sees me."

Nia side-eyed Jillian as she spread her samples on the bed. "I'm feeling green for this room, but I can't make up my mind between these three shades for the walls. Do you like the minty one, something slightly more dusty, or this one that is almost gray but green enough not to be gray at all?"

Jillian pushed aside the mint green. "One of these other two. The mint would be way too much on the walls. In my humble opinion."

"Do you think it would be overall too dusty to use this plum color in the bedspread and drapes? I haven't found the print I love yet, but I'm weirdly tied to the color."

"The person you really want is Veronica," Jillian said. "Doesn't she usually help you decide what would be authentic Victorian colors and patterns?"

"I respect your taste as well." Nia spread out her fabric swatches. "See anything you especially like more than the others?"

"You don't have to decide that today, do you?" Jillian glanced at the time again. "Just the paint, right? So Leo can get started?"

"I figured as long as you're here, I might as well see what you like with the wall color."

"I promise to come back for another consultation," Jillian said. "If I don't get going I'm really going to hit rush hour traffic out of Denver."

"Oh sweetie pie, it's too late for that. By the time you get to Denver, the interchanges will be a mess already. The construction on I-25 is never-ending, and they'll have everything shut down to one lane somewhere and it'll all back up clear to the south end of Denver. I hate to criticize, but this is a silly time to be heading out when you don't even know if Cate will be there."

Jillian flopped on the bed. Of course Nia was right. "If somebody would just take my call. How can they all be so busy on the same afternoon?"

"I know what would make you feel better."

"What? A search party for my AWOL father?"

"Nah. Dinner out. Let's get spiffed up. I have a new dress that would look fantastic on you."

"I just live up the street, Nia. I have clothes. All this business lately about new dresses is creepy. Besides, I don't feel like going out to a fancy dinner."

"It'll make you feel better."

"No, it won't."

"Yes, it will."

"No, it won't."

"I know for a fact we wear the same shoe size, and with the right dress, the difference in our height won't matter in the length."

"Nia, really." Jillian sat up on the bed. "You talked sense into me. I won't drive to Trinidad or even the Springs. I probably would have turned around before I got to Denver anyway. But dressing up for dinner—I don't think I have it in me."

Nia grabbed Jillian's hand and tugged. "Come on. Let's go raid my closet."

"Nia."

"I'm so stuck on plum that even the new dress is a deep plum."

"I'm not doing this."

"Just come look at the dress. It's that flawless shade of not red, but not purple. "

Jillian gave in and let Nia drag her downstairs and through the house to the private quarters she shared with Leo. From a hook outside Nia's closet hung the rich, silken folds of perfection. The exquisite drape from shoulder to hem stopped Jillian's steps.

"It's gorgeous, Nia! Where did you find it?"

"Veronica and I went shopping in Denver. She needed a dress for her cousin's wedding."

"I remember. She wanted me to go."

"You should have. I went along, and I found a couple of things."

"You both get gussied up a lot more than I do." Jillian stepped toward the dress, allowing her fingers to brush its beguiling supple gloss.

"That new dinner place across Westbridge has opened," Nia said.

"With the view of the creek?"

"That's the one. Let's do it up right and go there. I want you to wear that dress."

Jillian gasped. "I couldn't! It's brand new. Have you even cut the tags off?"

"It's perfect for your coloring. We'll put your hair up. All those great natural curls—you'll look fabulous and you'll feel fabulous."

Jillian hardly ever dressed up. Even her six months of dating Drew consisted mostly of deciding who would make the drive to visit the other or a quick meet-up in the middle in Colorado Springs. Their time together was cozy and casual. They rarely had an occasion to dress up unless it worked out for Jillian to attend one of Drew's performances. Then, a nice pair of slacks and dressy top usually did the job. Most of the time she didn't give a second thought to the boundaries of her wardrobe. But tonight maybe Nia was right. Tonight maybe it would turn her restlessness around to dress up and go out. And if someone returned her call during dinner, she could always answer the phone.

"If I wear the new dress, what will you wear?" Jillian said.

"No fear," Nia said. "I bought another dress from the discount rack that I like almost as well."

CHAPTER TWENTY-NINE

THE ANKLES THAT SERVED JILLIAN perfectly well when she ran miles in the hills nevertheless wobbled in three-inch heels. She didn't wear heels often enough to master the pacing and balance.

"This may have been a bad idea." Jillian felt for steadiness in every step across the parking lot outside the restaurant. "I feel silly dressing up for no occasion."

"Nonsense." Nia was undeterred. "You look stunning. I look fabulous, if I say so myself. We'll have a great time."

When she dressed from her own wardrobe, Jillian wore her mother's pearls. Today—it was barely the start of evening now—a silver chain with a sapphire cross accented her neckline, and her hair was piled up and held in place by unseen mysteries at Nia's hand. The shoes—brand new also—were silver as well. Her makeup was done with a light touch. Jillian's last glance in the mirror in Nia's bedroom assured her that she did, in fact, look stunning.

If only she felt stunning.

If only she had some idea where her father was.

If only he would answer her messages.

If only, if only, if only.

For Nia's sake, she tugged out the corners of her mouth.

"That's my girl." Nia pulled open the door to the restaurant.

Inside, Jillian took the glittery shawl Nia had loaned her from her shoulders, folded it a couple of times, and hung it over one arm.

"I'll just check on our reservation." Nia stepped toward the hostess stand for a hushed conversation.

Jillian was unprepared for the visage before her. The last time she'd been inside this space it had been a bargain furniture store hawking shelving, desks, and other items that could be packed flat and required assembly by the owners. Because Nolan could capably build attractive shelving or small tables from solid wood and was humble enough to seek advice from master craftsman Leo Dunston when necessary, he quietly shook his head at the idea that they should have any prepackaged furniture at the Duffy house. After a decade or so, the store closed, and the space was empty for several years until new owners purchased it to renovate for a restaurant. Jillian had half expected an industrial setting for the dining establishment, but the place was completely done over with lovely soft colors and ambient lighting. White linens draped round tables of various sizes to accommodate parties, and an elegant buffet lined one wall. At the front, a small band played live music.

Nia returned. "They're just about ready for us."

"This place looks fantastic!" Jillian said. "Have you been here before?"

Nia shook her head. "I've heard good things about it from friends."

"There's quite a group of people over in that one section. Are you sure we're not walking in on someone's private party?"

"Positive."

Jillian squinted and looked more closely. "That's Marilyn, isn't it?"

"Oh is it?"

"And Carolyn." Jillian pushed her eyebrows together. "Marilyn and Carolyn don't hang out with each other."

"We don't know everything about them."

"Wow. Dave Rossi in a suit. Nia, are you sure we're not crashing a party?"

"We are expected, Jillian. We'll get a table. We'll explore what I hear is an amazing buffet. And I'm sure you'll hear from somebody. Try to relax."

Jillian blew out her breath. "You're right."

"That's better."

Jillian shifted her weight and looked in another direction, catching herself before she tipped too far on the unfamiliar heels. Then her arm shot out and grabbed Nia. "My dad's here."

"Are you sure?"

"Over there. Look at him. He's got on that new suit he's only worn to court three times. You have to take me home."

"I will not! So what if Nolan is here? You can find out why he hasn't returned your calls."

"I think I know."

Nolan's head was bent toward Kris's as they stood near one of the smaller tables, and Kris bent her toward Nolan in an conspiratorial way that made Jillian uncomfortable. If they had something to tell her, she wanted to hear it straight out from them, not because she discovered it when she wasn't supposed to.

"Your table is ready now," the hostess said.

"We have to leave," Jillian said.

"We are not leaving." Nia looped her arm through Jillian's elbow. "We will follow this nice young woman to the table, and we will have one of the best nights of your life."

"I can't."

"Yes, you can." Nia tugged.

Jillian felt as if people were staring at them, so—for the moment—she surrendered.

As they walked farther into the dining room, she realized people were staring. People Jillian knew. Smiling. Making eye contact. She still couldn't figure out whose event would have brought this disparate group together. Clark Addison and his niece, Joanna Madden, were there. Luke and Veronica O'Reilly. Leif from Catch Air, the ski shop. Ben from the bakery, the only person on the planet who made pastries even close to Drew's creations. Lizy, from the bookstore. Rachel from Candles & Cards. The librarian who had never been too busy for any of Jillian's questions. At least two dozen people from church. And Leo Dunston. Why hadn't Nia mentioned he had a dinner event to attend, and why hadn't Nia gone with her husband? But what did Leo have to do with all these other people that didn't also include Nia? This didn't add up.

"Here's your table." The hostess set out two ornamented single-sheet menus. "If you prefer to order off the menu, you are welcome to do so, but we always recommend the buffet. The items the buffet includes are listed at the bottom. Miguel will be taking care of you tonight. Enjoy your evening."

"Did she just wink at you?" Jillian said after the hostess left.

Nia shrugged. "It's annoying, but some people are like that."

"This place. I don't know."

"You're going to love it. I predict it will become a favorite."

Jillian blew air out her nose. "You can't know that."

"I have a good feeling."

"Are you going to have the buffet?" Jillian was tempted to order off the menu and avoid risking an encounter with her dad or Kris while reaching for the salad tongs. Even if they were just here with that larger group, did they have to look quite so friendly with each other in such a private way?

"Let's just soak up the ambiance for a few minutes," Nia said.

The band wound down, changed instrumentation slightly, and started another number.

Jillian looked up from her menu, scanning for Nolan.

"Relax, Jillian," Nia said.

"Did my dad put them up to that?"

"What?"

"That's Verdi. Is the band taking requests? Why else would they start playing "La Traviata" for a buffet dinner crowd?"

"It's just music, Jillian."

"It's opera. The tenor always gets the girl. Did you know that's how opera works?" Jillian realized no one in the large group of people she knew, gathered for an event to which she had not been invited, had started eating. Now more of them were drifting toward tables.

And then there he was, with his parents and sister behind him.

Drew.

In a dark suit. He was always handsome in Jillian's eyes, but when he wore a dark suit, his level of gorgeous ratcheted up to dazzling. When he donned formal tails to sing concerts, sometimes she could hardly breathe at the sight of him. This suit was right on the line between the darkest navy she could imagine sliding into black, with a crisp bright white shirt and a plum tie.

A plum tie that matched her dress exactly.

Her mouth opened and the air went out of her as he came to her table and went down on one knee.

With a grin, she found her voice. "Hello, Drew."

"Hello, Jillian."

Everything inside her burst into glittering light. "You're awfully confident."

"Please don't make me look like a fool in front of all these people. I haven't got a contact lens I can pretend to be looking for down here."

The light shimmered in silver radiance. "Then I guess you'd better ask a proper question."

He took her hand. "Jillian Siobhan Parisi-Duffy, I have spoken to your father, and while he gives me his unfettered blessing, he also reminds me that this is the twenty-first century and your hand is your own to give. I would very much like to have it to hold in my own as your husband for the rest of our lives together. Can I be your husband?"

She choked at his sweetness and understood now why Nia had insisted on the no-run mascara. "I would very much like to have you for my husband."

Drew stood and pulled her by both hands to her feet in a moment that stopped time. She received his deep, long kiss, one gentle hand behind her neck, the other lacing fingers through hers, while cheers and applause flared around them.

Nia cleared her throat and tapped his jacket pocket.

Drew broke the kiss and fumbled in the pocket for the ring box. The diamond and sapphire in a silver setting were purely and wholly right. Simple. Understated. Nothing that would make Jillian self-conscious to have on her finger now and the rest of her life.

Nolan and Kris stood a few feet away, grinning. Now she understood everything. Nolan must have read at least one text—the one saying she was leaving town—and made sure Nia stopped her immediately. Kris had been busy helping to make sure all this happened. Nolan was in on it from the start. The planning must have been going on for weeks.

Jillian turned when someone tapped her on the shoulder.

Cate was there. "You look amazing!"

"I can't believe you're here." Jillian released Drew in order to embrace Cate.

"I tried to get Min to come, when I found out she didn't come with Drew's parents, but she just didn't feel up to it. She's very happy for you."

"She knew I'd say yes."

"Of course! Unfortunately, I can't stay much longer, but I really wanted to be here for the big moment."

"I'm so glad you were."

"Sorry to ignore your messages. I'm just not good with a straight face. I guess you know that."

Jillian laughed. She did know. "We have good news from the sheriff. I'll forward you a document later. But you need to tell Patrice her services are no longer required the first chance you get. Don't leave her alone in the office. I'll make sure my dad calls the sheriff for details."

Cate's eyes widened.

"I promise I'll call soon." Jillian hugged Cate again. "It's going to be okay. I'll come down in a couple of days. My brain is exploding on so many levels right now, but one of them is your exhibit."

"Don't worry about me." Cate's eyes shimmered. "This is an amazing night for you. Be right here, right now. I've known Drew as long as I can remember. You couldn't have found a better man. Love you, cousin."

Cate scooted out of the party without eating. Jillian watched as Cate left and a man in a gray suit came in, scanning the room. A few seconds later Kris found him and offered her cheek for a kiss. So this was the man Kris was taking it slow with. Not Nolan. Not her father. Mick Sanderson from the new gelato shop. Jillian laughed softly.

"What so funny?" Drew leaned into her again.

"All of this. Funny and wonderful. Every minute of it."

Jillian scanned the room herself. She didn't have to look far for the open arms of her father. "Dad, thank you."

"It's nothing, Silly Jilly. Your young man was the genius."

"Something tells me he had a lot of help from you." Jillian wished this fancy dress Nia had put her in had a tissue tucked away somewhere. "Dad, I've been self-absorbed, worrying about whether I was making mistakes with Cate and you've had my back. Like you always do. Planning my engagement party in the middle of watching me find Mom's family—"

"It was the pleasure of my heart."

Jillian wriggled her fingers into her dad's hand. "I wish she was here for all this too. Hearing about the man I love, watching us get engaged. When I was growing up, you must have thought she would be here too. The wedding." She choked. "That will be hard without her. I don't tell you enough how lucky I feel to have you."

She leaned into her father's kiss on her forehead.

CHAPTER THIRTY

Friday, May 1, 1914
Outside Pueblo Colorado

GEPPETTO STOPPED SPRING DIRT off his shoes and met Caterina's eyes at the back door of the little red house.

"Do you have them?" she asked.

He dropped the newspapers on the small table, the thinner one from Pueblo and the thicker one out of Denver. Out in the main room, they reminded Peppy six times a day not to play with the growing stack of newspapers chronicling events of the last ten days. Celestrino read very little English. After her months on the davenport absorbing English, Chiara read more. Most days, Geppetto read the accounts and Caterina translated into Italian so no one missed anything.

"Is it over?" Caterina side-eyed the headlines.

"Yes. For now."

"What does Carrick hear?"

Geppetto shrugged. "Some people are cheering. Some are indignant."

"I'm glad it's over. Even this way. It had to stop somehow."

Geppetto nodded.

They had gotten Celestrino out just in time. After the militia guards looted their way through the Ludlow colony as they set it aflame, striking miners in other colonies went to war. Miners attacked and dynamited mine tunnels where they had earned their livings a few months earlier. Fearless, they raised battles against mine guards and militia along the stretch of forty miles between Walsenburg to the north and Trinidad to the south that ran through Colorado's southern coalfield. At Forbes, where so much violence had already occurred, three strikers were dead, along with six miners who did not belong to the union. Several company towns were hardly more than uninhabitable rubble. Near Walsenburg, from a position above the McNally mine, a gunfire battle took the lives of ten guards, a striker, a militia doctor, and someone not connected with either side of the battle.

Every day, for ten days, the headlines screamed of the violence. Every day.

By the time the Parisis and Rillos reached the safety of the Kyp ranch, dawn was breaking. If Chiara had not been desperate for her husband that day to the point of unstoppable irrational decisions, would Celestrino even be alive? Or would he be one of the twenty-six who died on April 20 in Ludlow or thirty-nine more since then in the ten-day war?

Caterina was glad it was over.

Chiara wept constantly, and who could blame her?

In Ludlow, on the morning after, a telephone lineman was picking through the ruins and lifted an iron cot to discover a cellar underneath. Inside, Mary Petrucci, Alcarita Pedrogone, two other mothers, and their ten children had taken refuge from the gunfire. Only Mary and Alcarita survived the burning. Everyone else suffocated from the smoke.

Little Joe, only four years old. Lucy, only two. Frank, only six months old. And Mary had already lost Bernard, five, in February because keeping small children healthy while living in a tent in the harsh winter was near impossible.

Every time Chiara thought of her friend's heartache, she burst into tears again.

And every day it was in the newspapers. The "Death Pit," the reporters called it now. The "Ludlow Massacre." They meant the massacre of those poor children and their mothers in the Death Pit. Repeating the story sold newspapers, Caterina supposed, but she wanted it all to be over. The fighting. The dying. Just over.

"I guess we should go read to them." Caterina threw her dish towel at the kitchen table, picked up the papers, and marched into the main room.

Celestrino, as he so often did, wiped Chiara's tears while she nursed the baby under the blanket over her shoulder. The days still began and ended with fires in the hearth, but in the middle of the day like now, the little red house held enough spring warmth that only occasional poking at coals was needed to keep the home cozy. Giuseppe was on the davenport beside Chiara, patting her cheek. A week ago he had many questions. "Why Zia Chia sad?" Whether any answers Caterina offered satisfied him, she did not know, but now her sweet little boy simply offered his Zia Chia comfort in the best way he knew how.

"It is done, yes?" Celestrino said.

"Yes."

They knew the confrontation would come.

Three days after the Ludlow Massacre, a striker was shot and killed in a street battle between mine guards, militia, and strikers in Walsenburg. The next day, a thousand armed strikers from the Aquilar colony gathered just south of Walsenburg expecting General Chase of the militia guard, who had left Denver with reinforcements at noon the day before. His train halted at Walsenburg and unloaded horses so that the train could continue to advance into the forty-mile battleground under the defense of a cavalry guard. Women and children in the region around Walsenburg scrambled into cellars and other places of safety. Already terror was rampant through the coalfield, and the battles continue to rage up and down the mining corridor. General Chase was unsuccessful at putting down the strike before reaching Ludlow and unsuccessful at containing the violence after Ludlow.

Then the women of Colorado marched on the state capital three days after the confrontation in Walsenburg. Geppetto had read and Caterina translated how the Denver Times praised the women. "Their hearts rung by the unnecessary bloodshed and suffering." According to the papers, Governor Ammons first refused to meet with the women, but they refused to be ignored and prevailed on him to wire the president of the United States for federal troops.

U. S. soldiers came from Fort Leavenworth, Kansas. For two days, they'd waited, reading newspapers and knowing that not only had the Colorado National Guard taken the side of the mine owners during the strike but now the federal government was sending in troops not to ensure justice for the violence against the strikers or uphold the laws mine operators had been violating, but to quell the uprising.

And now it was done.

"They did stipulate that the militia working for the Colorado Guard must leave," Geppetto said.

"They took our guns," Celestrino countered.

"They took the guns from the Guard too. They closed the gun shops and the saloons so that no one on either side can start up again as soon as the federal troops leave."

Celestrino closed his eyes and shook his head. "The militia will get more guns if they want them."

"We hope they won't need them," Caterina said.

"No one will do justice for my friend Mary Petrucci," Chiara said. "Her four little children! How does a mother recover from this?"

"The newspaper says there will be trials." Geppetto refolded one of the newspapers. "Investigations. Finding out exactly what happened that day and who is responsible."

"Not for Mary's broken heart. Not for the mothers and children in that cellar who did not stand up and walk out. Who will remember them?"

"A strike turned into a war," Caterina said. "Now the war is over. Other mothers and children will be safe."

"But the strike?"

Celestrino shook his head again. "It is not over. The fight with guns may be over, but the fight for fair work is not over. The union will not stop here. They will get more tents and put them up somewhere. Maybe even Ludlow again. They will still try to stop the trains bringing in strikebreakers to work the mines."

"Surely they do not think the mine operators will listen to their demands now," Geppetto said. "Not after they have blown up tunnels and torn apart company towns."

"We cannot go back," Chiara said. "Celestrino, we cannot go back."

He gripped her hand. "I don't want to. Not anymore. You heard what Geppetto read in the paper. Strikers are already being arrested. I don't think I will be—I was here for the last ten days. I had nothing to do with destroying the mines. I didn't even have a gun to fire that day in Ludlow. You know I was here. I have been stubborn about supporting the union, but not anymore. I would never have done these things."

"Thank you, Celestrino."

"I am a papa now," he said. "My Chiara and my Gianni are here. I will find some work. I am young and strong."

"And brave," Chiara said.

"I am sure you can work on the ranch," Geppetto said. "I will speak to Carrick. He is worried about you. He always hires extra hands for the summer."

"Thank you. If he agrees, this will give me time to make a plan."

"Caterina and I have our own plan." Geppetto glanced at her and she nodded. "I worked at a hotel in Denver. I dream about opening a small hotel in Pueblo, maybe with a restaurant. A family business. Maybe you come and work with me when the time is right. I have already spoken of this dream with Carrick. He may even want to invest!"

"A hotel?" Chiara said. "With a restaurant? I am a very good cook, you know."

Caterina smiled. "I need some air."

Peppy scrambled down from the sofa. "Mama? Go out?"

Caterina took his hand. "Let's go, Peppy!"

Chiara handed her sleeping son to Celestrino. "I'll come too."

They walked a few yards outside in the afternoon sun, shawls around their shoulders, and leaned against the slipboard wooden fence to gaze at the Wet Mountains in one direction and the San Isabels in another.

"I will cook tonight," Chiara said. "I know the smells are hard for you."

"Not always," Caterina said. "It will be better in a few more weeks. It's nothing like what you went through."

The creek bed flowed with spring runoff from the unusually heavy winter snows, and birds had already begun filling the trees again with their chirping and warbling. Peppy found a sturdy stick and banged it against the ground, his favorite thing to do when they came outside.

"My grandmother's rosemary bread will be a favorite in the restaurant," Chiara said.

Caterina smiled. "You sound very confident."

"You will see. I will make it for you soon."

Peppy pointed. "Elk!"

Caterina nodded. "That's right." The herd had come down out of the mountain to the summer ranges. The ranch was a route for elk and deer passing through in spring and fall. This was the first season Peppy paid true attention to them.

"Will you miss the ranch?" Chiara asked. "When you open a hotel in town?"

"I hope we will visit often. Ela and Carrick have become my friends as well as Geppetto's."

"Do you hear from Geppetto's cousin? Aldo?"

"We get letters from his parents sometimes."

"Perhaps Aldo will come to work at the hotel, yes?"

"Perhaps." Aldo was old enough now. Or nearly. He had started working at the hotel in Denver with Geppetto when he was only nine or ten. Geppetto might like to have him. Salvatore and Annamaria might send him if they thought it meant he would have a career in a family business.

"Caterina," Chiara said.

"Yes?"

"You have been my friend. My amica in hard times. I am a wild thing. Celestrino says this. But you love me anyway."

"Yes, I do. And you are my amica." Caterina squeezed Chiara's hand.

They turned their gazes back to the mountain peaks that were farther away than they seemed.

"Do you remember Italy?" Chiara asked.

Caterina shook her head slowly. "I don't think so. I was so small when we left. My parents think I should remember, and I don't want to disappoint them, so I don't say anything."

"I wonder if our bambinos will ever go to Italy."

"Maybe we will take them." Little Peppy had never even been on a boat. It was hard to find a lake in Colorado, much less an ocean. Did he even know the word yet?

"We will make a little Italy in the hotel and restaurant. Our bambinos will know where they came from."

"And if I know you," Caterina said, laughing, "their bambinos will speak Italian."

CHAPTER THIRTY-ONE

JILLIAN'S FINGERS HAD BEEN INTERLACED with Drew's for the last forty miles, ever since they got out of the maze of Denver interchanges and onto the clear, straight, south-heading lanes of I-25 between Denver and Colorado Springs and he could drive with one hand. The views of the front range of the Rockies were always spectacular on this drive. Today, though, she was more interested in the view of the driver. The curls over his collar. The dimple in one cheek. The glances he threw her direction that she didn't want to miss even from two feet away.

They'd been engaged for thirty-eight hours and twelve minutes.

Drew grazed her ring with a finger. "I'm glad you let me drive you down."

"I'm glad for the company. Yours in particular."

"Your dad said he would come fetch you on Saturday."

"Apparently you two have gotten into the habit of scheming to arrange my life."

"I didn't hear any complaints the other evening."

"Not a one." Jillian squeezed his hand.

"You've been driving back and forth a lot." Drew's glance carried concern. "And you're always dragging your work with you. I know you can be a night owl when you get deep into a project. The stuff with Cate and all the shuttling around—I worry you're not sleeping enough."

Drew was going to be her husband. There was no point in minimizing the truth of what he said, so for the moment Jillian said nothing.

"How late were you up last night?" Drew asked.

"Yesterday was crazy." Jillian twisted her mouth. "You were there." The news of their engagement had rocketed through the shops up and down Main Street, reaching anyone who hadn't been at the party. Jillian's phone rang nonstop. She barely had a chance to speak three sentences in a row to Drew, who had stayed to spend the day with her, much less respond to the messages stacking up in her work inbox or voice mail. She'd done her best in the evening to tidy up the essentials before being away yet again. Then that list of names of couples and families who had stayed in the hut on the ranch had stared at her and she couldn't resist.

"You could take a little nap, you know." Drew raised his eyebrows.

"I don't need a nap."

"Because you had coffee in the middle of the night."

Drew had wandered downstairs at one in the morning and found her back in her office. She couldn't deny the evidence.

Her phone jangled. Startled, she released Drew's hand to find it in the bag at her feet.

"What's that tune?" Drew asked.

"The Italian national anthem. Cate put it on." Jillian answered Cate's FaceTime call. "Hey cuz."

"Hey." Cate was in motion. Jillian recognized the trappings of the hallway outside her office suite. "I'm about to give Patrice the ax."

"Does she know anything's coming?" Jillian angled the screen toward Drew. "We're in the car."

"I don't know." Cate was in the shared waiting room now, across from Epic EduKids. "Yesterday, I emailed her that I wouldn't need her but that I would meet her here today. So this is it."

"Are you sure?" Drew leaned slightly toward Jillian's phone. "We can drive all the way down to Trinidad if you want to wait for us."

Cate shook her head. "I want it done and over with. I don't want her anywhere near any of my files another minute."

"My dad spoke to Deputy Pesko," Jillian said. "They're going to figure out what to charge her with and make it stick."

"He told me. But in the meantime, she's history. I have her last check ready and everything. She'll have no reason to come anywhere near me. But I'd like to keep you on camera while I do it, if you don't mind."

Jillian and Drew exchanged a glance.

"Sure." Jillian nodded. "If that will make you feel better. Try to stay calm. Keep it short and sweet."

"Maybe not sweet." Cate stood outside her office.

"Short and firm then."

Cate turned the doorknob.

Jillian put her end of the call on mute while Cate found a discreet place to tuck her phone in her bag, allowing the camera access to the room.

"Is this legal?" Drew whispered. "Us watching?"

Jillian grimaced. "We didn't make the call and I don't think she's recording. Besides, it's her own office. Should her employee have an expectation of privacy there?"

"Does this opinion come with a caveat that I should not construe it as actual legal advice?"

"Thanks for the extra day off yesterday," Patrice said. "I really needed it to catch up on some things."

Cate pulled an envelope out of her bag. "I have a check for you here."

"But it's not payday."

"This is your final pay."

"Final pay?" Patrice made no move to take the envelope. "We have a contract."

"A contract that includes termination clauses either of us can use." Cate set the envelope on the desk. "Take it or leave it. Makes no difference to me. I have refrained from deducting any amount for your betrayal, but the gig is up."

Jillian winced. "I wish she hadn't said that."

"And I think you realize there will be no reference," Cate added.

Patrice snatched up the envelope. "If you thought the pittance from your grant was paying my rent, you're more of a sap than I thought."

"You may go now." Cate gestured to the open door. "Just leave your key. And there's no need to stop and see your friends across the waiting room."

Patrice glared, but she took her jacket from the back of her chair and a large purse from the floor and exited.

A moment later Cate's face filled the screen again. "Well?"

"Well done," Jillian said. "It's in the hands of the sheriff's office now. She probably doesn't know what's coming."

Keeping his eyes on the road, Drew leaned toward the phone again. "Are you working tonight?"

Cate sighed. "My mom is nagging me about filling in."

"Do it. Make her extra happy by staying the night so you can come by the ranch tomorrow."

"I could come by the ranch tomorrow even if I didn't work and stay the night."

"Yes, but peace on the homefront could come in handy right now."

Hesitation flickered through Cate's features.

"Would your grandmother come with you to the ranch?" Jillian asked.

"Nonna Benedetta?"

"I have a feeling Min would like to see her."

"I guess I could ask. I might have to see what my dad thinks. Oh, I see. Peace on the homefront."

"And the journal." Jillian flashed an expectant smile. "Min. Benedetta. The journal. Those photos of the hut. All in the same place. Aren't you a little bit curious?"

"What if Deputy Pesko needs me?"

"That's why you have a lawyer."

"Oh, you're smooth."

"So you'll come? And bring your grandmother?"

"I'll try. Maybe I'll see if I can just stay with Nonna this time."

Cate turned and picked up a stack of mail from the desk. "Uh oh."

"What is it?" Jillian's heart rate jumped up.

"An actual letter from my grant board. This can't be good." Cate ripped the envelope open and scanned the letter. "I have until November 1 to submit a final revision to my business plan, and if it is not approved, funding will terminate December 31."

CHAPTER THIRTY-TWO

THE BREAKFAST SPREAD MIN MANAGED with one good arm and one healing wrist made Jillian feel underdressed. She gave Nolan's full traditional Irish breakfast a run for his money. Buttermilk pancakes—which would have been crepes if she'd had two working wrists—strawberry syrup, bacon, sausage, melon, Greek yogurt and three kinds of berries layered in stemware and topped off with whipped cream. The dining room table was laid with a tablecloth and fancier dishes than those Min used in the kitchen. In all her visits to the ranch, Jillian hadn't seen these before.

"Goodness, Min, how long have you been up?" Jillian tugged at her blue plaid button down shirt tail, glad that at least she hadn't schlepped to breakfast in a hoodie at eight o'clock.

"You deserve an engagement breakfast." Min's eyes were bright with pleasure. "A proper welcome to the family."

Jillian swallowed past the lump that instantly made speech difficult.

"Drew won the prize when he found you," Min said.

"How could I turn down a man I first saw on a white stallion?" Jillian recovered her voice. "And one who lives in a little red house and sings like an angel."

Min chuckled. "We all know you are far more sensible than to be carried away by the cover of a romance novel."

Now Jillian laughed. "I suppose I am. But still. I'm glad you're pleased."

"I am."

"This breakfast is too much! Didn't we just have an engagement dinner last night when we got here?"

"Pish posh. That was just Drew pottering around the kitchen the way he does."

"It was a pretty amazing meal."

"Be careful, or you'll put on twenty pounds the first year you're married, the way he cooks."

"True fact." Jillian glanced at the clock on the dining room wall. It was just shy of eight, when Drew had promised to come up from his little red house—probably in his truck rather than astride his white horse. "Shall I make coffee?"

"Already made, but I'd be happy to have you pour."

Jillian fetched the pot, just in time to open the back door for Drew and stare into his gray eyes waiting for a morning kiss. His cheek dimpled. He knew what she wanted.

"Hello, wife-to-be."

"Hello, husband-to-be."

"I got the better deal." Drew kissed her, and Jillian tried to hold onto him with her lips and not spill the coffee pot.

"Come on, you two," Min said from the other room. "Pancakes are getting cold."

Over breakfast, Min wanted to see more photos of the engagement surprise in Canyon Mines, and Drew and Jillian took turns passing her their phones. Since yesterday, both Kris and Nolan had forwarded their shots, so Jillian's album was bursting.

"Is Benedetta Parisi really going to come here today?" Min said, finally surrendering Jillian's phone.

"Aunt Min, she's been Benedetta Polombo for more than sixty years." Drew added another pancake to his plate.

"What are you going to do about your name?" Min looked at Jillian. "It's already hyphenated. Parisi-Duffy-Lawson would be a mouthful."

Jillian had a mouthful of yogurt and berries, which she swallowed. "I haven't thought about it yet."

"Think of your poor children."

"Aunt Min!" Drew wagged a slice of bacon at her.

"I'm an old woman. I don't have time to dance around the questions everyone wonders about."

"Well, you'll just have to," Drew said. "If we have something to tell you, we'll tell you."

"It will be nice to see Benedetta." Min raised her coffee mug. "It's been years. I can't think when it was. She stopped working at the restaurant a long time ago, even before Cosmo passed. Mateo and Cinzia never had much interest in being the ones to run things. I think Benedetta and Cosmo always knew Vincenzo would be the one in charge."

"Do the others still work in the family business?" Jillian asked. "I know Cinzia helps keep the books."

Min nodded. "She became an accountant."

"And Mateo? I think Cate said he goes by Matt."

"I'm not sure. I guess you'd have to ask her."

"I know who he is," Drew offered. "He works for a builder. They built Mary Lou's. And they did the last interior upgrade at Peppy's. Vince calls him for all the repairs."

Jillian exhaled. "It sounds like no one completely cuts the ties."

"You're thinking of Cate," Min said.

Jillian nodded.

"I quite enjoy Cate, and I think I will quite enjoy seeing her grandmother again. I suppose if I went into town more, I might still run into her."

"I'll clear up." Drew picked up the now-empty pancake platter and arranged the nearly empty berry bowls on it.

"I'll help." Jillian stacked her plate on his.

"Rather a dull ending to an engagement breakfast." Min handed over her plate.

Jillian caught Drew's eye and then glanced at her glinting ring. "A portent of old married life."

They cleared the dining room table, loaded the dishwasher, wiped down the griddle, washed assorted small pans, and generally straightened up both the kitchen and dining room. They plumped pillows in the front room and pestered Min about whether she needed anything to be more comfortable. A pillow under her sore wrist? A glass of water? Fresh coffee? She was starting to give them dirty looks.

Cate was thirty minutes late and then forty. And then an hour. Jillian fetched her laptop and a couple of file folders from her room, partly to be ready for Cate and partly to have something to do with her nervous energy while they waited. She and Drew both kept checking their phones.

No messages from Cate.

No answers to the ones they sent.

After Cate's victorious sacking of Patrice followed immediately by the threat to her funding, it was hard to read Cate's moods.

Finally: SORRY. BE THERE SOON.

When Cate pulled up in front of the house and got out of her car, she was alone.

Jillian met her on the porch. "What happened?"

"My grandmother wouldn't come."

"Why not?"

"She woke up this morning feeling awful. She says it hurts too much. She has terrible gout, and she's completely unreliable about taking her medication when she's supposed to."

"She'd feel better if she did."

"We all know that. But she doesn't, and she won't let anyone look over her shoulder about it either. Then she ends up like this. She's so stubborn."

Jillian couldn't keep her face from falling no matter how much she tried.

"I'm sorry, cuz. I did my best to sort her out before I left, but she just wanted to sit in her chair."

Jillian turned toward the hand on her back. Drew had come out to the porch. His hand slid down her arm to enfold her fingers.

"Sounds a little like someone else we know." Drew's other hand still held open the door. "We'll have to tell Aunt Min. She had worked up to what passes for excitement at the thought of seeing Benedetta."

"I did bring the journal." Cate pulled a thick bubble-wrap package out from under one arm.

"I guess I'll to save my questions about its provenance for another time." Jillian fingered the package.

"I promise we'll try again."

In her recliner, Min took in the explanation of Benedetta's absence while Jillian gingerly opened the journal for the first time. She couldn't read any of it on her own—it was all in Italian—but just holding it and turning pages was spellbinding.

"Where is her gout?" Min wanted to know.

"Both feet," Cate said. "Her big toes."

"Yes, it's a common place for gout to afflict. Hurts like the dickens to walk, they say."

"That's what my Nonna says, but she says it in Italian, and I think it's a stronger word."

Min slapped a knee and laughed. "Let's go to her."

Jillian glanced at Cate. "What do you think?"

Cate shrugged. "Her medication should have kicked in by now. It's usually pretty fast, if she would just take it."

"She might still like to visit the ranch another time, but in the meantime, isn't she a little bit curious about me? Or seeing Min, at least?"

"She's very curious about you. She figured if you were marrying Drew, you weren't going anywhere."

"I'm not sure I know your grandmother," Drew said.

"She knows you make the best desserts in Southern Colorado," Cate said, "because my mother brings them to her, and she knows you're Min's grandson. What else does she need to know?"

"Indeed."

Jillian side-eyed Drew. He'd picked up saying *Indeed* from her father.

"I guess I could call her." Cate took out her phone. "The worst that happens is she says no."

Jillian hadn't expected Cate to launch into Italian. When her parents or brothers spoke Italian to her, she responded in English, as if she wished they would forget the ways of the old country none of them had ever visited. Listening to Cate speak to her grandmother, Jillian realized the degree of her fluency. She spoke. She listened. She spoke. Clipped tones. Higher pitches. Lower soothing pitches. There seemed to be some resistance and then some coming around. Cate was nodding and a plan was forming.

She ended the call. "She says yes."

Jillian laughed. "It seemed like she said a lot of other things too."

"Italians. They need a lot of words."

"Are you sure she wants to do this?"

"She says yes. My father is picking her up to go to Peppy's at lunch time. He doesn't like her never getting out of the house. I wanted her to stay home. I said having visitors is almost the same as getting out of the house. I don't really want to go to Peppy's and deal with family drama again."

Ah. The resistance was on Cate's end.

"But she said she already promised my dad, so it is Peppy's or nothing." Cate exhaled heavily. "So I will deal with my family. I owe you.

Also I want to help."

"Peppy's." Jillian tilted her head. "I haven't been there yet, and I'm curious."

"There you go, then," Cate said. "Benedetta, Peppy's, the journal. It's a trifecta of curiosity."

Peppy's. Named for Giuseppe Parisi, son of Geppetto, cousin to Aldo, son of Salvatore, great-great grandfather of Jillian. Mentally she was double-checking—again—the family tree. She still had trouble thinking of the person whose leaf on the tree was labeled Giuseppe as Peppy, a nickname. But in the restaurant that bore his name, perhaps several stories would come together. The ranch, the journal, the families from the hut, the restaurant.

"We have a few minutes," Drew said. "I need to go down and let the horses out into the pasture for the day."

"I'd like to see the horses." Cate's eyes brightened.

"Then come along." Drew glanced at Jillian.

"I think I'll sit with the journal," she said.

"We'll be right back."

Drew and Cate went out the back door, and Min left for her room. Jillian turned pages with care, wondering how much her Grandpa Steve might have been able to make out of the Italian script. Probably very little. The handwriting, it seemed to her, suggested an older thoughtful child. Whether a boy or a girl she could not discern. The writing was square and methodical, the lines straight and schoolish. Could it have been a school project? Jillian flipped back to the front cover, outside and inside, back and front. No school name, no child's name. It bore not even an initial. The outer reddish brown leather looked anonymous, but no doubt the pages, filled from top to bottom and front to back, were far from anonymous. They told a story. Jillian just had to find out what it said. Surely Cate had read it—probably her grandmother as well, though Benedetta's reading might have been years ago.

Jillian found the center pages, where the journal fell open naturally.

Sketches.

She recognized a portion of the house that must have been the original. The trim was different and the porch not as large as it was now. Somewhere in the house's history the windows had been changed. But the bones were there. The drawing of the little red house looked just as it did now, with different plants in front of it. A barn, a pasture, out-buildings, another drawing of the little red house from a wider perspective with a second, smaller structure across the way.

The hut.

The child whose story these pages told had lived in the hut. Jillian was sure of it. If the child was in one of the families photographed standing in front of the hut, the options would narrow, since many of the children were too young to have filled this journal.

Letting the journal fall to the sofa, Jillian went to her room for her folders and narrow-ruled yellow legal pad. Those sleepless nights Drew was festering over had been for a purpose, and a couple of pieces were about to slide very nicely into place.

If Jillian was right, Cate had a historical jewel on her hands.

Jillian insisted Min ride in the front seat with Drew. The first time she came to the ranch the distance from Pueblo had seemed long and rural along the narrow two-lane highway. Now she'd traversed it enough times to mentally mark off the miles and the minutes, and it didn't seem any farther than driving from Canyon Mines to Denver. Of course Pueblo was much smaller than Denver. Once you got to Pueblo, any destination was easy to reach. She gazed out the window at the rolling landscape.

"We lost Cate."

Jillian's attention snapped to Drew's eyes. He was watching the rear view mirror. "What do you mean?"

"She's been right behind us since we left the ranch and now she's not."

"She can't bail on us now." Jillian's stomach clenched.

"We don't know that she did."

"We do know she wasn't wild about running into her parents at Peppy's." Jillian twisted around to look about the back window. "Did you see her leave the highway?"

"Sorry, eyes forward and all that."

Jillian slumped. "Should I text her?"

"She's driving. She shouldn't answer."

CHAPTER THIRTY-THREE

"HONESTLY, YOU TWO," Min said. "Give the girl some space. I thought you would be over thinking the worst of her by now."

In the rear view mirror, Drew's eyes flicked toward Jillian's.

"You're right." Jillian tapped a couple of fingers against the side of her knee. "She said she'd be there."

"I'm surprised at you, Drew." Min's voice carried exasperation. "I may not drive into town on my own as much as I used to, but I don't get lost. You know good and well that we just went past the turnoff a lot of people use to avoid that series of long traffic lights. She'll probably be wondering what took you so long."

Drew erupted in laughter. "Jillian, she's right."

Outside Peppy's a few minutes later, Cate greeted them with her palms turned up.

"I know, I know," Drew said. "I'm driving like a tourist."

Jillian blew out her breath.

"Don't be nervous." Cate nudged her elbow. "It's my nonna. She's going to love you. And the rest of it—well, I'm just not going to let it get to me. I promise you."

"Maybe your parents aren't here." Was that the right thing to say? Jillian wasn't sure.

"Oh, they're here. My dad already called while I was driving. He thought Nonna was confused about what was happening."

"Well, then."

"He did ask if that Nolan guy was coming."

"That Nolan guy?"

"Your dad did give everyone something to think about after what happened at Mary Lou's."

"Is that a good thing or a bad thing?"

"Maybe just the presence of Nolan's daughter will be enough to make them stop talking about making me quit my grant."

"Okay then. We'll go with that."

Jillian glanced up at the sign, brightly lit even at midday. Peppy's. It was a feel-good name for a restaurant, she decided. The perfect place to be meeting Peppy's daughter. Cate marched toward the door and held it open. Inside, they all paused. At least Jillian did. Behind her, the others had no choice. Cate, Min—even Drew—they'd all been here countless times. This was her first view of the establishment Parisis had founded and sustained. Peppy Parisi. Had he gone by that name even as a grown man, or had it been only a childhood nickname? When had the interior last been renovated? It was charming, but not at all shabby as Jillian had supposed it might be. The exposed dark ceiling beams heightened the sense of space. Classic Italian street scene artwork adorned the walls, but Jillian knew immediately these were not prints ordered from a restaurant supply vendor. They were handprinted, each one using the same rich palette to evoke cobblestones and arches and narrow passageways, but the canvases varied in size. They hadn't come off an assembly line, and no effort was made to correct the size differences at the framing stage. The irregularities drew the eye in a way that standardizing never would have. There were no stereotypical red and white checked tablecloths, but only crisp white linens with generous drops, and the dishes laid on the tables carried the scenery theme on through not with overbearing grapevines and gold rims but countryside views in sturdy blue and white stoneware.

Against one wall, sitting alone at the head of a table, was a stout gray-haired woman who could only be Benedetta Parisi Polombo. Cate confirmed this by pushing past Jillian and rushing toward the elderly woman to kiss both her cheeks. Benedetta obliged, but her curious eyes were on Min and Jillian as they approached.

"Wilhelmina," Benedetta said.

Min chuckled. "You always insisted on calling me that."

"It's a lovely name." Benedetta gestured they should sit. "It has been a long time."

"Yes, it has."

"Old people like us do not mean to stop seeing people we used to know. Somehow it just happens."

Min nodded.

Drew pulled out a chair for Min and Cate sat beside her, closest to her grandmother. He pulled out another chair for Jillian, smiling encouragement as they took their places. Under the table, Jillian reached for Drew's hand.

"My Rini has been talking my ears off about all of you." Benedetta tugged an ear. "Yes, at least one is still attached."

"Do you know Drew?" Cate asked. "He sometimes fills in here. He used to manage the other restaurant when it first opened, as well as being the chef."

Benedetta nodded. "I remember Wilhelmina was very pleased when he was born. Her sister's grandson!"

Min waved off the thought. "Don't give him a big head."

"You make very good desserts, young man." Benedetta pointed a gentle finger at him. Her movements were focused but slow, as if the gout in her feet was not the only pain that hindered her daily activities.

"I'm pleased to meet you," Drew said. "I'll have to make sure you get some extra confections."

"This is Jillian," Min said. "They've just become engaged."

"Jillian." Benedetta nodded. "The cousin with many questions."

Jillian and Benedetta met eyes, peering across generations, examining decades, gathering the features for recognition.

"I can see you favor Aldo," Benedetta finally said.

Jillian's breath stilled, and something fluttered in her belly. "You knew Aldo? My mother's grandfather?" Musty air of dry, long-ago decades stirred.

"He was my grandfather's cousin." Benedetta tilted her head and inspected Jillian's features. "Sometimes he would take a train down from Denver for a visit. I was small, so I may be imagining, but there is a Parisi look about you."

"Nonna," Cate said, "Jillian *is* a Parisi."

"You think I do not understand this, Caterina? Of course I know this. She looks more like a Parisi than you do."

"Nonna!"

"Let's hear your questions, Jillian Parisi. Rini tells me that you carry questions with you everywhere you go."

Jillian glanced at Cate.

"Well, it's true!" Cate said. "What do you have in your bag right now?"

Jillian shifted in her seat. "A few things."

Benedetta tapped the table. "Let's discuss."

At the end of the cluster of chairs, Vince Polombo slid into a spot.

"First of all," Jillian said, "it's incredible to meet you. I'm so grateful. I wish my mother and my grandfather could have known there was a branch of the family just a few hours away."

Benedetta gave a stately matriarchal nod. "What a reunion that would have been."

Mary Lou Polombo stood behind her husband now, a hand on his shoulder.

Jillian forced herself not to fixate on what their behaviors might be. Somehow she thought Benedetta's no-nonsense demeanor would carry some weight in these circumstances and no one would be asking Cate to grab an apron and bus a table today. She withdrew the journal from her bag.

"Caterina brought this to me. We haven't had a chance for her to read any of it to me yet—I'm sorry, I don't speak Italian. But I'm fascinated about why you had the journal all these years."

"It was my mother's. I don't mean to say she wrote it, but it belonged to her. You have things that belonged to your mother, yes?"

Jillian nodded.

"This is the reason. My sisters and I were not supposed to touch some things, but Wilhelmina will tell you that I could be naughty."

Min laughed.

"When my mother was out, I used to sneak into her room and read this book. It was my favorite."

"But why do you think she kept it?" Jillian asked. "If it wasn't her journal, why was it so important?"

Benedetta shrugged. "This I do not know. My mother was a tender woman. Her mother was a tender woman before her. Emotional. You understand this? You do not throw away things that tell the story of a child. This is what you see, yes, Caterina?"

Tears sprang to Cate's eyes as she nodded. Jillian glanced at the Polumbos.

"I have a theory." Jillian opened the journal. "One of you will have to read to me from this journal later and we can figure it out together, but I think this is the journal of a girl who was about ten or eleven years old when the Ludlow Massacre happened and lived through it."

"I've read it many times," Cate said. "It talks about worrying about a father who worked in the mines and hardly ever seeing him, but it doesn't mention Ludlow a single time."

"Because she doesn't want to say that word. It was too horrible. But I bet she misses things she had to leave behind. I bet she misses the friends she didn't get to say goodbye to. Maybe she even misses when she used to get to go to school."

Cate's face scrunched up. "That's exactly right. How did you know any of that?"

Jillian flipped to the drawings at the center of the journal and laid it in the center of the table.

Min gasped. "My house."

"But I was at your house many times when we were girls." Benedetta reached for a better look at the book.

Two gray heads bent over the sketches older than they were.

"You knew the house after my parents had to shore up the foundation," Min said. "They decided to put on the larger front porch, and my mother insisted they do something about the drafty windows."

"I don't remember that."

"Neither do I. I was very small." Min traced a finger over the drawing. "This is before the changes. I've seen old photos. My daughter has them now. She wanted to see if someone could enhance them and digitize them. This sketch is quite good for a child. They all are."

"Is that the hut?" Jillian asked. "Across from the little red house?"

Min tilted her head. "I've only seen photos, but that's where it was."

"Wait!" Cate hunched in. "The hut from the photos we found in the suitcase?"

Jillian nodded. "I've been trying to track down some of the names. There was a family with an older girl and an infant son who was on the ranch in late 1914. The Marcheses. I wonder if this is the girl's journal."

"Min," Cate said, "I could kiss you!"

"Please." Min held up both hands. "Contain yourself."

"Those photos you found are the missing link for everything."

"Someone explain, please," Benedetta said. "What photos? What is this hut?"

Min turned both hands up in a shrug. "It was after the Ludlow strike your Rini is working on. I understand that long before either of us were born, my grandparents helped some former miners get a fresh start by keeping them by turn in the hut while they got on their feet. We Kyps have always been good people."

"And the note we found from Chiara Rillo—she was there and helped too," Min said.

"It looks that way."

"Chiara Rillo?" Benedetta's pitch rose. "You have a note from my grandmother?"

"Rillo?" Cate was puzzled. "I thought your mother's name was Julie Ricco."

Benedetta shook her head. "Giuliana Gabriela Rillo."

Mary Lou spoke up. "That's why your name is Caterina Gabriela."

"But Julie Ricco," Cate said. "Where did I get that? I'm sure I've seen it on documents."

"Writing it down does not make it so." Benedetta's tone left no room for dispute. "I know my mother's name. And her mother's name. This note? You are sure it is from Chiara?"

"I have a theory." Jillian inserted herself. "Census takers didn't always hear things accurately, and they didn't have the best handwriting. Even officials who record documents like marriage records or property transfers didn't always pay attention to consistency of a name spelling, especially if they were dealing with language accents. In my line of work, I've seen more than one name morph in and out of spelling variants, yet I'm sure it's the same person. *Ls* can looks like *Cs* or vice versa. In the family tree Cate gave me, there's an entry for C. C. Ricco. I can't quite match that up with the census records, and it looks like it's only one part of a married pair. Maybe it's meant to be C. G., for Caterina Giuliana"

Benedetta waved her hand in front of her face. "C and C."

Jillian's eyebrows went up. "Like separate people?"

"Celestrino and Chiara. My Rillo grandparents."

"My great-great-grandparents. How did I not know this?" Cate shook her head slowly. "I just always heard about the Parisis because of the restaurants."

"I don't know the names of my great-great-grandparents," Jillian pointed out. "They would be Sal and Lou's parents. It's quite common

Now That I Know You

for people to lose the names that far back."

"I suppose so." Shock still shaped Cate's features.

"Then Giuseppe Parisi married Giuliana Rillo?" Jillian turned back to Benedetta. All the C and G initials could so easily be mixed up in records.

Benedetta was nodding. "Yes, Celestrino and Geppetto opened the hotel and restaurant together. Later the Rillos moved away, except Giuliana, because she married Peppy. After growing up in the restaurant business, my Uncle Gianni wanted to try his hand with a food truck in Denver, a bigger city. He asked my grandparents to help him. My grandmother was a very good cook, and very fast."

"Fascinating!" Cate's eyes were alight.

"Lili," Min said.

"Who?" Jillian asked.

"Giuliana. Zia Lili, we called her. I told you we just called all the Peppys zia and zio. It's coming back to me now."

"Yes," Benedetta said. "She was Lili to the family."

"Jillian, you just have to make us one of your fancy family trees with all of this straightened out."

"I will," Jillian said.

"The note." Benedetta thumped the table. "It's from Chiara?"

Jillian nodded. "We think so. The note mentions Celestrino and Gianni, so it fits. She writes to Ela Kyp thanking her for her kindness and returning some things that other families might use while they found work outside the mines."

"My grandmother was very fond of Mrs. Kyp." Benedetta looked at Drew and Min now. "I would like to see this note."

"You will. It's in safe keeping, just as you have kept the journal safe all these years," Min said. "And your granddaughter will keep it safe as well."

Cate's eyes widened. "I can use the note?"

"Of course." Min answered without a hitch. "It belongs to your family as much as it does to mine. And you are going to do great things with your exhibit. The stories you tell to the children of Colorado are important. If our ranch and our families were a part of them, I am proud to give it all to you."

At the end of the table, Vince cleared his throat. "You really think

Rini can do this?"

Min glared. "She already is doing it."

Benedetta scowled. "Pay attention Vincenzo. You too, Mary Lou."

"Mama, let's be fair." Vince squirmed. "We have a thriving family business, and Rini can contribute in many ways if she would just buckle down. She could have a secure share of the business. This grant is precarious. I'm only thinking of what is good for her and the family."

Jillian tensed and moistened her lips. Cate's eyes narrowed, but so far she showed no sign of jumping out of her seat or even opening her mouth in retort.

Benedetta shook an arthritic finger. "Nonsense. Think of where Caterina can shine. You accuse her of not caring about family, but she is caring about many families and showing the best of ours. Your daughter has a sacred calling."

Cate's dark eyes gleamed with dewy luster.

"I will see these photos on a day when my feet don't hurt so much," Benedetta said. "Perhaps I will make you drive me to Trinidad, Vincenzo."

Vince squirmed again.

"I can bring the photos to you, Nonna," Cate said. "And you can see them, too, Pop. We'll make copies."

"We will see your work, Caterina, wherever it is. Your family will see your work about all the families. And we will be proud of the stories you will tell the children. We will all be proud of you." Benedetta's scolding stare bore into his son and his wife.

"Nonna, I love you." Cate stroked her grandmother's hands, tenderly circling around the arthritic knots.

"I know this. But it is good if we say this, yes?"

"Yes, Nonna. Yes."

"Yes?" Benedetta looked at Vince and Mary Lou.

"Yes, Mama." Vince nodded at his daughter. "Good job, Caterina."

Drew's lips brushed Jillian's cheek and he whispered in her ear. "Well done."

CHAPTER THIRTY-FOUR

"ARE YOU SURE YOU DON'T want to stay for supper?"

This Saturday had been an overflowing day. Min's engagement breakfast ten hours ago felt so distant that it might as well have been a week ago on another continent. Benedetta and Min both tired easily, it seemed, so lunch at Peppy's was not a protracted event. Mary Lou brought a variety of pizzas to the table and they ate—some of the best Jillian had ever had—while old memories seem to gush out of both of them. Eventually Jillian admitted she had a notepad in her bag and took it out to at least jot down some brief descriptors of what they were talking about. Then Caterina returned to the ranch, and Jillian and Caterina indexed all the items Caterina had to work with to enrich her exhibit and they backed them back in the original leather case, itself an artifact of the time the items would showcase. Now, after a rest, Min had banished the "lovebirds," as she called Drew and Jillian, from the kitchen while she prepared a light supper.

"I can't stay," Caterina said. "You heard me promise I'd be back to work the dinner rush. I left things in a good place with my parents. I want to keep it that way."

"Good choice." Jillian glanced at the clock. "My dad will be here soon. He'll be sorry not to see you."

Caterina grinned. "He's stuck with me now. We're family. My family doesn't distinguish cousins by marriage. Bella's husband would just be a cousin, same as her."

"He'd like that."

"I've never had an Irish cousin before."

"If you say that to him, you will be fast friends."

Caterina slung her bag over her shoulder and picked up the case. "I'd better go."

"I'll walk you out."

They paused in the kitchen for Caterina to say goodbye to Min, who wasn't technically a relative but might as well be. It was her family that sheltered the Parisis all those years ago—and the Rillos and so many other miner families.

Drew was outside, and when he glanced up at them, his gray Kyp eyes danced with the light in his slightly scruffy face. It wasn't hard to see why Jillians friends called him Dreamy Drew. Jillian had stopped insisted they not.

"Just checking your tires," he said.

Jillian puffed air out with her smile. Drew actually did have a tire gauge in his hand.

"One flat tire ten years ago," Caterina said, "and you won't ever let me forget it."

"How many pressure gauges have I given you in those ten years?"

Cate rolled her eyes. "Six."

"And how many are in your truck?"

"I am not discussing this." Cate opened the passenger door and arranged the case of keepsakes safely on the floor.

"Drew," Jillian said, "stop picking on my cousin."

"She was my friend first."

"She was always my cousin. I just didn't know it."

Caterina jangled her keys. "Now children, no fighting. There's plenty of me to share."

"I'll find the Marcheses," Jillian said. "When they were on the ranch, that little girl was old enough that she would have been listed in the 1910 census unless her family hadn't come to the U. S. yet."

"And I'll read the letters again," Cate said, "looking for any reference to where her family might have gone when they left here."

"Together, we'll get your proposal done by your deadline."

"Just what I wanted."

"Sounds like the Parisi cousins have the presentation well in hand." Drew draped an arm around Jillian's shoulder.

"That's it!" Cate clapped twice. "My new business name. Parisi Presentations. The story of the Parisis becomes the story of the strike through the eyes of a child who knew them."

Jillian grinned. "I like it."

Jillian stretched her arms around Drew's midsection, latching them together by crossing her wrists, to watch Caterina's departure. He pulled her closer and set his chin on the top of her head. Jillian had lived her whole life with a postcard-worthy mountain view right outside her home and restored her spirit by running the hills of God's glory and feeling the pulse of creation in her stride. Yet this view, of the Wet Mountains in one direction and the San Isabels in the other, was a distinct sensation every time she visited the ranch. And so they stood, arms around each other, watching the sun find its way down behind the sprawling western landscape.

"There's such a sense of expanse here," Jillian murmured. "Such bigness. So much room for hope. I can see how families could come here to figure out what's next."

"A great place to stare out at your own soul," Drew said. "Or walk until things start to make sense."

"Or pretend to walk while you are really calling your daughter's boyfriend to arrange an engagement party."

"Yes, that's been known to happen." Drew kissed her forehead. "But here we are, engaged, with our own future to figure out."

"This feels like home to you as much as Canyon Mines is home to me."

They were silent for a few moment. Then Drew audibly took in air.

"We have an offer on the ranch."

Jillian drew back far enough to look at his face. "I thought you've only been trying to sell off a few acres to stay afloat."

"That was the plan. No one in the family wants to sell the place out from under Aunt Min as long she wants to live here and is able to."

"So? You can't really entertain an offer right now, can you? Is that really what everyone wants?"

"We didn't expect this offer. It's from the same person interested in the acres we have on the market."

"Wow."

"The family foundation owns the ranch. No one can singlehandedly decide to sell."

"But you're on the ranch because Min shouldn't really be out here completely on her own, and now we want to get married. Is the family worried?"

He tightened his embrace. "We haven't even talked about when. And living here was always meant to be an interlude. We have all the bigness we need to figure out our future."

"But the ranch, Drew. That's a big thing, after over a hundred years."

"It is. For now, the buyer may be willing to take the acres we're selling with a little extra earnest money to have the first option if we decide to sell the whole ranch within a certain period of time."

"I could see that. You've already decided to let those acres go to somebody."

"Nobody's deciding anything now. I just thought you should know. Your dad should be here soon."

"Come to fetch me and ferry me back home."

Drew gestured with his chin toward a pickup ambling down the ranch's private road toward the main house. "Here he is now."

"He had so many questions about Benedetta. Someday I want to introduce them."

"Would your mother have liked her?"

"Very much."

"Then Nolan will too."

Jillian spread the fingers of her left hand, letting her ring catch the sunlight. "Now it will feel even stranger to go home and not to be with you all the time."

"So we'll have to figure that out."

"We will. My friends are already pestering me about the date."

"Maybe I should plan a surprise wedding."

"Maybe this time when my friends want to take me dress shopping, I should say yes."

AUTHOR NOTE

I HAVE BEEN DREAMING OF WRITING about Ludlow for nearly twenty years.

When my son was a freshman in high school, he joined the mock trial team, and my husband and I entered the league of parents who watched versions of the same competition over and over. The state bar association selects a case and provides every team with the same set of documents to study as the basis of preparing both prosecution and defense. No other information is allowed. Team members play roles of prosecution and defense attorneys, and prosecution and defense witnesses. If a team does well and advances through the regional and then state competition brackets, parents know the case very well by the end of state competitions.

That first year, the case was trying a particular individual in connection with his role in events that culminated in the "Ludlow Massacre." My son played a witness for the prosecution, and even though his team was made up largely of first-year members, they advanced very well and went to the state rounds. (My proudest moment was when one of the scoring judges—who are actual judges—singled him out for his skill in recognizing and dodging the opposing counsel's interrogation strategy. He avoided having his testimony construed as something he in fact did not say.) Somebody hold me in my chair, because you really are not supposed to jump and cheer at mock trial!

The Colorado Coal Field Strike had lasting impact for workers' rights. The Ludlow tent colony did rebuild after it was burned, and the strike continued for another few months. Ultimately, it seemed like the workers gained almost nothing. None of their demands were met when they went back to work in the mines. The mine owners still had a tight grip on the industry that kept power and profit in their hands. Yet in historical perspective, this strike did lead to some reforms in labor relations, especially because the deaths at Ludlow and the ten-day war that followed received national attention, and opinions galvanized about the way workers had been treated. From a public relations perspective, it was difficult for mine owners to simply go back to their old ways as if the strike and violence had not happened. They became more open to negotiated settlements with workers. The United Mine Workers of America maintains a monument at the Ludlow location as a testament to the struggle of organized labor in America for safe working conditions, fair pay, and other principles that bring dignity to workers' lives.

Thank you to all the readers of the Tree of Life series who reached out to ask me, "When is book 5 coming out?" I would not have done this book without you.

Olivia Newport
September 2021

CPSIA information can be obtained
at www.ICGtesting.com
Printed in the USA
LVHW012146200122
708836LV00006B/314

9 781737 671800